THE HORROR OF THE

ORDINARY

Stories

by

Richard Krause

THE HORROR OF THE

ORDINARY

Attention schools and businesses: for discounted copies on large orders, please contact the publisher directly.

For information contact:
Unsolicited Press
Portland, Oregon
www.unsolicitedpress.com
orders@unsolicitedpress.com
619-354-8005

Editor: S.R. Stewart
Cover Image: Bruce New
Cover Design: Kathryn Miller

ISBN: 978-1-947021-96-9

I wish to thank Mandy Davis and Sharon Whitehead, who were always willing to read my work, for their encouragement. Also, I wish to thank Rubie Grayson and S.R. Stewart who took a chance on this collection.

Table of Contents

Gregor

You'd think this kind of thing would come easily to me, but it's not easy. You'd think Gregor was innocent, a dusty old dung beetle living with his family, a traveling salesman. If truth be told, everyone is a salesman, has to sell themselves sometime. I should know. I was an orphan and you quickly learn to please people. Walking into their house for the first time asking, "Who's gonna be my boss?" doesn't come out of thin air. I knew where things stood. I knew what I had to do so they'd keep me in their home, so I wouldn't be out on the street shining shoes like my mother had wanted.

The pathological cleanliness I still insist on to this day, not like Gregor with the dust balls collecting on his legs, the rancid cheese neglected, the sour milk. Granted his family never knew how to please him, what his diet should be, for he was a housebound beetle who kept his eye on the hospital across the way, who tried to win sympathy with the three o'clock crucifixion and those electric apples that his father threw that rotted on his back. Poor Gregor!

But at least he had a father. Not like me who was just left with the legacy of being German, and all the twentieth century guilt associated with that.

How was I to escape the mindlessness of being born afterwards, of decades later finding myself in Kentucky and watching them strip the cherry trees, every last leaf, dally with the fig at their leisure, but then leave the birch tree bare? But at the grape vines, ah, that's where I got them! That was the last straw! There they brought it out of me, there they weren't out of reach but at chest level.

I staggered compulsively in the dazzling afternoon sunlight

from tree to tree, just the time of day when they congregated the thickest, when they doubled up on each other at midday, hugging themselves, mounting each other shamelessly there right in front of my wife and children. They had to be stopped! I hate to say it, but they increased my ardor! I know that, but they gave a fine point to my rancor at taking their pleasure so openly. The movements of their bronze backsides and their little legs struggling for entry, the energy of their mandibles too, their coppery green shimmer, all admittedly dazzled me.

And I know Gregor had nothing to do with it, pathetic creature that he was, getting excited only by the picture of the furred girl on the wall. Little wonder he defied aerodynamics dropping periodically from the ceiling for the sheer pleasure of it, the stubborn willfulness of not opening his wings, absorbing the concussion of each fall out of spite for being so neglected. Smash, he'd smack the floor and delight in the stunning blows he administered to himself if he couldn't have their love.

I know of his fondness for Grete, his sister, and yes that should have humanized him and made me think twice about what I did. The way she entertained the boarders and he grew emotional over her violin should have softened me.

Who do I think I am? Yes, that was asked of me by others more than once, and I had too much to say to answer them. It would have required a thousand-page monograph, I told myself.

Gregor's author took pity, because needless to say he identified with him, but I identified with the whole race of people responsible for the murder of so many. His sister in a few short years would go to the camps. But I wonder if that unspeakable murder is less horrid than this reduction for my own family, keeping the insects at bay.

Snap! I just closed the lid on another one. They fall in as I tease them off the leaf till they lose their balance or grow alarmed and try to use their wings. Mostly they slide down the leaf as I close the lid and continue panting around the tree, my heart pounding wildly with midday palpitations. In a matter of minutes, I'd have ten, fifteen, twenty beetles. At the height of the season, hundreds by early afternoon. They'd all be buzzing, disoriented, clinging to each other in thick clusters. There'd be so many that I'd have to break off leaves to feed them, the very leaves they'd strip bare in no time, like the most efficient exfoliant. I'd cover them with leaves, so they couldn't see to fly out. Though some would get away when I'd open the jar up for others. Then I'd stand there stunned, musing on all the permutations of freedom.

I went from tree to tree like a hunter, a sanitation worker, a forest warden, an exterminator whose methods didn't give them much of a chance. I prided myself on using no chemical agents or gas, though sometimes out of sheer anger and frustration I'd pinch them between my fingers, sometimes with enough force to make them dust.

Mostly I'd open the jar, work the lid just enough to slip it between the leaf and a Japanese beetle eating in peace without the rest escaping. I became an expert at this, at bumping him gently and quickly clamping the lid down and he'd join the others.

I'd watch intrigued at the degree of sociability, the eagerness with which the new entry would attach himself to a mate, or the simple dismay at being suddenly trapped in a closed environment, flying towards the lid or into the glass.

Though I grew dizzy and a little fatigued at my labors, drained almost of a compulsion that at the same time pumped me up with enough adrenaline to continue, my skin itched with the feel of a gray wool uniform I didn't realize I was wearing and my legs grew heavy as with boots.

More than once I tried to make my way towards the house, wobbly from the sunlight beating down on my head, staggering from the indecision of which tree to visit next, but I remained at my task going from tree to tree.

It is rarely accounted how the sunlight beats down on us, eroding our resolve if we stay in it too long, making us question ourselves, our circular whereabouts, sapping our energy and our sense of direction.

How often I doubled back, like it was a blazing narcotic,

addicted to the six or seven chestnut trees they had a mild appetite for, never voraciously stripping a whole leaf but leaving a teasing patchwork of unsightly holes, or I'd go all the way to the property line for the blackberries that I knew they were fond of and had to share with giant golden green, everlastingly stubborn, yellowish blue beetles that I ignored even as they'd reduce each pip to juice, bruise each berry till it looked like mush, so when'd you'd pick them they'd dissolve staining your fingers.

My preoccupation was with the Japanese beetles that stripped our cherry trees entirely and left the birch eerie skeletons against the white bark, left in the leaves of grape hopeless fenestrations that barely hid the Concord grapes. This roused me to battle and was the excuse I told myself for the jars, the glass boxcars, vitreous enclosures for them to swim in their own watery exhalations, reason enough for my going out every day rounding them up.

Gregor was guiltier than Kafka let on. How many trees did he strip in his heyday, how many crops did he destroy, keeping the fruit from coming, rotting in the bud; how many trees died because of him and his kind? Whole forests were denuded by the infestation, entire seasons of crops totally ruined, villages left in famine, was it not right that I at least was here, the first line of defense on my own property?

He must have been responsible for some serious crop damage. Kafka himself must have been responsible for more than he let on, for guilt doesn't come out of thin air. The inscriptions on the chest are there for a reason, for how could he have abandoned Gregor to such a thankless family giving him absolutely no past? That's suspicious. There must have been forests he denuded, plagues inspired that devastated countrysides. Yes, Kafka kept this from us, hiding it in a tale of pity for a dusty old cockroach.

The message that he never received from the Emperor must have been about those very beetles, about the timid mice in the ground. Little wonder he invented Gregor, his crowning achievement, it was more than the bedbugs he claimed in his own family. It was the famine of a whole people he was dealing with. Little wonder too the inscription on the chest. The guilt had to be engraved. Someone had to take responsibility. Gregor, and his kind we know, was the scapegoat for such plagues on people but buried in a past that humanized the insect. But someone had to stop them!

All this I had to factor in as I tightened the lid and set the jar in the summer sun and watched the beetles crawling atop each other, converting the green leaves to a brown liquid, soaking everything in the condensation from their collective breath in the rapidly rising temperatures. Some of the beetles drowned face down in their own fluids, but most continued crawling over each other, going nowhere, clinging stubbornly to their mates for one last embrace or to gain a footing, balling up into clusters of five or six.

I watched in amazement the rapacity of devouring leaves, the multiplication that coated me with a film of guilt about my own appetite and sexuality. I stood stunned at the pleasure I took, at the cruelty of daily collecting Japanese beetles in a jar and leaving them to bake as their movements slowed.

Collecting them off the leaves of my trees, I knew they had to be stopped, but nevertheless I felt guilty at such large numbers, at my dogged compulsion to eradicate God's creatures. Maybe one or two or a handful I could live with, but not the swarms that infested the trees.

Even when I was dog tired, and there were days that I didn't feel like going out at all, I staggered outside with jar in hand. I was clearly uninterested in continuing, but I forced myself. Even when I was downright disgusted at the hundreds of beetles baking in the afternoon sun to preserve the acre of trees in my own backyard, I soldiered on.

Uppermost in my mind were the tender green leaves they devoured. Maybe that accounts for it. I'd walk from tree to tree, I couldn't help myself. Even when my wife called me for a late lunch, I'd stumble on ahead deaf to her entreaties; sometimes I imagined only to resist her, out of sheer stubbornness.

Yes, they all deserved it I tried to tell myself to rationalize

13

the slaughter of so many, and then I thought of Gregor and how he got off scot-free from any such accusations. In fact, we were miles from accusing him of anything!

Neither were they innocent victims, for what they did to me. So efficiently working their mandibles, so efficiently eating leaves clean, stripping the cellulose between the ribs of their favorite foods, the venation of the leaves spread out like live skeletons while they fattened for reproduction on the very trees where they sunned themselves. Openly, right before my eyes! Such smugness was unbearable! They deserved what they got!

Poor white birch, poor Bing and Tartan cherry, flowery Kwanzan, Yoshino cherry from their homeland even, and poor grape, chestnut, and blackberry! I'd come to their rescue! Be there for them!

Why all this mealy mouth guilt on my part? Why this ridiculous confessional! Who else is going to save my backyard, rescue the fruit and flowers from their greedy mandibles! If I wasn't the first line of defense, then who was?

But rarely was I, for all my tough talk and mea culpas, able to even keep up with the infestation, until all at once the season changed, until there was a subtle alteration in temperature. The axis of the earth came to my aid changing the tiniest receptors in the beetles' bodies, slowing their metabolism, making my incarceration, the baking of hundreds daily seem crude, barbaric by comparison. They grew too lethargic for it to be a sport any longer. Nature has such a light touch it is astonishing. We are Goths, vandals by comparison. We only know how to destroy en masse, not by subtle alterations of body chemistry.

I couldn't tell the changes at first, but one day their numbers diminished, though I like to think that it was due to my campaign of attrition, emptying the trees every day. Or maybe the beetles one day ate their fill, grew sated, or like Gregor just died, desiccated slowly in time from a declining appetite. I'd like to think too that I was as efficient as the bold cleaning lady who with a dustpan and brush just swept Gregor up in the end. But I suspected it was beyond me, that they

14

disappeared of their own accord, stopped coming from the change in their metabolism.

Yes, I was the landowner only protecting his crop from well-armed invaders, from the oversized mandibles. I did marvel at their sheen, the beautiful brazen colors, the bronzes and purple green iridescence, and their incomparable articulation, so neat, clean and precise. It was a model of creation compared to my wanton daily destructiveness where they virtually came apart, disintegrated into a wet mess then dried in oven temperatures by the time I'd open the jar.

I could see why they were so fertile, attracted to each other, for just such as the likes of me and hosts of birds that never came around. But as they dried in the sun, as the hot rays flooded the jar, and after a few hours when I'd open the lid, the overpowering smell would rush at me that I'd turn away, quickly shake the clusters of Japanese beetles like dry flowers that disappeared into the grass. Burying so to speak the evidence of what I had done. They'd make good compost for the grass, I rationalized. Yes, that's what I told my wife as I tormented myself with another whiff of the empty bottle. Even today the stench stays with me, occupying a permanent place in my nostrils.

"Here, smell this!" I said holding the bottle up to her trying to share the guilt as my wife stepped back and refused to participate in the horror, giving me instead an odd look.

I sensed I had done something wrong. Maybe because she was Japanese and carried burdens from her past. Or maybe because of the open assault on things Japanese. Should the beetles have been exempted? Didn't I have a right to protect my property? What if this infestation was a fact of nature that I was interfering with? But so is cancer, cholera, the destruction of a season's crops. They were vermin, pests, they had to be eradicated!

Their struggling in the sun, visibly in the jar, all the appendages moving a mile a minute, the struggle for breath through tiny spiracles in their abdomen, admittedly it was creepy to watch. You couldn't help thinking of people.

I alone was the architect of such torment, that by the time they were thoroughly desiccated a few hours later all I recognized was stench and lightweight bodies pouring on the lawn to make the grass grow or fattening passing birds that may have seen me.

I was disgusted with myself as much as fascinated with my compulsion to continue this every day. Pruning was the same thing. Once I start on a tree I can't help myself. It's therapeutic to keep cutting, causing the sap to bubble, cleaning out the growth, limb after limb, simplifying the trunk till the branches come to mimic me! More than once I've left only two of them!

The six-legged beetles I assaulted because they had too many legs and wings I didn't have. Not to mention their outrageous appetites and their joy of sex compared to my fussiness. I've always been a finicky eater, a finicky lover. Doing it on a leaf, just anywhere out in the open in the afternoon sun before my family, was degrading! Doing it with only one partner was bad enough, but with a whole cluster. Who'd put up with that! Ugh! It was outright lewd.

Why am I trying to defend myself? Who needs a defense of such outright gluttony? And to strip my trees, you might as well take the shirt off my back! Who do they think they are?

Yes, I felt tainted somehow interrupting their reproductive cycle. But should I have? I know, I know, who am I? This sad little proprietor. Own land, what a silly appropriation? Who can own anything? We thought we could own the bodies of others a few short years ago. Little wonder I rounded up these beetles on an inconspicuous plot of land. Wasn't I readying myself for the horrors of the 21st century?

It was then that the most famous beetle in literature leaped to mind, and I thought of myself, neglected, desiccated of late, almost needing help out of bed, my bones so stiff, fearing finally being swept up by a dustpan for getting smaller than anyone can see. As the cells in my body lose moisture daily, I know I've become a husk of the man I once was.

Killing Japanese beetles every year in my own backyard restores me. Yes, I thought to myself, it was very fortunate that

I had the trees on my property, that I wasn't let loose on the general population.

Crossing State Lines

I don't know why he ran all the way to Baltimore, or what was there. He got a room and just waited because he needed the distance. He said he didn't know what he was waiting for. Just to sort things out, he said. The decision was so big. He didn't know if he could make it, if he was man enough. It was momentous and might end insupportable. He was only one man after all, he said. He didn't know if that was enough, or if it would ever be enough.

He knew others had done it, and some had the same qualms but didn't know if he was at all like them. And the repercussions, could he handle them? He said it as if he were already carrying the burden of the whole world on his back. What a burden, just the thought of it was unmanageable. He half expected me to help, but he knew I couldn't. I was out of his league. He was on his own.

He just didn't know, he said, but he couldn't remain away too long, or they would all get suspicious. He didn't have anyone to talk to about his fears, he said, that's why he wrote the letter. He said nothing about my understanding him, nor even assumed I would. He just wanted to inform me that he was on the run, in a hotel room, that he had crossed over the state line. He was having second thoughts. In Maryland, if you could believe that, he said. The name was enough to follow him around, bring up questions. Both his parents had committed suicide separately, and he was raised by his grandmother. I knew him after he was dumped in the orphanage. Was there a family history in Baltimore? Or was it Poe that disturbed him? Did he end up running from where he'd end up, a full circle like a noose tightening around his neck? She wasn't Mary, not even Phoebe whom we all heard about after high school. She had gone to the same college. Where was it, the Mennonite college in Virginia whose name escapes me. But they split up and then he met Marilyn, and now this letter. It has come down to this. I remember he was the only one who didn't go to the prom for religious reasons, taking the prohibition against dancing seriously.

I remember too how he balanced chemistry equations before anyone else. Read Günter Grass when we thought only of mowing the front lawn, loved Steinbeck and Kafka, the latter we had never heard of, moved to New York City and got an apartment on the Lower East Side. He returned too to the Holland of his ancestors, purchased the great coat as if he still endured the freezing European temperatures of World War II. He wrote to his relatives condolences when the Queen Mother died. It was from his apartment that he saw all those foreign films that were over our heads but appealed to the searching intricacies of his own brain.

He just didn't know if he could go through with it, he said, or if there was any light in the end. He didn't mention a tunnel, but there was a lowering darkness about his decision so that he said he was tentative, fearful about the outcome, but still he didn't know if one, two, three days were enough to decide, or if he ever would. How do you come to such a decision with the burden of such crushing hours? It was then that he wrote the letter to see for himself, he said. But I knew it was only half the story. Like his ancestors constantly under siege from the Nazis, everyone was mum. He imagined always a fascist at his door. He was unable to assert himself except in brief, frenzied outbursts like the Führer. Every weakling loves to mimic him. Maybe that's why they are only a blip on the screen, magnifying what makes everything lopsided. He had made the decision, but he capitulated to the moment, ignoring what he really felt. Sometimes it takes a lifetime to approach the moment of honesty, then at the very end a true word is finally uttered.

What do we really want deep down, ignoring all our own shallow breathing? How can we decide on anything? We talk about our deserts, but who really feels they deserve anything? Our thoughts keep tearing us down, exposing one layer after another. Who else in the end are we afraid of but ourselves? Those terrifying revelations about us. Max had to face them in Baltimore, to avoid being crushed by expectations that magnify the least step, it's monstrous. Each appendage appears disproportionately outsized. We shrink before the hairiest joint. Our fears mind a body that is not really ours, but yet we are attached to it. Someone else has to say our name to assure us of our identity. Otherwise it escapes into the nearest insect. We alone can whisper it. Gregor. We do, ever so low, so no one can hear, so no one knows what is going on. The transformation is all our own. Sometimes we don't know it ourselves, our own shadow jumps out at us in the least light as we pass compounding our loneliness. It is always waiting, lurking there in our loins, folding back on us for long moments of speechlessness. Placing us in the pockets we have our hands in. Some of us positively can't face ourselves. We look like we are dawdling. We put on a happy, cheery face, we whistle, to convince others, even ourselves? But deep down we don't believe in anything we say or do, despite being seduced by our own appearance, despite our grouches. Max had many of them. How could he not, living with himself? But here he was trying to face it, the metal-rimmed glasses, the round face, the high shiny forehead, the florid cheeks, the incipient stomach pouch.

He had told no one, just up and left. He had tried to eat through it, but it didn't go away. He thought crossing the state line would enable him to get his bearings from the formality of a boundary, its statutory demands. The Mason-Dixon Line too if the decision were not so powerfully private. If it didn't close in smothering him. The room was waiting, a compartment in his own mind locked away. How could his brain house it and the walls not collapse before giving him access? He imagined his skull paper thin, the lamplight inside revealing each suture. It could be crushed so easily with the wrong thoughts. Something would stave it in. Sometimes he wished for the concussion if only to find himself in prewar Holland at the end of a nightstick.

We imagine we are remodeling what houses us, the furniture of our mind, changing location. Ignoring the suggestion that we should just move. It's easier to cross a state line, check into a motel, the roomy extension reaching to another state. The thoughts there can finally be alone. He can be his own man. But Max needed help, so he wrote the letter. He couldn't face a telephone call.

The decision overpowered him. His fear was profound. No more solitude, no more city jaunts, no more foreign films, solitary moments with Günter Grass, Kafka, and Steinbeck. How would they decide on the music to be played? He might have to give all that up. Then where would he be? Marooned. How could he suffer such a dislocation?

I didn't know what to say but saw the comedy in how he fit the stereotype like any other guy, taking off at the last moment. Still he felt obliged to go through the motions. Real men did it, even if they were on the run. At the last minute checked out leaving everyone standing open-mouthed.

Max reached out with his letter, "I just don't know, Jack. It's such a weight, a change. Maybe I am just getting cold feet. I know, I know, you'll bring up the foot massage again! Someone every night to fill my loneliness with her warm hands. What am I to do?"

Before Jack could reply Max was back. They went through with it, Marilyn and Max. You had to admit the names fit.

The funny part of it was that I knew what it was all about. Like a bachelor party in disguise before getting hitched. The sigh of relief from the last few days of freedom. The soul searching all men go through before the ceremonial loss of that freedom. Even I had waited. Maybe Max thought we were alike, that I was an ally. I had never told him I looked over at Cindy in the car for years and panicked, felt absolutely smothered by the prospect that I was trapped with one person. I hate to bring up Prometheus bound to the rock; it is not an apt metaphor for an unheroic age, but it fits. Even driving I gasped for breath, felt sharp pain in the pit of my stomach that could have easily been my liver, clutching the wheel I more than once had the impulse to turn it sharply going seventy miles an hour to see what would happen, turn my life upside down in response to being so harnessed to the sheer stupefying monotony of what could only be addressed by this random violence. I too had no

21

one to talk to. The shame overwhelmed me. The sheer lack of wiggle room, being caught with only one person my whole life long made me panic and was only relieved by the most violent thoughts. My wife strung up in the basement, stuffed in an exhaust vent, all manner of thoughts about hiding her body plagued me. So I understood Max. Gradually these concerns subsided. I tolerated their intensity, but I couldn't say "wife" for ten, fifteen years without wincing.

Yes, Max did get hitched. His problem wasn't the marriage as such. That was my own projection about the freedom lost. I guess I wanted to throw you off the track. What was it then? It makes me a little queasy about bringing it up. My own digestion has never been very reliable. Why did he cross the state line, and the Mason-Dixon Line? Why a hotel in Baltimore, incommunicado for three, four days, except for the letter to me?

Marilyn sang in the church choir, worked for a religious organization called Friends that relieved the poor, and did community charity work. She was perfect for Max in that regard, mildly critical but docile and chastened by an inexplicable love for him. His past, his crochets, grouches, occasional self-destructive tempests of inexplicable anger, his attachment to his long European coat and trips to his ancestral homeland, and to the Lower East Side where they always visited; she tolerated it all with even a measure of what appeared to be genuine enthusiasm. Max this, Max that, his name was always in every other sentence out of her mouth. Yes, she was perfect in that regard, so why the flight? He must have sensed how good she would be for him. Was it just a man thing, something dull and predictable? Then why didn't he just throw a party rather than go off by himself and write to me? Me! How could I help him?

Here's the problem. I know. I know. I have been keeping it from you. What would happen if he had a child? He was absolutely terrorized by the fear of that. You could say that is a fear many of us have, to bring a new life into this world with all the horror already existing. Imagine that! Another human being with the capacity to feel pain just like us, to feel disappointment, heartache, the constant plunging of self-esteem.

Who would be so irresponsible? Every day his declining self-respect, or a limb maybe pinned under a car, ninety percent of his body burned in an airplane crash, electroshock to the genitals from imprisonment in a foreign country, the loss of eyesight, of the mind over concentrating on a simple ashtray. No wonder it gave Max pause, anyone would be mad to produce a child. Who'd want to expose their own flesh and blood to wars, to chemical agents, famine, nuclear accidents, radiation poisoning, and worst of all to the debilitating envy of others. The pain of associating with people, the lack of honesty in daily life, the betrayals necessary for his own survival, never plumbing the depths of anyone but wallowing in his own jealousy, the spite, the lifelong confusion about ourselves, the sharp stings from assumed friendship. Finally, his exposure to us, the changes of his diaper, dressing him, observing the incipient pubescence. The soft down of his body hair. What would we do, who knows? It'd drive anyone like Max across state lines. Avoiding the law inevitably comes into play, big, bruising lawmen fearing their own fathers in hot pursuit for a crime that may not even be committed yet but is there every time he lets his guard down. No wonder Max ended up in Baltimore, with all those laws still on the books. He foresaw what might happen and he was terrified. Little wonder we avoid the formal ceremonies that might produce our pride and joy, the source of all horrors. Yes, that's what I said, gentle reader. You heard correctly. I know what I am taking about. It isn't a misprint. That is the word I want. Horror! I am not talking about the world itself. Sure, there is enough of that in the world, but when it is found inside of us who could stand it? I know, I know, you ask, what are you talking about? Make yourself clear. It is just an innocent jaunt across the state line. That's what you tried to picture, the man thing, totally innocent. Why complicate it? But no, it isn't totally innocent. How much a deity is culpable, if you believe in that, we still don't know. I am not going to change your mind, I know, or even try to. But there it is. You can't avoid it. You might as well be avoiding yourself. Something in all of us. *I am sorry, but I don't know what you're saying, we are not all the same.* I know, I know, you'd dissociate yourself from Max completely if you found out. But he is just like you too; he is probably more sensitive, has deeper feelings than you do, but you'll not believe it. I admit, maybe not quite like you. But those feelings terrorize him like they never do you. Still he pretends a quiet acceptance, lives in the community just like you do, but then something like this ceremony pops up and he is totally on the block, at the mercy of himself, of all of you; he's not what everyone thinks he is, and there is the rub. He knows it if you don't. That is what drives him across state lines. Of course, you take someone like me to task, but I don't condemn him because I know he suffers more than you ever will. You couldn't experience what he does every hour of every day looking over his shoulder. It makes me wonder how he carries on his life, how he doesn't follow his parents or seek refuge across fifty state lines and change his name in every one to hide from you all in the endless spools of colored thread in a haberdashery shop, or the bottomless inventory in a hardware store, in the nuts and bolts of the exigencies of daily life where our feelings get submerged with enough detail to forget ourselves.

Do you get my drift? Have I been clear enough? Maybe he had a vague feeling that the law is everywhere, or that he was living outside the law already. He hid behind his thoughts and we don't know who he already befriended. Perhaps he thought he could get locked up by a police state always listening, ferreting out our deepest secrets, entering our bedrooms, the parks, or the movie theaters where we meet young strangers, even the thoughts in his own mind would be revealed. So his brain wasn't even a boundary, but something to pass as easily as the Mason-Dixon line. Nothing can be hidden enough when it comes to us, and a letter crossing the state line is only a diversion. It mentions nothing really, only the doubt shrouding the real fears about something larger, deeper, and that you or I could not live with. Max's fear is that he could be discovered with his flesh and blood, that he'd be his own detective. Perhaps he already brought himself up on charges. That is the fear Max wrestled with every day of his life, something so subcutaneous that no physician could hope to find the vein of it. He was at the mercy of himself, his own worst enemy.

Yes, Max was afraid of having a child of his own. How can I put it more clearly?

Could he imagine that, watching it grow? Would he have to shield his eyes, hide behind the customary jokes, paternal pride? He didn't know. Would his love be enough, that blanket of pure snow melting when his boy came of age? Would there be the attendant coldness to stop him? That's what was so frightening. The innocence, the trust, and then bang there's his true self, naked. He'd not even know himself what he was doing. Oh, he would, but the horror! Would there be enough state lines to cross after that, enough lawmen to elude? Or would he just find himself crumpled, drooling, mumbling in some corner of a motel, or would he end up in a wilderness where he belongs, untraceable, his bones found decades later. The mere skeleton of the hand that reached out to his own son, the other hand clutching his free hand, the molten one, once red hot to the touch but now bone dry, the thought was disastrous, who could live with it a second?

He'd have to stop it beforehand, or they would surely come after him. There wouldn't be enough motels to go to, enough anonymous names, enough cellars to crouch in when the front door is broken down, or enough stairs to descend. Yes, the combined body of local, state, federal, even international law enforcement did he decide to cross the ocean to Morocco, Interpol, would be waiting, tailing him and for what may not even be his email, but in his own mind that he'd run from so it wouldn't be picked up on a scanner at some airport, or on a city sidewalk. Could he keep that from anyone? It was why he was running now, before the technology caught up to him. But how could he keep it from his own child? The love would be routed by his fear, tainted by such thoughts. He'd have to touch him at some point, pick him up. What a balancing act. And when the boy is of age, entering pubescence, that was Max's dilemma, what he sought foreign films and books for, the absurdities of Kafka, or Grass's aberration, the screaming dwarf Oskar, so he wouldn't catch up to himself. So his impulses could be rerouted. Before everything got hi-tech, he dreamed of the creakiness of an imagined vehicle, a bulky trailer already in flight so he would not have to sign the register in motels. He need only tell Jack about the man thing, not the boy thing. His boy, how was he to avoid him, what could he do? He couldn't bring it up but thought instead about travel.

Yes, he took the plunge, recrossed the state line. He thought he could stave it off. Who knows what happened all those nights when they were together, his headaches, back pain, his fatigue, the hypochondria developed to an art form, he and Marilyn finally eschewing intimacy altogether, age catching up to them. Nothing happened in the end.

Marilyn confided in me that Max wasn't "keen on having children," more than once.

It told everything. He did everything he could to avoid having them. His early flight testified to that. Even if other children weren't immune, he was keen that they would never have a face resembling his own. Max assured it wouldn't happen, and it didn't. End of story that only purportedly is about the simple fear of marriage. Who knew how to resolve it? I mean you'd have to live in his shoes. Max deserved to be like everyone else. Our fears are always less complicated than we are. Sometimes they can barely be expressed unless we squeeze out a narrative about something else. It seems almost trivial to put the cuffs on someone for just the thoughts he has about his own son.

Hamid, the Water Carrier

Hamid was the tallest man that the Afghan villagers had ever seen. He was called El-Hamid for his stature and enormous strength. He was slow and deliberate in his movements, and, though he came from one of the poorest families in the village, he acquired a dignity because of his size and gentleness.

When there was a broken water main, or the falling lintel of a house needed propped up and repaired, Hamid with his broad shoulders was called. Whenever anything required heavy lifting, Hamid was the first on sight. When someone's goat was trapped in a stony crevice and bleating for dear life, Hamid's gentle touch and strong arms were required. Animals and children grew calm around him. Perhaps it was his sheer size, the overwhelming presence of a man magnified who could eclipse the sun or provide shelter from the rain. Perhaps it was, too, the softness of his hands that were so deft for so big a person, that ordinarily you'd expect them to smash stones, skulls, or be used in anger, not so obligingly for the collective good.

Hamid appeared almost like a physician, for the laying of his broad palms on someone would immediately comfort them, whether it be for a lost sheep, or the young child who looked up to the splendor of Hamid's great size and felt his extraordinary energy flow into his body.

The fact that Hamid was just the opposite of what they expected, calmed people almost like morning dew, like the hush at twilight, or the sedative fumes of the poppy. It awoke in the village a special pride at having such a large, powerful man among them, whose huge capacities set him apart from the ordinary run of men.

The whole village drew from Hamid's strength as if it was an extension of their own, like the atmospheric lightning somehow harnessed, or the deep reassuring quiet of the star sprinkled sky. It was as if the village was one flesh with Hamid, who embraced children when they were ill, or in trouble, or at festive gatherings when they could feel secure in the wingspan of his giant arms. He was their shield and protective umbrella. They crowded round him for group photographs; all with radiant smiles on their faces, proud of being in his presence.

And his occupation was nothing more than that he brought water to the village. Hamid had to walk daily five kilometers to Farah to fetch fresh water. Sometimes when his cart was near full he carried two extra buckets on his own shoulders to relieve the exertions of his donkey. The strength required appeared almost effortless to Hamid and enabled him after he disburdened himself to walk with an added uprightness, giving his posture the impression of royalty, so graceful was his carriage.

Hamid was worshipped, too, by his loving wife, Myra, and adored by his five children. The sweets he bought for them, the quiet devotion to each of their needs, and his powerful size made him seem a tall god walking the earth.

In fact, for the whole village Hamid was the cornerstone, the solid underpinning, the center of love and activity, a community resource much like the water he carried, and almost taken for granted until something had to be moved. He never inspired the envy of cleverer men, the shrewd who are always focused on their own advantage.

When people looked into each other's face they inevitably saw the reassuring shadow of Hamid behind them, and his smiling daughters and sons. The water the villagers drank, the community projects, all bore his reflection, even the foundation stones of buildings, the heaviest of which had always been lifted by Hamid and still contained the memory of his exertions.

That Hamid would one day be caught in the crosshairs of a country ten thousand miles away was unthinkable to anyone in the village. That he'd be the object of a thirty-million-dollar aircraft, developed by some of the best technical minds in the West, cruising over southwest Afghanistan that day, would certainly boggle the minds even of American taxpayers.

Captain Wainwright caught the tall man on his target finder. Hamid was traveling with a wedding party for his nephew, Karim. He was dressed in a long white robe of coarse cotton and stood out among the party of travelers even from the air, locked onto by the most delicate cockpit instruments known to man.

"It looks like him!" Captain Wainwright said to Major Moore.

"By God, it does!"

Above Wainwright was clipped a photo of his wife and three children back in Wichita, Kansas.

"Lordy Mercy, we got him!" Wainwright exclaimed.

"Yes, sireee, it sure looks that way, Captain!"

Both officers got excited as promotions already raced through their minds. The deck the Moores would build in their backyard, the swimming pool they could finally afford. And little Bobby Moore could get his braces. His son, Kevin, could get into Norton Academy, the private school in New England, and Kathy could buy Susie her Viennese violin, and Robert could buy the fur coat he had always wanted for his wife. Overnight, with one shot, their careers would be launched.

Wainwright, too, was the consummate family man. Up on the cockpit ceiling and inside his wallet were the same photos of Darlene Wainwright and their three kids, Mickey, Mindy and Jackie, all Tennessee born and bred. Wainwright came from a long line of volunteers, hunters who insured the safety of their womenfolk back when bear and Indians were the only threat.

Wainwright already envisioned surprising Darlene with his promotion, for early on she had fallen in love with his chest full of medals and looked with admiration to the bravery of her husband flying through the clouds for the protection of his country and family.

The warm glow around Jack suffused the Wainwright household, even when he was away, with a sense of their own importance and sacrifice. It was a family ritual on those mornings when Jack was on active duty to raise the flag in their front yard. Little Mickey blew on his trumpet while Mindy and Jackie stood proudly at attention, as Darlene Wainwright slowly raised the American flag.

"Request permission to fire from Central Command," Major Moore said.

Computers in Kuwait checked the coordinates, matched it with data of troops on the ground and other aircraft in the area.

"It looks like it's all a go, sir."

"It sure looks like him. He towers over the rest."

The sky was pink, streaked and with bronzes and a scarlet underbelly, the blues darkened to velvety black at the fringes drew in the lemony yellows. The chlorotic greens bore the beguiling chloroform hue of another era of trench warfare.

"They'll give you an oak leaf cluster, Sir." Wainwright said.

I got him, Moore thought, in smothered jubilation.

Wainwright already pictured the ceremony of his promotion to major and the adoring look on Darlene's face, not to mention the pride of his three children.

"Permission granted," General Booth at Command Center crackled over the intercom.

Moore squealed in delight and reached towards the control panel, oblivious to the deafening roar of the jet engine.

The release code was accepted, and the missile engaged. Then in a split second it launched with whistling speed at the slow tread of the gentle giant moving on the ground.

Hamid was joking with one of his uncles about the antics of his youngest child, Asa. He wore a smile on his face that the only surviving member of the party would remember.

The next moment the missile created a small puff of smoke on the ground. It had hit its target and blew almost everyone apart. The concussion threw Haji so far that just before he lost consciousness he was able to picture Hamid smiling at his uncle.

"Target engaged!" Wainwright whooped.

"Mission accomplished! Goodbyyye Osama!" Moore added.

The shock would be repeated after the body parts were returned to the village. Stunned villagers stood around with an angry, but defeated incomprehension.

"Why," they asked, "were they attacked? Why kill Hamid? What did he do to them?"

That morning at two-thirty, suddenly, from out of the night sky like extraterrestrials, precise cones of yellow light appeared, then the quiet hum of an airship whose shape had never been observed by the local inhabitants, as four black ladders dropped figures with the most advanced gear in the world and matchless night vision who pointed their weapons at the roused villagers in their white tunics. Their cloth turbans and sandals were no match for the sensors on their helmets, or their Velcro vests and thick leather boots.

They demanded to see the village headman, and quickly cordoned off the village into occupied sectors. They reported on their radios that they had made contact with the enemy, had secured the site and met with no resistance. A few goats bleated in their pens, and children in their mothers' arms screamed in tears at the strange spectacle of the special forces, fearing what would be done to them.

The soldiers' faces were blackened, and their fearful looks terrorized the astonished villagers, as did the unfamiliar equipment silhouetted in the dark, creating such eeriness that there was now barely a murmur of resistance.

The blowing up of the wedding party, of Hamid, seemed like an act of God, and the villagers thought it was the end for all of them, a judgement from above.

The translator wanted to know where the dead bodies were, and the soldiers were led to a small makeshift morgue that had never had so many dead at one time.

"Where is the tall one?" they asked, and the village headman pointed to a torso of Hamid that had only one leg and the remnant of a face whose large features now seemed like a floppy rubber mask.

Way was made for a medic who worked through the crowd of huddled villagers and soldiers. With his bag he bent down before the corpse, unzipped it and took out a small glass vial and a scalpel, then scraped two skin samples from the remains of Hamid for DNA.

The special operations personnel withdrew as efficiently as they had come, as the airship disappeared mysteriously into the night.

It would later be determined that Hamid, the water carrier, that extraordinarily tall man in the wedding party, was not the famed terrorist Osama bin Laden after all, but that would have to await final lab analysis.

The promotions of Major Moore and Captain Wainwright depended on those lab results, not to mention the personal benefits to their families. Needless to say the deck, the swimming pool, the fur coat, the private school, even Bobby Moore's braces, and of course the personal ambitions of the two servicemen, would all have to be put on hold.

But Moore and Wainwright were in for the long haul, and in their own way happy to be flying the skies over Afghanistan, eager for the opportunities that awaited them in what was now being described as more target rich Iraq where they hoped to shoot some real terrorists from the air, not just innocent water carriers who had the misfortune to be born taller than the rest of the local population.

Reparations for Hamid's children, and for the other villagers, were never even considered, being that the dead were casualties of a war that had never been formally declared.

The Splinter

A splinter pushed into the soft tissue of Jacob's finger. He was charged with disposing of the wood, breaking it into small pieces. A wedge was hammered into the beams and, after successive concussions, the timbers separated into one chunk after another. Most of the scrap was burnt and the tiniest pieces were raked for future kindling.

The authorities wanted the site cleared, and Jacob had to dispose of every last piece. One piece he picked up and pocketed for good luck, whistling like it was his lucky day. For his aged uncle had gotten him the job.

His finger where the sliver of wood had entered was never the same. The splinter inflamed the site, brought forth memories that later tormented Jacob. Just like when Jacob was with women he pushed into another dimension, a shaft of darkness sheathed by moist walls that dilated his nostrils and involved all his senses, as if he were drunk on the penetration of wood that closed cleanly, inexplicably, leaving the embedded darkness all to itself.

Jacob soon found himself a simple day laborer cleaning up others' messes, sweeping the ground of every bit of debris, staring into the small fires he'd built as if his finger were not the counterpart of all the burning in the world, the ever-present renewal by purgation. Despite the eye-watering fumes, Jacob cleared the air, so he thought, after each particle disappeared.

The piece that he absently pocketed he didn't think about. The rest he raked in neat piles for tinder, as the shavings swirled on updrafts that finally vanished back into the earth.

For the remainder of the ash Jacob dug a large hole. In fact, he loved digging, as the counterpoise to the giddiness of the open sky.

Jacob dug holes for trees to compensate for the wood he cut up. He had planted over fifty trees in the year after; it was a frenzied series of replacements on his small parcel of land. He dreamt of the almond, cedar, oak, pomegranate, olive, and fig, as if he were trying to imitate the Creator himself, for the vanity of so much building, like the Tower of Babel reaching all the way to the heavens.

Just breaking ground, digging round holes, squaring, placing the seedling, or root ball, or dwarf tree in the earth, lengthened Jacob's step. Feeling the soil between his fingers, smelling the moist earth as he dropped to his knees, made his arms divining rods insuring the nourishment of what he had planted.

Jacob compensated for all the ignoble purposes wood was put to. He insured for the future, trees that mocked the straightest most utilitarian boards, and he imagined a fruitfulness that would bring a halt for a few growing seasons to the cutting of all the forests of Lebanon, the dustbowl the world was being turned into destroying the mighty cedars. Jacob trusted that mysterious force of nature reaching heavenward with every tree he planted, absorbed as he was in the passing clouds, trying to decipher some hieroglyph of meaning. Jacob felt the trees that he planted were the closest he'd ever get to heaven, their trunks swelling to the topmost extension of their branches.

Jacob himself couldn't explain all the trees in one year. He had used up all his savings. It was as if he alone were cleaning up everyone else's mess. For despite bouts of gross intemperance, he was a capable and studious worker.

Jacob loved wood, the swirl of pine and the smell of cedar. And while the weight of oak burdened his spirit he couldn't help admiring the tree itself, such stunning reach out of a remarkable acorn. Maybe it was the immobility of an oak dresser he had once moved. The beautiful blond wood almost gave him a hernia lifting it up steps to his friend's apartment that he concluded it should remain in the ground to do the soaring itself. He admired the rich grain in cherry from the north and felt apprehensive of denting the soft pine. He loved too the stains, varnishes, the dizzying euphoric smells of the resins, sawdust even, and the cozy warm curls of honey-colored wood. The supple waviness and dark rings he thought told more than his own life span.

Jacob was now past middle age and content to live alone. He had no immediate family to share the trees that grew like guardians around his house. The silvery underside of the olive trees caught the light like so many coins. Even the blackberries he had tried unsuccessfully to plant grew wild in an astonishing abundance, spiting the stock he had planted.

One day word got out about the splinter still embedded in Jacob's finger and the night sweats he had. Some claimed Jacob was even having visions. For afterwards his finger was never the same; a private agony seemed to have attached to it quite different than the prick of even a sharp thorn. The embedded black, almost indigo, spot appeared as unthreatening as an isolated dot on the shaved underarm of a woman. The wood had reached down past any jagged surface pretensions and lodged cleanly in Jacob's finger as a kind of permanent reminder. Maybe the wood carried bacterial properties from the rust of nails and that's what made his jaw lock for a time, promoting a disinclination to talk about what he had experienced. Soon hardly a whisper came out, so that Jacob chronicled nothing of what he had done, but earned the suspicion of those around him, and retreated to the muteness of his trees. In fact, it could be said that even Jacob himself didn't know exactly what he was hiding.

At night there was a banging in Jacob's head, vaguely jogging a memory that couldn't take the next step without cleaning up. He had visions of giant timbers reduced to shavings, honeyed curls and the radiant smile of a child and the wet noses of lambs, wooden pillars pushed against and collapsing, giant arks, and ceilings that turned blood red with a man reaching through, naked from the waist up, saying he'd give anything for the splinter, for the wood in the glass by the bedside.

"Here!" the torso from the ceiling said and held out a bundle of money that when Jacob reached up the man retracted it grinning, as if to say it wasn't going to be that easy.

"One condition, one condition!" the man repeated. And

Jacob was bathed in blood until he woke up and found his bedclothes soaked in his own sweat.

Whenever Jacob drank in the local tavern he maundered about his past, about the splinter still in his finger and fevers that had lasted weeks, then dwindled to a dark spot until every spring it grew inflamed. Most took this as evidence of Jacob's loneliness, having no wife, no family, only a splinter in his index finger, and the piece by his bed, and the trees he had planted, so they laughed and poked endless fun at him. All except for Joseph the Baker. For him Jacob's story was the yeast, a literal rendering whose significance grew with each telling.

The groans Jacob said he heard from the wood conveyed the spikes crushing the cellular tissue for all to see, especially Joseph who watched every morning the rise of dough. The baker knew that like the miracle of bread, history, legend, the stuff of myth surrounds us all the time, if only our instruments are keen enough to detect it.

The axe to cut the timber down, the tools to shape it, the dripping sweat distributing an array of electrolytes, are all picked up when the mind is ready. The cumulative weight of any whole can be extrapolated from a tiny sliver of wood in the finger, reconstructed in its entirety, down to raking up the mess.

The massive cross rested on the shoulder that bore the heft of the wood, defying gravity under one man. The bloodstains, the sweat and tears, the dust gave everyone an unearthly mask of being enshrined in a pantomime for all time.

The wood's lightness in the glass testified to the wedge driven into the timber, conveying the uncertain significance of this strange cuneiform. Its driftwood lightness testified to the dragging, to how the extraordinary burden on the shoulder of just one man had changed everything.

Jacob imagined the stiffness of his desire going soft and tender once satisfied, and he couldn't reconcile the two except by the shoulder on which this wood had rested with an accumulated weight that was unimaginable to the little man who had cleaned up the mess of an empire.

The baker sensed that middle age can get airy, brittle, the

36

bones hollow, tormented by the power they once had. The will remains, the imagination, Jacob describing the sunlight playing on the glass by his bed, reddening it with tiny prisms of salty vision from the utter oppressiveness of the heat recapitulating the climb.

The baker at his oven saw the bloody indentations from the lashes, the massive wood making the footing treacherous, the rag offered to wipe the face, the spitting and curses hurled, the rotten fruit thrown that stuck to the thorns.

How everything would come to be glamorized he had no idea. The crawling would be forgotten, his abandoning the cross altogether, hiding in a ditch, covering his head, refusing to move, the prodding, his rising reluctantly, having to be forced to take it up again. Then stretched out, held down by so many men, and the spikes, the screams even had seasoned soldiers wincing.

"Heave ho, heavenward," someone mocked, "you're almost there, King of the Jews!"

It was all there in Jacob's dream, in the wood swirling daily like wreaths of blood in a water glass, the sunlight playing tricks on him. And the pain in his finger had him gripping his bed, his brow beaded with sweat, an agitated pulse at his temples. Jacob would squeeze his finger to reproduce the agony up the hill, being nailed and hoisted up for all to see.

The baker, sensing all this on Jacob's face, was lifted like Jacob in the air, outstretched himself.

One night there was a banging at the door, and Jacob awoke startled.

"Who is there?" he called.

"Open up! Open up!" voices demanded.

And Jacob couldn't have thought he was entering the gates of paradise, a dream involving ladders. His wooden bed told him otherwise.

There he was in the tiny house surrounded by so many trees on this small plot of land with what he thought was an insignificant splinter in his finger, despite the suspicions of the baker. The full moon gave no indication of what was to come.

It was the villagers, absent the imaginative baker, who arrived in the dead of night.

What had they come for, what did they want? A passport to the afterlife, indulgences for their sins; did they know all along, or had they just heard Jacob rambling at the tavern, and had finally come to believe him? Anything to enter the gates of heaven.

The villagers broke open the door and fought at the passageway for entrance, surged into Jacob's room, believers, doubters of every stripe, necromancers, those who wanted to gain an edge in the afterlife. They rushed to the small stand by Jacob's bed.

"There it is!" one screamed, overturning the glass, fighting tooth and nail for the gray wood as one smashed the glass against the head of another, and others jumped on Jacob himself beating him down, grabbing at his bedclothes until someone tightly gripped his index finger.

The rest wrestled on the dirt floor for the piece of wood, rolling around in bits of broken glass. The room was soon a wreck, the crude little stand had overturned, Jacob's one chair was broken, the coverings on the windows were torn down. The fighting spilled out into the front yard under the moonlight with the trees Jacob had planted mutely passing judgment on the cursing, spitting, and kicking up of dust, at everyone trying to get that one little piece of wood that grew so abundantly in their trunks, driftwood that the stream of time had deposited in a clutching fist as a passport to heaven. A powerful kick in the groin, to the front teeth, made it change hands any number of times. Soon the wood disappeared but villagers continued their attack, stepping on each others' faces, noses, kicking eyes that swelled shut losing sight of each other, but still kicking and swinging blindly.

The wood could have been splintered into a hundred pieces had reason prevailed, and not the greed, as they pummeled each other, bit a chunk of nose here, a whole ear there, took a mouthful of soft cheek, the better part of someone's Adam's apple, twisted fingers limp, tore at scrotal sacs till they all lay groaning on the ground with the wood nowhere in sight.

The villagers grew forever suspicious of anyone who afterwards had any good fortune, each thinking the other had secretly reaped benefits from the wood.

Jacob himself lost consciousness and bled to death in his bed where his finger had been so violently removed that no one ever found it either.

The Orthodontist

The animals' heads were on the walls of the orthodontist's office. He was trying to straighten out his own life, the three marriages that had failed. He's loose again on the women who come to his office. He shot a zebra this last trip. Quick-footed antelope the time before that to match the impala already there. An elephant when he went for the overweight beast in Tanzania to compensate for his own expanding waistline. A monkey too, actually a lemur, in Madagascar that surprised everyone he was so unbearably cute, and small. He's completely stuffed. The little expressive face and the tiny hands amazed the children and parents alike and left them in raptures and squeals of excitement. The lemur looked like the cutest children that came to his office for braces.

Most mothers were flings that ended up disappointing the doctor. The animals always seemed to intervene. Their presence almost compensated for the thwarted beast in him. The heads alone that were so massively immobile for never being attached to the fluid grace of the animal again still had a presence; their eyes caught your attention. It was almost as if you could hear the thunder of the pounding feet and feel the charging bodies bursting through the wall, anticipate too Dr. Caudill's fear, see the sweat beading his brow, experience the trembling of the rifle, the determination of the trigger finger, the squint through the scope, the clenched jaw and finally the slow squeeze, see too the native guide backing the dentist up if the shot went up in the air, then boom, the bullet entering the animal, exploding, blood everywhere, raining over the body crashing to earth, and then somehow the papers filled out, a veritable carpet of floating transportation that ended up with these stunning creatures on the dentist's wall back in rural Kentucky.

His puma head had such a strikingly clean outline of mouth and defined pink nose, broad whiskers, and gimlet stare that the face seemed almost unreal, an artist's perfect rendering. Who knows what canyon the good doctor climbed, the absolute danger he placed himself in for the shot at the marvelous cat who too watched his every movement. He loved the animals' bodies so much that he dreamed about them being in his possession for all to see, in this case the expressive yellow eyes and the sleekness of the remarkable tawny coat. The doctor just had to have the permanent companionship of either the entire animal, or their heads mounted on his office walls. With the same exactitude that he tightened his patients' braces, gave the final twist to bring into maximal alignment the crooked teeth in their mouths, he too had a hand in the exact positioning of the heads on the walls.

Even the smallest patients with their little squeals of pain the next moment he'd remedy after an extra twist by then loosening the metal braces, not any different than the pleasure he took after the hot lead had entered the animal's fast breathing body to then put it out of its misery as it finally stopped dead in its tracks, with the dentist's shadow looming overhead. He already pictured his trophies on the soft pastel walls of his office and the stunned admiration of his patients. Too he pictured the hot semen streaming into the women on his bed who could at the same time observe the multiple heads around the room.

Even without a rifle in hand he tumbled back from exhaustion after he spent himself and threw his outstretched arms with a sigh that took all the wild world in, experiencing the final pleasure of the hunt, the kill that unlike the animals with the women came back to life, despite for the moment their too not moving from the great hunter's bed, shocked that the sex was so good.

Few women looked up and identified themselves similarly mounted above Dr. Caudill's bed. True he had their heads severed and almost single-handedly supported the local taxidermist Jake Motes as the animals were rushed back before the facial structure would collapse from decay. The heads were mostly immediately frozen. Business was good as the orthodontist continued to straighten the teeth of America's children, cousin to the crooked outcropping of pronghorn sheep or impala whose horns identified them like a thumbprint. They looked down from the walls with zebra, tiger, and the elephant that no one saw but in his private office with a privileged tour. The African elephant had its full complement of tusks. How Dr. Caudill was able to get it out of Uganda no one knew.

His own children he handled with care, never gave them evidence of the bleeding hands, the sweat on his brow, the soaking of his underarms, the trembling, the cowardice, for even with them he had the sure touch of someone so deft at twisting metal, who in his dental training demonstrated that he could tie a knot inside a matchbox with only his two fingers. Though as the children grew up they sensed a trail of blood from the office that was so at odds with the sanitized heads that looked down almost alive, mounted as if they were silencing screams, the earsplitting shrieks of being shot, the hot lead puncturing vital organs and rupturing arteries. The grimaces were eerily gone, the protruding tongues, as the animals now stared down at the patients calmly reminding the good doctor of all the women he took to bed, their faces too twisted in pain, like the pressure of metal in his patients' mouths, and then the pleasure of release they took from the good doctor's weight as he tooled around their bodies and oral cavities, sometimes bleeding down their jaws, a trickle of blood an assistant quickly swabbed away, or down their legs, not unlike the bloody appendages of the animals. The women were privately hoping the good doctor would choose them permanently, like the animals mounted on the wall, to become part of the life of someone with such an astounding successful practice and such an astonishingly exciting hobby.

That the doctor himself deserved to be shot for all the dead animals probably never occurred to him or to his patients, at least as far as we could tell from the calm looks on their faces while sitting in the waiting rooms. The most recent elk just seemed like another trophy that took its place among the pantheon of animals the doctor killed. He had gone to Montana for it and since it was newly mounted had placed it as the centerpiece in the main waiting room. The rack of horns dominated the entire wall. One could hardly imagine the rest of the body of such a huge animal, or the remarkable mind that saw the animal through the scope, that squeezed the trigger sending the hot lead whistling through the air, bringing such a magnificent creature crashing to the earth.

Of all the patients sitting there in the dentist's waiting room, would there not be at least one patient feeling stunned, dry-mouthed, at a loss of breath at what happened to such splendid creatures that the wall despite its powder blue grew splattered with a live map of dripping blood from hemorrhaging vessels escaping the animal's body, coming out the ears, the mouth, soaking the nose, so uncontrollably that for this one patient the other patients too were doused, swimming in the animal's blood, not the tiny trickle from a brace too tight bleeding at the gums, or leaking down a woman's leg, but a massive assault from arteries severed, a fountain of blood so that there was no escaping for anyone? The waiting room would be awash with it, patients wading through it to leave, tracking the blood to their cars in collective footprints. Telltale signs of what the dentist had done. Everyone would be floating as a consequence on a sea of sticky red. Was there at least one patient so affected that he could imagine this for the rest?

Elementary school classes made field trips to the orthodontist's office for the sole purpose of observing the animals from Africa, Asia, Australia, the midwest United States, and up to Alaska. No one knew of the private room for the grizzly, or the surprise of the kangaroo with his small forepaws extended as if he wanted to shake the children's hands, reaching out just for them.

"Go on, kids!" Dr. Caudill insisted. "You can shake hands and pet the little joey at his side. Here, take some candy from the basket he's holding."

The elephant tusks in his office he encouraged the kids to step up and touch them, so the animal almost came alive under their fingers, as the doctor pushed out his chest and strolled with pride beneath his trophies.

43

What kind of reprisal was in store no one could guess. Certainly not one of his small patients who were themselves blown away by the animal heads, though maybe someone who could actually hear the sounds, the shrieks, the blood curdling screams, the squalls of the young, or see the unborn when a mother was opened up, or imagine the separation of mates and offspring as a desperate stampede trampled one of the herd, the whole drama of almost unregulated killing and then the hunter's victory dance, while with open mouths patients gave themselves to the dentist and his assistants, and braces were seated and tightened. How the tightening metal hurts when suddenly the bulging eyes of a rhino reflects the little patient and somehow the pain disappears because of the mystery of the animal's head mounted on the wall as the little patient's eye proceeds to travel the length of its white horn. In that regard the animals on the walls really helped.

What father of a little boy that his mother had mindlessly made the appointment for in the dentist's office was blown himself away, totally floored by the heads? He must have been someone who had never seen anything like it.

"The slaughter" he probably mumbled to himself as he looked to the floor then buried his head in his hands and couldn't look up. He grew dizzy at the spectacle, as he went around and around and couldn't stand up. Is he the one who envisioned the spilling of blood over everyone? In the room for the moment the blood rushed to his head as he felt the hot lead in his own body for the impassive gaze of such remarkable creatures on the wall. It was all he could do to keep from collapsing in the waiting room, to get to his feet to schedule his son's next appointment, and place one foot before the other to finally exit the dentist's office.

"Dad, what's wrong?" his son asked.

The father himself didn't quite know what was happening.

Did the good doctor calculate what all this killing deserved? Could the patient hear each individual scream, and would he have a fraction of the doctor's courage holding his own before a stampeding or charging rhino? Was it a matter of courage? Or would the guide behind him open up in time as was often done and save the good doctor's hide? The man tried to explain it to himself. How did this man get away with it? he asked. Who allowed their wildlife to be spoiled, condoned such obvious brutality? Only for money? Courage, it wasn't that with today's technology where a big game hunter couldn't miss the broad side of a barn.

Did Dr. Caudill deserve to be hunted down in reprisal? Would some such patient one day be the agent, sanction a personal hunt, or like a true game warden would he even after the fact protect the animals? Who'd expect that logic if the deeds were already done? Nobody.

But shouldn't he pay for his actions, for this bold display of such outright slaughter? Who was he to decimate God's creatures and then mount them so unashamedly on his walls?

Did the moral consideration get lost in the overweening pride of a pumped-up chest as the taxidermist's skill each time masked the horror in the calmly mounted heads? Did it get lost in the women the dentist singled out and seduced, the hunt each weekend the dentist wasn't in the bush, the high ground of the Rockies, or in the far reaches of Asia? In the throes of that passion did the animals' heads pop up, the fast zebra, the lion whose ruff showed Dr. Caudill not at the tail end but King of the beasts he killed taking all the marbles, reigning over such magisterial heads adorning the walls; all bowed to his command, and now below him spreading their legs in his bed, beautiful women looking up at those animals.

Did he or anyone imagine Tony Gilliam, simple plumber, one day coming into his home, a man who had walked in disgust into Dr. Caudill's office, been thrown for a loop, dizzy and blood splattered, did he ever imagine the plumber pulling out a puny handgun in his bedroom, nothing like the elephant gun or high powered rifles he used for pronghorn sheep, or rhino, or even the crossbow the doctor owned? He never imagined that little weapon held to his head, as Tony told the naked doctor to get out of bed and get down on the floor on all fours to see how it felt. Who would have imagined that?

45

Certainly not Dr. Caudill!

Tony Gilliam then takes the revolver and sticks it in the doctor's rear, pushes it past the reluctant sphincter muscle, cornholed him with the snub-nosed barrel saying, "In my next visit I am going to splatter your insides out your mouth if every wall is not dismounted and there is not a mass disposal of this crime."

"Do you hear me?"

The woman was cringing in the corner of the bed and the doctor then started to cry, "Please, please."

Tony in a ski mask disappeared almost as soon as he came. No one knew whose father he was, or whether he was even a patient, for the doctor had had over the last ten years thousands of patients.

The animals were removed from the walls, even the elk whose dominant horns had been Dr. Caudill's most recent prize.

Goodness

Sister Mary was eulogized by everyone when she was going to leave our town after thirty-five years. The only question Jack had about her was what did she want? His mother never imagined people would take an interest in you without wanting something. If someone liked your work, the reason was that they liked you, but the work never stood alone, unmolested. There was a reason for anything being preferred. No goodness existed in and of itself. Everything was connected, even the least kindness.

The newspaper article reports that the sister likes to stay in the background. What inspires her but a natural predilection to do the good that lurks within us, that stays in the background, that swells some deadly, sumptuous sphericity.

She'll be missed by all, the writer says, but most by the downtrodden. Yes, those in the dirt, bemired, that she touched. Isn't that suspicious, the outcasts favored by Christ, those ejected from comfortable pods, wombs, from the everlasting warm beds that nourish us all?

Why is it that some of us reject feeding the homeless warm meals every Saturday in the local park before sending them on their way, having no need to commune with them the rest of the week?

She's leaving December nineteenth, just before Christmas, abandoning the luckless, the article doesn't say, the Christmas suicides, the beatings over so little money for presents, the deadly depression of the blue holiday. The good sister is leaving for Iowa. That's where she's from, returning to some sin in the Great Plains that she must be atoning for. What horrors did her ancestors commit on the native population, how many were shot, riddled with settlers' bullets, hacked to pieces making even scalping look innocent? Could the good sister have seen the lingering horror on the faces of her ancestors, bred in their genes, or did she observe the downtrodden Indians, their smell that runs through the Christian settlers making the women sick

47

and fearful and putting the wrath of righteousness in the men? Is that why Sister Mary took the name of the mother of God and traveled east to do her life's work of repenting for the barely recorded massacres, knowing that the only relief is through compassion and good works?

The grip of the sister, for her body was of moderate size, was strong, even with prominent arthritis, enhanced by surprisingly large bones that could use the Indians' own tomahawk on a squaw, or on the soft skulls of children where the incomplete fenestration fits the smaller stone head wedging it into the imperfectly closed skull. A massacre like what took place at Spirit Lake would spark violence for generations, igniting an eternal conflagration in the hearts of their offspring. But the good work of Sister Mary confounds, an "icon" the paper calls her. Doing good over and over again, how does boredom not enter making anyone want to break the cycle with some violence? Or is there a family drama whispered in hushed syllables? Everyone has done something, making it only right that the Sister Marys of the world have come to Kentucky to help, maybe because of the state's reputation for family scandals.

The article says the Outreach Center she started is legendary. Do its tentacles start with an inappropriate touch, some family fondling? Was Sister Mary trying to reach past that to nullify what happened to her or her sisters while her mother looked the other way, or was asleep in the next room?

Goodness is always the antidote to any ill. It will make everything go away, wallpaper it with repeated floral patterns, soothe the moment, assuage the victim's guilt. After all what was done wrong for the adults to act that way, and how should they act groping for warmth and tenderness themselves? Our behavior is always being revised, just cross a border and the interpretation changes, Marquis de Sade says. How should we act? Christ disappeared from age twelve to thirty-three? What was he up to those two decades after reaching puberty? He must have sown his wild oats? Did he need to repent so hugely for his very own sins, for his persuasiveness with women? How many broken hearts did he trail; his progeny must have been scattered all over the Holy Land, for who couldn't love Jesus, and how many young women must have turned on themselves and their own children when he moved on, those generations that spawned two thousand years of Christianity? Did Casanova pale before Christ, and did Jesus have to be crucified to repent for what he did to all those women for twenty years? After all he was the very personification of love. Today we love too easily, at the drop of a hat. Why must the yearning flesh of those young girls in Bethlehem and Jerusalem not have wanted to take advantage of the only real pleasure life offers, and what powerful need to repent did Jesus have for keeping such secrets that he'd have to enlist the support of twelve disciples to broadcast to the world that he was crucified for the sins of everyone? Likewise, Sister Mary must have been drawn to Appalachia for similarly mysterious reasons.

The Outreach Center is a spacious room on the ground floor of the picturesque Holy Family church. The "small wood-carved sign at the rear door marks the unobtrusive entrance," the newspaper tells us.

It is noted that Sister Mary doesn't have an office. How could she? What office could contain Sister Mary? An office is a nod to the world, but we are dealing here with goodness. Its entrance may be a wood-carved sign, a nice rural touch, and a room is okay to do good in, but an office is confining. Sister Mary would be trapped into an accountability she's not ready for despite secret compartments to house even family molestations. Might there be worse than the scalps taken from Iowans, native American body parts nailed to walls, or framed under glass? Would there be trophies in Sister Mary's office, and is that why she didn't want one? Her goodness was designed to be forgettable because of what it hid. One walk through an office door and the past would close in on her like a mind exposed, and her work would be over. Even the thirty-five years would pass in a jiffy. The secrets of our lives are what keep the goodness going, the smiles on our faces, the everlasting charades. Out the secrets and life loses its purpose, helping others becomes a chore, and the cat let out of the bag starts scratching everything in sight. Sharp or blunt instruments will be picked up if the past is not hidden. No one would be able to live with anyone, but there would be universal mayhem. The good from what is suppressed gives us a rest from ourselves. Christ had to recover from his two decades of who knows what and he did it with a vengeance on all of us, making a religion of his hidings. Sister Mary was so distantly engaged for a reason. There was something buried back in the Plains states, but exposed to the sunlight and blue sky, unlike the uneven terrain in Kentucky. There was accountability in Iowa, the sins were magnified for all to see, to atone for. There were no hollows where lack of contact encouraged the most heinous behavior, where the will of a few was imposed on the many, polluting whole families, towns, ruining the reputation of the state, and then a Sister Mary arrives to minister to the broken, the defeated, and stave off what past must have plagued her. So she operated in the shadows, behind the scenes.

"I sit at that table . . . over there," she says, "out of the way, and let them come to me."

Well, what could she be but an appurtenance? How could she bring attention to herself? The steely gaze of her eyes would frighten the discerning away, but her glasses protect her.

"It's really the Holy Spirit at work . . . I just get to help, participate and watch," she smiles, referring to "the emotionally drained people who come for help." Could this also be the Great Spirit of the Sioux talking through her?

The hollow need rest from the screams inside themselves, from clapping their hands to their ears. The large barrels make you wonder what noises could be inside. Is it the horrid excesses imprinted on Sister Mary's genes, the slashing of ears, cutting of throats, all the blunt trauma, facial disfigurement, continual rape, all the bones snapped like twigs, the browbeating, the lifelong retreat to a table in the Outreach Center waiting for what lumbers or shyly steps through the doorway? What is it that Jack is bothering about uncovering? Is it that nothing is what it seems? Maybe if he backs off there will be a ledge behind. Innocence after all is what is taken advantage of, constant predation defines it. You can't stop it or repent by coming east to escape your destiny. In the end the sunrise will not be halted. You can soothe it, assuage it, bandage it, but in the end no emollients help.

Sister Mary is sitting at her table in the shadows for all who carry their crosses.

With her strong body she sits there to talk.

Maybe she'll take them down afterwards, sponge the flesh, but that's something she'll not let Jack or anyone see. Maybe her bed is as modest as the table she sits at and all the furniture she has is a hardbacked chair in the corner where she says her beads, though Jack has never seen her with any.

She says she came to Kentucky for its reputation for poverty. She wanted to be at the bottom rung, among the "broken, desperate, and lowly, without love," she says.

Here at the Center she says, you can "get a cup of coffee, sit a spell and renew your spirit."

Jack tries not to read into that, the exploitation of the Columbian and Brazilian workers on the coffee plantations, or the sheer witchcraft of sitting a spell! Or think of the renewal of the spirit, conjuring up relief for some atrocity on the Great Plains.

Maybe Sister Mary has no idea what she is party to. Could this be the opposite of an insurrection, her own private warpath leading to finally laying down the weapons of her ancestors, or even a reaction to all the drownings say somewhere in Salem?

When asked about her accomplishments, the good sister says, "I'm not sure," and then after a moment of silence adds, it is "being with those in their sufferings, their hopes, their struggles, their joys, and offering the Lord's strength, His forgiveness, His guidance and His peace." The Lord, she says, "initiates the conversation in any situation." She then quickly credits all the volunteers.

Sister Mary fades into the background to do His work.

Is her grandfather the same Gerald Buckmaster who executed a four-pronged attack on an Indian village at Medicine

Bow, wiping out hundreds of Sioux in one afternoon, burning their teepees to the ground, scattering their culture to the wind, breaking every earthenware jug in sight, stealing their beaded clothing, blankets, and furs, bludgeoning the children, and making sure their pregnant squaws never gave birth?

Captain Buckmaster was promoted in rank, credited for ridding Iowa of Blackfeet and much of the Sioux. His rampages are indelible even in the games children play today, and in the curious silence of Iowans about the past except for rustling cornfields and nuns traveling east.

In the back of Sister Mary's mind, Grandfather Buckmaster was transformed into the one who answers all the questions of the tormented. He had become the Lord who alleviates what he once destroyed. Does Sister Mary compensate the Sioux and Blackfeet by ministering to poor whites with Cherokee blood in Kentucky? She must have noticed the same high cheekbones right off, the downcast looks, and so feels at home.

She tells of doing housing repairs, plumbing, electricity, installing septic tank systems for those "down and out . . . who don't know where else to go."

"We listen . . . ask how they are . . ." she says, "what's going on and how we can make a difference in their lives, especially the homeless . . . the outcast, kids whose parents are in jail . . . or where there's violence in the home." "Some even live in tents," she inadvertently adds, probably not reflecting on the teepees her grandfather burned to the ground.

Here the inadvertent goodness rises and shines each morning. She is the light streaming through the window accompanied by good works. How a terrorized Plains comes to this baffles the mind. It's almost as magical as the fields of corn hiding all the Sioux hunting grounds today and drawing every drop of moisture from once sacred ponds.

The conversation is so assured that Jack himself could scream for all the lost war whoops, for the horror blended into such polite speech. It takes a Munch to properly bring it back to life.

Looking at Sister Mary and listening to her makes Jack

scream for the smothered wailing, for what's muffled in the hollows, the collective sigh of all conquered people, for polite society absolutely thrives on goodness like the peanuts it can't stop eating.

Oh, forget me. How are you?

All the horrors that get tolerated when help is here almost brings you to tears. Instead of anger there is Christianity!

"Would you have it otherwise?" anyone might ask.

And even Jack'll say, "No."

But still he wants to know what's going on behind all the goodness, to find some evidence of the open wounds of lost generations. There is too much sweet crystallization, not enough bitterness, the agony is too muffled. The screams are too easily wiped away by the soft voice of a nun. The uncertainty of the next step becomes too sure on the right path, then stops altogether. It becomes a still life of the good even though people go about their business. Sometimes they'll watercolor three yellow pears in a dish to capture it.

Okay, maybe it is that Jack is not a part of it. He searches his mind to keep from screaming, is tormented by Munch's black hole threatening to suck him in. He can't really identify what's behind Sister Mary. The emptiness of all the goodness draws him inside its parted lips. The screams of men, women, and children make him want to jump out the nearest window. It's never out of earshot. We constantly drop our eyes at bodies riddled with bullets, torn by bayonets, blown up. You have to go right at the Buckmasters of the world, with the walls in their homes covered with deer heads, and hunting trophies from Africa. Sister Mary is carrying her grandfather inside her like a twelve-point rack looking down at her, a devastated landscape of burning teepees behind, that's why she's here at Holy Family Church in our community.

This unspeakably soft-spoken repentance makes you want to tear your clothes off and run screaming into the snow. The stench of bodies burning you can't get out of your nostrils, human hair and nine-month-old flesh. Sister Mary let your hair down, don't cut it short. You are not man enough to erase the past with the tentacles of your Outreach program. You'll never be able to gather all the Blackfeet children inside your embrace. I know you wisely refused an office. That could help. Maybe the one room has hope, but after the morning light it grows gloomy sitting in the corner, whispering, ministering. I don't even have to be there to see for myself. It makes you seem like you didn't know what is going on. I know they are all gone, it's ancient history. I know that you see the same submissive looks in these people like those your grandfather huddled together and shot. And the secrets of your own life I don't want to speculate, but I'm tempted, Sister Mary, I'm tempted.

What is it that grates on me about goodness? Is it something inside like the snowball with a rock at the center? Something about soft-spokenness packs a wallop. It's not innocent, something's amiss, Sister Mary. I want to pin it down, but you're in the way. I can't get around you. Maybe it is my own tightfistedness, something I can't let go. Maybe I think people should help themselves. There, that's it. But at yard sales, I virtually give what I have away to the needy, am scolded by my wife and daughter.

Maybe my sensitive nostrils get a whiff of sanctimoniousness. But if truth be told it is not that either, although my suspicions keep the thought alive.

I know we are all one, but not garbed in good deeds. There's the rub, that won't let Jack rest, or me, but the article exposes you unfairly. You don't realize all you are taking from the people you help, trapping them with your good will and fine deeds. You might as well clobber them over the head with a blunt instrument. The goodness encourages servitude, ensures their property rights will be generations away. You need to scorn them a little so they rise up, detest you, and help themselves, and rebel on their own, so you too will be a little afraid of your own neck being wrung like those nuns periodically murdered in Central America.

Milton Hershey, the chocolate magnate, is reported to have stood in the shadows, awkward at visiting the orphans he helped. What was his secret? To this day, I don't know. I tried to trace it to Cuba, the sugar mills, to a secret life without Fanny. Goodness bothers me. It keeps squeezing you with its back turned. Makes you gasp to catch your breath running away from it. The indignity alone makes you breathless. When you see the beneficiaries caught, shot through the heart until they are drained of courage, your own fails.

Goodness should do what it has to do and be done with it, not stay thirty-five years in one place. It should look away, embarrassed for others. It shouldn't show its face. Its left hand shouldn't know what the right is doing. Granted it's like evil, a necessary part of us, but it is not scorned enough or even questioned. Otherwise it's unhealthy. In fact, we foolishly fall all over ourselves to reward it. But what we do is encourage the stumbling of others and would be lost ourselves without it. Maybe people occasionally need the pity stops, though not the transfusions of will, the paralysis of being helped. Maybe being a human being is degrading for all of us. This give and take of kindness and ruthless disregard. The latter in an odd way restores our dignity when it inspires a twisted vengeance that thrives on ingratitude. That's the only way to hold your head up. Rectify the imbalance. Maybe it's both sides of the same coin, the expansion of an Outreach program and contraction of Buckmaster's leveling a village to a carbon footprint. Maybe life weighs too much for such a transformation not to take place. We put on the extra pounds ourselves to hide behind the material difficulty of not knowing how the spirit goes soft and steely at the same time. The way fat adheres, we can barely do anything about it, but enjoy the warmth despite the growing burden to the heart. There is too much of us to end lean and hungry. How do we want people to be, shadow or substance? Neither good nor ill, always trying to keep their heads above water. It is about drowning, isn't it? Our marine origins are no accident. We are not the landlubbers we think we are, but fish out of water. Maybe that's the problem, the smell in a few unwelcomed days, the inutility of our gills, caudal appendages, the stereoptic vision that can't resolve any image into one though we force them together.

What Jack resents about Sister Mary is the artificiality, the fake flotation devices she offers, the brevity of all the coffee breaks, and the scattered pieces lying in the shadows afterwards. What he resents is the dishonest attempts at unity. For a moment it holds, but in each really private moment it falls apart. Such a dangerous goodness masks what we are that strikes out of the blue with crushing thunderbolts and you have a holocaust, a Gulf War, three million Vietnamese dead, a million Iraqis and Cambodians, Afghanistan invaded and occupied while the good sit on their hands and spout platitudes about love, democracy, or take refuge in their houses of worship and helping people.

When there's violence in the home, parents in jail, imminent death when Hospice stops all medicines, Sister Mary steps in. When Jack's mother was dying Sister Mary came and listened, visited regularly, that's when Jack got to know her. Well, not really know her. You can't know Sister Mary through the impenetrable wall of goodness that discourages familiarity lest the goodness starts to crumble like plaster. Goodness, in fact, only exists at a distance, uninvestigated. She was all one could ask for, good, kind, listening, always making appointments to come again.

She relieved Jack's burden and his ambivalence towards his mother for dumping him with foster parents and then into an orphanage by the time he was ten. He lived with his mother eleven months of his life and moved her down to Kentucky in her eighties after she was found wandering in the New York City subway, but Sister Mary came and Jack was surprised at how attentive she was.

Jack tried to detect in her soft voice something in her own life that brought her to this dying woman's apartment. Maybe she wanted part of the inheritance, Jack thought, but later dismissed that.

Jack felt the care was genuine; even after his mother died Sister Mary came to her art show. Perhaps Jack needed that to get over the guilt of not treating her better when she was alive. He clearly remembered how he scorned his mother for telling his students in Tokyo that she was an artist.

Sister Mary wrote Jack a note saying that she was glad she met his mother, for she gained more than she gave. Still there was something that bothered Jack.

Maybe it was a suspicion of the shallowness of the feeling. Jack didn't know at the time that goodness can't survive depth, those rapid alterations of emotions, for when goodness is threatened it transfers to someone else without missing a beat. Goodness sinks no roots, and never has a true sense of outrage coating everything with a film of itself. To survive it has to be divorced from deep feeling. Its shallowness is a mask for everything, while deep feeling in its presence stumbles being itself. Goodness is so readily identifiable that it takes up the whole room that you want to run from it. But something was missing in Sister Mary and all the do-gooders who help families, who seem like ministering angels, for underneath the feathers, the extensive wingspan, there is no heart, nothing aches for all those that they soothe. It is as if they ward off their own pain at the expense of those they comfort.

The vacancy of Sister Mary's face, despite strong features and extraordinary calm under a consummate friendliness, looks kindly at people to the extent that her own feelings are kept secret, to the very extent that there is no scream. You plumb Sister Mary, and there isn't even anything erotic. There is no sexuality, but only that eerie calm of the good like the final stage of anesthesia taking effect. Sexuality disturbs with the sloppy mixed blood that goes into creating any new life, but with her it is a ghost town, an abandonment on her pale face. Maybe a black and white habit would be better, for something at the center of her is unoccupied. She is always there for work but only gives the impression of just rolling up her sleeves. That is why an article can appear about her. It'll never mention any demons, but that's the key. Her presence is predicated upon an absent past, the eerie silence that comes with her. Only the wind whistles and nobody is left. The past thirty-five years are like tumbleweed. She is a paradigm for the evanescence of all feelings, for the deceptive substance of goodness like the dew on the grass. No wonder she wants to remain in the shadows. She doesn't exist any more than the feelings do in time, transparent as gossamer we can pin them down no more than what we can pin down when she has left. An icon is a definition of her departure. She's transparent like all goodness that nobody is behind. Our agony punctuated by this feigned concern only wants to get back to licking its wounds and then go on the attack. All that's in between is a pity party, contrived, paying someone back for the horrors that have been perpetrated. People can be walked right through; it is a miracle that we have as much substance as we do, but you bring in the feelings and everything starts to turn false and a lifetime adds up to the wind blowing over a vacant prairie, behind the blue eyes of Sister Mary you know from the first look that you'll never come to the end of her. No black hole haunts her, no scream. It is a headline, an icon, leaving. The people stay, suffer, die, they've had to put up with each other every moment of the day, not bask in helping the needy, not have that aesthetic distance on the suffering of others, the poor, the downtrodden, the lonely. We are all in the same boat. The unerasable smile of Sister Mary is like the horror of a deity, a pitiless red horizon, like the leather harness of Commander Buckmaster under the sweaty animals he rode into the ground, like the countless heads of deer on his wall, so that Sister Mary does good works in Kentucky and is now leaving after being woven into the fabric of the community for thirty-five years like a guilty thread of goodness, shinier than the sweat on the backs of her ancestors running the screaming Indians off their lands.

Why he singled out Sister Mary, Jack still doesn't know, except to hide further inside himself by condemning others for a familiarity he can't bear.

The homeless, the outcasts, the parents in jail, violence in the home, Sister Mary steps in in an odd way, then caulks the gaps with her presence. She'll never gain weight or lose it. Weight is not the issue with her.

Still Jack wants to pin the tail on her when he sees her walking one day with an attractive Mexican girl.

Aha! She's lesbian!

But it is not that easy. Still there was something more buried.

I must find it, Jack tells himself. Am I approaching her easy tread with clodhopper steps, her skipping over the downtrodden, a skating that barely moves except to help? What drives Jack crazy is her helping, what he can't pin down. The suspicion that the feeling has no depth bothers him to no end. The papery shallowness of it insults him, the mask is what he resents, the consummate mummer. He counts four rosary beads hanging on the map of the county in the photo of Sister Mary in the newspaper. Is it not the Lord at all, but Sister Mary who lords over the fallen, the maimed, the needy? What is she after? Certainly it is not the goodness that in Mexico, India, the Philippines gives beggars coins perfunctorily looking away. How can Sister Mary look them in the eye like she does? The pride must be steely-eyed. It is not the invisibility of motive that is so refreshing, but that we can see through anyone to ourselves. Jack doesn't see himself in Sister Mary, that's the problem, he can't find himself. He's lost around her and feels a grudge for her goodness marginalizing him. Goodness has an uncanny knack for that. It is so possessive, so greedy, and ministers to something in itself so thoroughly that no one can see. It grows like a solid, no matter how much it wants to be transparent, like a rock of Gibraltar that no one can question.

"The good that she does, it is splendid, astonishing, we don't have adjectives for it."

"And she's leaving."

"No, I can't believe it."

"Stay, Sister Mary, stay! Oh, get her to stay!"

"I'm afraid her mind is made up."

"Oh, it's her hometown anyway."

"Can't we do something to keep her?"

"No, I'm sorry."

"I'm afraid when Sister Mary's mind is made up, no one can change it!"

59

The crude alternative of the awl will summarize everything about goodness, bring it to a conclusion. Somehow it should be used on her to bring everything together with quick stabbings, for thought won't do it.

Jack has always feared the sharp points of knives, the blade tied into his frustrated reaction to her. That is the only way to resolve this apparent contradiction of human nature, by unearthing the opposite in himself. It has to end like this so he can explain everything by the principle of contraries. In truth he knows there are no opposites, only the singularly misunderstood. The newspaper said Sister Mary was an icon. He wants to prove that she has clay feet and expose something fraudulent. He couldn't find it beyond the day he saw her walking with the attractive Mexican girl. Eureka! he thought. He had figured her out. But that faded when he never saw her with the girl again. And what was wrong with that anyway? Perfectly nothing unless it exposed a secret motive. It would make the goodness acceptable even, humanize it, so it couldn't stand like the authority of a Deity that was, well, just good. Although even He got angry, jealous, possessing all the attributes that define us. But Sister Mary couldn't be defined, so Jack sought to unlock her.

That's why he went to her house that night to find her secret. He thought the awl would do it, that frightful tool he was never comfortable having in his house. But he found she left and concluded that he couldn't summarize her for what it left of himself like the unusable minerals in hard water. He was always burdened with the residue. He was worth nothing if he couldn't figure out what inspired such calm self-assurance. It gave the lie to his whole life and polarized him from himself. He thought he knew who he was, but she threatened that that he wanted to plunge the awl back into himself. It'd be the end of him not able to figure her out, get to the bottom of her, overturn every stone with one gesture and find the obscene low life in himself. His hand was sweaty on the bulbous black head of the instrument inside his pocket. He always knew low life intimately and accepted it, but the goodness upset the scales. He recognized the slithering in himself and had no illusions he would be found out. Even to think of the awl was lower than serpentine. It wasn't even a man's instrument like what bludgeoned the heads of Blackfeet. The sneaky awl under the clothes threatened everything hard, determined to be its skinny self. The contempt made him second guess himself, his own treatment of his dying mother. At the time he didn't revolt, but it brewed, simmered, stewed inside him. In fact, he had forgotten about the nun until he read the newspaper. The very contrast to his own behavior by Sister Mary bothered him. He was desperate to find her Achilles' heel, for her coming to the apartment made him unnecessary, threw him out into the cold. His mother waited for her, not for him. He had completely forgotten wanting to strangle the sister for her goodness. It was downright evil of her to replace his mother's feelings and soothe her with her presence. What did she have to be there for? His mother being a nurse recognized compassion, but Jack saw through it with a laserlike precision that burned to uncover the truth. Such an excited emission of photons taken for compassion was the lie underneath. He couldn't identify it but he was going to find out. Maybe it was the simple jealousy in Jack that informs everything, but kindness seemed milkish compared to what Jack was feeling. He scorned the size of her breasts. He was going to get to the bottom of her, Jack thought as the awl poked his leg when he moved. He knew the irony of his mother sewing fresh pockets into his pants. Despite the stiff coarseness of the material that was how she showed her warmth! And so what was Jack getting angry at Sister Mary for? Maybe it is a conspiracy of Marys. After all both are to blame, they have the same name. "Mary is the mother of God," his own mother would always say, before cackling in her high-pitched voice exhibiting her human frailties all the more. Maybe Sister Mary was the lightning rod for all the ill feelings he had always had towards his mother, though he knew that similarities of name are enough to make you dive headfirst into the grave, or into an empty pool.

If he could only prove a motive, and leave the rest for others. He'd intensify it by sticking her, but beneath the habit she didn't wear, absent a white wimple, through the mannish clothes she always dressed in, that sweater that came up to her neck even in warm weather, proving there was no body there. Didn't she sweat like the rest of us? Was she no more real than a single fly on the wall, always listening, reflecting us in her glasses that almost hid her face that you had to hunt for the features through the dazzling light, ferret out some shameful agility that she was keeping from you, hiding her body inside the clothing except for the noticeably defined breasts. They weren't unassertively large but so well-concealed in the turtlenecks that their function was perplexing. They didn't seem a fortress, yet they served as a kind of barricade. She was the dike he was trying to puncture while holding back the water with his finger, so she could go about her work while he was pained trying to retard her. Or was this so much sophistry for not being able to live with himself, for the giant charade of goodness that gave the lie to western civilization, the white man's burden to native populations, to the Sioux, Blackfeet, and Cherokee? Jack saw in Sister Mary all the mysterious smugness beneath a confusing film of piety. The myth of the last being first, of the rich man no more likely to get into heaven than camels can pass through the eye of a needle. Jack wanted to puncture all that, at the same time keep his finger in the dike. But she was gone. He couldn't even draw blood, be equal to the violence he feared.

Sister Mary metamorphosed into Kurtz crawling on all fours, but he couldn't prove it to reassure himself. If he could only live with himself, not have to endure the torment of being like someone else, an impossible icon! No wonder he wanted to smash through the goodness we mask a hundred times a day, that stifling superiority that pulls us all down. That was it! Sister Mary's calm goodness pulled Jack down, but because of its sheer shallowness his escape was hopeless. He feared drowning in the feelings he couldn't show his mother, in their personality clash, while Sister Mary sashayed in and just took over, filled the void, diminished Jack, made him feel like nothing, not even a son for his dying mother whose wheezing in the end he was unsympathetic to.

He remembered clearly when he wouldn't help her out of the car at a rest stop in West Virginia on the Interstate, refusing to play valet and hold the door for her. He wanted to teach her a lesson. She promptly fell down at the curb that a stranger rushed over to help her up.

All Jack could manage afterwards was to whisper, "You did it on purpose!"

He had so much anger towards her and here comes the sister in dungarees with her always off-white turtleneck sweaters. She must have a whole closet full of them, open, friendly, warm, and intelligent; she had to be hiding something! He'd find out, he'd penetrate it even if he was drowned in horror. Underneath they were the same! He wanted to plumb Sister Mary to find the injuries bandaged over with smiles and such an exemplary understanding of others. Compassion is such a false accompaniment to the awl that tells the truth with one thrust. She is so far from real passion that she should be ashamed to pretend to feelings she doesn't have. And here Jack thought he was going to expose her! Instead he threw the awl away into the darkness of the abandoned lot beside the Southern Belle milk processing plant.

His life had been a living hell with Sister Mary in it. She upset the order. Christ too must have gotten away with murder those two decades. He had to have changed his name not to leave his bloody footprint. He must have been nothing like the twelve-year-old in the temple, more like the one nailed to the cross twenty-one years later. Something went on, like with Sister Mary, some slaughter, some massacre in his past, if not a thousand indiscretions. He couldn't possibly be all things to all people, or we would have heard. Okay, he went undercover because like Sister Mary something was going on back in the Plains, if only a past that everyone even today is hush hush about. You think nothing happens under a prairie sky and that the blood cannot run for the flatness of the land, but it spills nevertheless. That's what the two were involved in, though you'd never tell it by the radiant countenance. Well not Sister Mary, but certainly artists' rendering of Jesus. But it is the mask of Sister Mary that Jack is trying to expose. She has it like everyone else, like the two decades the absent Jesus bears testimony to, that's why they are hidden. Uncover it and it will make your life's work satisfying, or better, we all can finally live with ourselves!

But Jack couldn't even draw blood, he wasn't man enough. Sister Mary he knew was a dead end to protect himself. Outside the newspaper article her departure was final. She left town early so people would not be snooping around her past, anticipating those with awls wanting to get at the elusive goodness she gave the residents of the town. The lesbian label didn't stick. Still it would have humanized her, made her one of us. There have to be corpses in the closet, for everything is too undistributed if they are confined only to graves.

All the goodness of the church of Jack's childhood outside real life, the smile of the Irish, the piety of the Italian, priests who had their secrets, was strengthened too by the nuns who smashed pupils' heads against the blackboards. Maybe it was that that Jack was trying to puncture in Sister Mary, but by that time she was on her way to Iowa as Jack passed the house she used to live in one night when it occurred to him that Sister Mary may never reach Iowa, and perhaps never really lived in their own town though she left the idea of goodness that everyone could read about.

Baseball

The sheer mastery, the craftsmanship of the foreign-born pitcher stunned all of us. The curves, the sliders, drops, the forkballs, knuckleball, and his patented splitter. He brought his kids to the ballpark just to see him, their heritage on the mound. The phenom from Japan captured the imagination of baseball fans everywhere. To watch him go through all the junk in his arsenal, to hurl it at the American players, was a pleasure to any lover of baseball. His fastball reached the nineties, but would speed up later in the game as needed when he bore down, or to get out of a jam. He had the habit of giving up to the first batter a hit or a home run to get his own attention, then he'd get down to business, tighten the screws, and get his ten strikeouts by the sixth or seventh innings.

By midseason he had completed the most games in the major leagues. He had opposing players swinging at pitches out of the strike zone that looked like they could be hit just before the ball dove into the dirt.

Some must have sensed the foreign players were getting back for the savage bombings of Tokyo, the invasion of the mainland, the long occupation after World War II. Japanese players had been coming over for a couple of decades, finding retribution, but here was truly the battleship *Yamato*. Hiroshi Akagawa was sinking one major league player after another with what one sports writer in the end called his kamikaze pitch, the splitter that fooled players not only from the US, but from the Dominican Republic, Cuba, Haiti, even players from as far away as Korea.

Dim suggestions also of the reprisal for Hiroshima and Nagasaki sometimes entered sports writers' commentary. Some even mentioned the internment of so many Japanese Americans during the war, America's outrage toward its own citizens that was somehow now being addressed by the heroics of Akagawa.

"The poor Japanese soldiers," I was shocked to hear one Japanese colleague say to me in Tokyo to show the powerful myopia that still exists about the role of Japanese soldiers in the war.

Then came the slider to almost erase all politics as another batter whiffed assuring no one would be stealing home. But the splitter like a divine wind fooled everyone as batter after batter struck out expecting the ball to be where the next moment it wasn't. Then when they least expected it Akagawa's fastball flew by them, left spectators stunned and batters devastated. Of course there were racist epithets hurled at Akagawa, but most fans even on the road marveled at his efficiency, at the stupefying control the Japanese pitcher had, and the clever way he mixed pitches, caught batters totally off guard, used the element of surprise attack that some called outright sneakiness that defined a whole people decades ago. Batters with wads of chewing tobacco in their bulging cheeks, or bubble gum, batters scratching their crotches or licking their fingers with a synchronicity that ill-matched the exquisite timing of Akagawa, undisciplined batters who despite their rituals in and out of the batter's box looked threatening swinging their bats, as if they were just short of attacking the mound. They too were mowed down by the Japanese pitcher. Big men, unlike the shorter versions he faced so successfully in Japan, looked foolish swinging at air chasing after Akagawa's pitches.

"Timber!" some wanted to yell, anticipating another home run that would bring everyone to their feet, that suddenly turned into a strikeout as one big man after another went down like falling trees.

Akagawa threaded the needle with astonishing precision and ended leading the league in strikeouts. Major leaguers were dusted off, like he was a housewife cleaning a baseboard; just when the player thought he had a fat juicy pitch to hit out of the park, the ball would drop from sight. Some even brought their bat around a second time trying to account for the missing balls.

The drop seemed never to hit bottom, but had players fanning the hot summer air, cooling the Yankee catcher energized by Akagawa's pinpoint pitches. The Japanese national seemed more than a baseball player, a clear reprisal by a people over sixty years ago terribly humiliated, a country devastated by war, ravaged by starvation, demoralized in the unspeakable aftermath of Hiroshima and Nagasaki. There was a cultural silence that Hiroshi Akagawa was now addressing. You suspected the war lingered in the minds of every Japanese, even those born after the events, that it was part of their collective psyche that no Japanese would ever forget. They were the guinea pigs of the world, the only country where a nuclear bomb had been dropped, not once but twice, and the consequences were so horrid that it was never used again. Who could tolerate that but by ignoring the black and white footage that is rarely seen today of flies on victims' bodies, an unspeakable lassitude the likes of which the world had never seen, and despite that the one superpower continues to build up its nuclear arsenal. It must be privately obscene to the average Japanese who remains unspoken in a world ruled by Americans.

How to combat that but by sending over the number one technician from Japan, the fixer, a man who hadn't lost a game in Japan all last season. Some thought he would never duplicate that feat in the States, that Japanese baseball was overrated, and could never compete with the major leagues despite earlier successes. But here Akagawa was with only one loss midway through the season who after eleven wins was leading all pitchers in the major leagues. Who could argue with that?

✢

Finally, when Akagawa's thirteenth game is almost history, a ball is hit. The crack of the bat echoes throughout the stadium. Most are paying attention, some are not. It's the sixth inning after all on a sultry night in Riverfront Stadium at an interleague game. Many fans have gloves at the ready to supplement those on the field. Many would die to make a catch, risk life and limb leaping over seats or under railings; it is what they go to the game for, to fulfill their dreams and be part of big-league play.

It is a slow game that has the kids dawdling over what is near at hand, a bag of peanuts, pestering their parents for ice cream, punching or scratching their sister or brother, children mesmerized over the antics of someone drunk, or quieted over their own parents openly arguing, youths horsing around, friends joking with one another over an opposing player, someone yelling insults at a batter. Some fans are so hopelessly intoxicated by the later innings that they get so loud, brash to the public's fascination or amusement, to the chagrin of their families or the prompting of their buddies. Some shame their families who vow never to come to another game. It is all in all a convivial atmosphere, the heat getting to everyone gradually relieved by the giant scoreboard displays or fireworks, by the alcohol, the iced drinks, or the occasional breeze through the stadium. Studs flaunt their beautiful wives or girlfriends, dressed to the nines, openly kiss despite the many families like Mickey's who bring their kids.

This case is doubled-edged. Mickey's wife, Reiko, is Japanese and so his kids Kenji and Keiko are what in Japan are called *hafu*. They straddle the bloodlines of two nations, the American and what has now become also the Japanese pastime. Mickey sits with his kids to share in both cultures. Reiko used to watch games with her father growing up in Japan and developed a passion for the game she is trying to instill in both her children. *Basebaru*, as it is called, invaded the homeland, and since the nineties Japanese players have been recruited by the majors. The influx of pitching aces has had the biggest impact though they often flame out after a year or two.

Pitchers with remarkable control, exquisite training, exacting discipline, and a work ethic second to none have had an immediate impact and inspired Japanese fans from Queens to Seattle to follow their favorite players. It has been nothing less than the Yankee pinstripes for Hiroshi Akagawa to match the storied Yomiuri Giants in his homeland. It is a marketing dream, and a veritable feast of baseball, with most all of Japan, over a hundred and thirty million people, watching their countryman's every pitch, his every at bat. The people rise early to catch the games that fill everyone's morning, housewives at home or husbands at work, for companies set up TVs for their employees, and schools get in on the act, and certainly it is carried on the iPhones of the kids. Everyone follows their national heroes in the majors.

Akagawa's popularity has been meteoric now that he is in his first season with the New York Yankees. In fact, he is meant to bring them back into playoff contention. One imagines like the Filipino boxer Manny Pacquiao, he could even run for Parliament and win a seat in his homeland. Everyone digs into their morning rice bowls and drinks their green tea watching every move of Akagawa. Each grain of rice cleaned up with the ends of their chopsticks employs a precision not unlike the cleanest strikes of Akagawa, and though a grain may slide off the chopstick they are readjusted in an instant just as Akagawa quickly readjusts his fingers on the seams of a ball to alter his next delivery and baffle another batter. The food is similarly delivered to every Japanese's mouth with accuracy in the complicated ritual of feeding themselves in front of the TV barely remembering the scanty rations immediately following the war.

"The bigger they are the harder they fall," the Japanese commentator translates an American saying as another batter whiffs.

"Gottem!" and the next one goes down in only three pitches.

"Ten pitches for the whole inning. No waste for Akagawa today!" the announcer bellows.

"Remarkable" a broadcaster exclaims for what Akagawa has accomplished his first year. "No rookie has ever equaled his performance. Not even Hideo Nomo!"

"It is truly remarkable. He's the man of the hour, a man among men, and look his size is good but not towering."

"He has the best splitter on the planet!" someone says.

"He's a craftsman, not flashy but workmanlike. A man of his people," the American announcer says.

"When the going gets tough, he bears down," another adds.

✻

One thing that has baffled Mickey about the game that he too loved as a kid, famous for his side-armed pitch, was seeing his kids play and thinking about, despite the helmets they wore, the danger of the ball. Secretly he was glad when Kenji stopped playing baseball, but now he is happy to take his children to see these extraordinary heroics of his wife's countryman.

The seats this evening are on the third base line, about thirty rows back. Mickey is absorbed for six innings, but then his attention wanders. He's telling Reiko about something at home. They start to argue. Reiko immediately picks up on his sarcasm, says something back. Keiko is meanwhile absorbed with her ice cream sandwich, and Kenji resentful that she won't share it is finishing his popcorn when there is the crack of the bat.

Akagawa had just streamed a fast ball slightly out of the strike zone. The right-handed Reds' batter jumped on the ninety-three mile-an-hour pitch. He got good wood on it, a solid connection that he pulls too hard. It's clearly foul, a virtual line drive just behind third base. The power of the connecting bat makes the ball a projectile that could have been launched from the barrel of a gun. It is faster than Akagawa threw it.

It catches even fans with gloves off guard. Instinctively they part when the ball comes towards them. It is so fast that the ones behind can't see, as many are standing for the runner on third. It is like the Red Sea parting for a projectile that by the sheer will of Akagawa's pitch toward home plate is now rerouted off the bat towards the crowd behind third base. The ball goes straight towards the place of vulnerability, not towards the left field that is completely empty except for the one Yankee fielder. It has been pulled too hard.

Could the magical Akagawa reroute his pitch, take it back, he surely would have. Could the architects have altered their blueprints of the stadium, surely someone's design might have

70

forestalled what happened. Or the nets behind home plate could have been extended. Or maybe had they not sold beer, or the player's timing wasn't thrown off by scratching himself, or fans were on their toes not drinking so much, that may have improved everyone's reaction time. A glove might have reached the ball first.

That is why they brought them, so many wanna be major leaguers. Had fans not been distracted but more attentive, not showing off their big mouths, their swagger, their women, her expensive clothes, low-cut dresses, maybe the outcome would have been different. Had it not been the sixth inning but the seventh inning stretch, they could reassemble their energies and focus better on every swing. Had the temperature not been a sultry ninety, but dropped a few degrees, and the humidity more tolerable, or the breeze more active making everyone a tad bit more alert. Had they all been more attentive on this warm evening at Riverfront Stadium, or had Akagawa's fast ball been late or a fraction early or a mile slower so the batter could have straightened out his swing so the ball reached the left field fence, even at the expense of a home run, instead of being pulled, the outcome would have been different.

Perhaps there could have been a flaw in the bat, dead wood that broke it, or had the batter connected at the trademark, the bat's weakest point, the ball instead might have dribbled back to the pitcher's mound, but no. It headed straight for the third base crowd that parted one after another, right for the little boy, Mickey and Reiko's son, the *hafu*, bridge between East and West, who absorbed both cultures, and buried the animosities of each, the arrogance of one, the sneaking surprise of the other with now its stunning arsenal of pitches.

The little boy's glove was in his lap as he scarfed down his popcorn to keep the bag away from the clawing fingers of his sister who wouldn't share her ice cream with him. Mickey was still arguing with Reiko when the ball struck his son in the forehead and his little drink jumped up in the air upset by his arm when his body rocketed back as the ball ricocheting from pitcher to batter found its mark and smashed into one of the most vulnerable foreheads in Riverfront Stadium.

What more can be said? Anything less would not describe the irony of everyone coming for a good time to worship their heroes. Nets are placed behind home plate but extend only partially up each baseline. After that there was nothing. Like Archibald MacLeish's poem about the big top, there was "Nothing—nothing at all."

The crack of the bat could scatter balls all around the stadium. Did anyone not think of that? Mickey himself, admittedly excited over Akagawa, had even researched years before to find just out how many fans had been injured, killed, by baseballs at major league stadiums, but he came up with nothing solid. Was there a history intentionally unrecorded? Balls are hit into the stands at least a hundred miles an hour. The laws of probability would have to pick someone out. Most likely the oldest and youngest, despite all the adult supervision. The balls could travel faster than their reaction time.

The heckling was sometimes awful. Maybe there was a private feeling of deserts among the players. Maybe the risks were calculated as acceptable, or there was some disclaimer on the tickets in small print or above the turnstiles.

"You bum, go home!"

"Cheater! You're a drugstore robot, Mathews!"

"Martin, you're a punk."

"You got a glass arm Kuroda, you won't last the season."

"Weaver, you're a disgrace to your uniform! Go back to Texas."

But the workmanship continued. Here was the best of seasons for a Japanese pitcher that Mickey had, despite the futility of his search years ago, taken his kids to see. Without realizing it he like everyone else in the stadium was playing the odds.

The ball struck Kenji smack in the forehead, and the drink and popcorn and unshared ice cream sandwich were nothing compared to how it drove Mickey's son straight into the seat behind where his body collapsed like a rag doll. His head hit the ground and immediately swelled to twice its size, spawn of a single hardball that seemed now to come out of his forehead.

It was astonishing that so careful a pitcher as Akagawa, on target for a Cy Young award, almost 12–1, slated to start in the All-Star game in a couple of weeks, a master on the mound, a perfectionist the likes of which baseball had not seen in years, could not control what happened to that one pitch that struck Mickey's little boy. That Akagawa threw the ball, that it was hit foul, that it ended smashing into the head of a little boy, come to pay homage to this phenom from his mother's country, was beyond irony that absolutely crumbles before what happened.

Who are these foreigners that have invaded our homeland, flooded our major leagues, found an ally from intermarriage, and now this? Does it not show something's wrong with the game? That people should not come together when there is such a horrifying outcome? What does it mean, so many sitting ducks in the stands, unwittingly arguing, loud, drunk, so self-satisfied feeding their faces? Actually getting on the best they can as human beings. Did they, do we all after all, just play the percentages? Someone's always going to get picked off, in a car wreck, on the battlefield, at a sports event! Should we not travel, go to war, amuse ourselves? Should everyone just stay at home and stop this irresponsible intermarriage that brings cultures together with such a horrifying scenario? The revenge factor after all is always there. But how is this revenge? This just happened.

Nothing just happens. There is a method to this insanity. Eating ice cream and popcorn, both parents arguing, the sibling rivalry, the heat and humidity, the fact that it was the sixth inning, everyone was tired, concentrating on their drinks on a warm evening in July at Riverfront Stadium, amusing themselves rattling ice in their paper cups, the game not grabbing their attention like it should, is this not certainly a sad commentary on the gathering? That the result should come to this? That the near perfection of an almost 12–1 record should be so devastating to the life of a little boy. Something is wrong.

Can Kenji be to blame for the surprise attack sixty years

before, for the internments of Japanese Americans taken from their homes to relocation camps, for the brutal fire bombing of Tokyo, for the cruelty of Japanese soldiers throughout Southeast Asia, for the Occupation, for the economic revenge on the American market being overtaken by Japanese carmakers, for the bubble bursting? Do you throw a little boy to the wolves for that? Do we have to speak in hushed whispers about the aftereffects of Hiroshima and Nagasaki, or the brutality of Japanese soldiers on Saipan? Is this little boy the upshot of that, and the carom off the bat from the Japanese national's fastball, did it hurry for its target with an added speed, a vengeful pace carrying all the resentment of two cultures that had built up to this? Is the Reds player responsible too? Who is he, by the way, what nationality? Is it a misdirected anger at the surprise attack all over again, abetted by Hiroshi Akagawa at the Reds Riverfront Stadium? Who'd have expected it, on a popcorn eater, a little boy, until you learn he is a *hafu*, a false reconciliation between both cultures.

All Japan heard about Akagawa hitting someone, first a little boy, then that his mother was Japanese and there was stunned silence.

"That'll teachem," some said.

Others said, "Teachem what?"

"They can't be mixed. What is he doing over there anyway but conquering the country like Japan should have done in the first place.

"But we were humiliated."

"We never should have surrendered. And unconditionally!"

"Now this. Akagawa himself, the most valuable Yankee! The turncoat!"

It made some people dizzy.

"But with a little boy, half Japanese."

"Still he's a *hafu*!"

"Who could get away with that?"

The pitcher's excellence faded with the horror of what

happened.

Akagawa was driven out of the All-Star game, scattering seven hits in the first eight batters he faced, and later he fell out of the Yankee's rotation in the second half of the season.

Kenji's swollen brain lasted for weeks, into late September.

Akagawa was done for, like the boxer Emile Griffith who killed Benny Paret. He had a reason for cornering him so savagely on the ropes, but he was never the same boxer after that.

Akagawa stopped pitching for the rest of the season. He visited the boy's bedside every day until the swelling subsided.

He never returned to the mound. The field was finally leveled for him and he was traded by the Yankees.

The Alumnus of the Year

Kalid and Hamid's family were nomads forced to relocate after their uncle was killed at a dispute over well water.

Their mother had died of childbed fever with their stillborn brother a hundred miles from the nearest hospital.

Towards evening their silhouettes darkened the dunes for what seemed an eternity as their father led his two sons across the vast desert to the bazaar at Basra to trade in dates.

As the boys slept under the night sky they dreamed of magic carpets, colorful fabrics, the ornate shapes of hookahs, shiny copperware, the whirling sounds of flutes, an array of scents, snakes and birds of every color, condiments, syrups, lotions for the body, veiled servant girls bringing pistachio sherbet, sweet melons, fruity bars of indescribable desserts glazed with syrup and dusted with coconut, grenadine drinks made from fresh pomegranates, a countless display of confections whose sugars speedily crystallized on the surface.

Everything vividly contrasted to the monotony of the hot desert, to the splay step of the camel, to the sag of its top load, to the fierce blazing sun before its last red rays disappeared into a cluster of cool palms. The night offered a reprieve of scenarios unimaginable during daylight.

The boys wondered at the stars sprinkled overhead before their eyelids involuntarily closed, while the small campfire shadowed the cheekbones of their sleeping father.

Biting into a sweetmeat, staining the near perfection of the rectangular candy, the boys were rudely awakened by the intrusive sunlight and gritty sound of their father's sandal. It was a daily balancing act, for those who had invented the zero, to keep their bellies from shrinking to naught.

Since their uncle had died the treks across the hot sand were more punishing. Another family link had been broken, as their father sat gazing for hours at the sheer vacancy of the desert.

When his wife had died, Kalid and Hamid seemed cut off

from his affections as cleanly as their camel's footprint was erased by the collapsing grains of sand. The two boys blamed themselves for losing their mother, as if their youth and preoccupation with sweets somehow caused it, just as any vitality insults the memory of those who have passed away. Their father's warmth was now buried like the imagined flanks of a woman outlining the next dune. The hot sands kept him going, yielding to the curves of his wife's body underfoot.

It is remarkable how individual dramas play out in worlds barely imagined, as we peacefully enter an oasis, a bazaar, forgetting the endless beauty of the stars and the sparkle of sand.

Suddenly there is an explosion of anger at a well, a well-calculated blow to the temple, collapsing a grown man like a house of cards, as a tiny rill of blood trickles out an earhole. And as there is no hospital, no physician that can help, what's left of the family picks up and moves on. The authorities comb the rubble for clues but end up running the teeth through their own hair the next morning after splashing aftershave.

Sometimes the unreality of a blast will send the tiniest fragments, or sharpest projectiles, hurtling through space with such accelerated slow motion that they seem unreal. Dumbfounded we look at the fragment of bone that travels so fast as if to reconstitute the skeleton before it lodges in the soft flesh of a palm tree, or bounces like a toothpick on a cobblestone demonstrating some elementary law of physics. Body parts follow almost unrecognizable as anyone's relative.

The family entered the bazaar. After selling their dates, the boys raced to the confection booth clutching the coins their father had given them. They could hardly sleep the night before, imagining the sweets they would buy.

The boys truly loved each other. They shared candy as if it were one mouth, taking pleasure in the sweets melting on their palates. The nougats, the thick-jellied colloidal suspensions, the pink dots and rectangles peeled off long strips of white paper one by one, the assortment of powdered juicy fruits and colorful licorice; their choices were dizzying as their poverty multiplied the pleasures on their tongue. The complex sugars, the fructose and the sucrose, educated every nook and cranny as they vacuumed and swirled the riot of taste around their mouths, each buccal cavity cornering a sweet before it attached to the roof of the mouth to release additional sugars, while the tongue stood sentry mixing the sweetness with saliva. The boys were masters of confection, as only the poor can be, and knew to the hundredth of a dinar the exact sensations a coin could buy.

After they bought their cache the two boys repaired to the nearest cluster of palm trees, and sat cross-legged to observe the procession of shoppers in the bazaar and await their father.

The boys were perfectly content, smiling blissfully through the succession of sweets in their mouths, truly in seventh heaven at such an embarrassment of riches. How lucky they were for the extended dry season, for this year's dates were sweeter as the translucent brown indicated a thinner tunic around the seed so their load fetched a higher price and their father was correspondingly more generous.

Their father had stopped at the bagman's shop to purchase an enlarged sack, next to one of the most expensive carpet merchants in all of Basra, when the explosion came.

He was lifted out of the bazaar along with the carpet merchant's patron, Karim el Har, a prominent Shiite leader. Both rained down on the earth in pieces. The bone that flew by the two boys was followed by body parts, torn bags, swatches of carpet, splintered tent poles, and an appalling unwinding of internal organs like pink balloons and twisted red ribbons.

Even the glass from the confection stand shattered through sweetmeats and into shoppers' faces.

The scattering of debris obliterated any memory of the tourist in khaki pants and shirt carrying a camera who had ducked out of sight only moments before. Though some witnesses reported him to the police, the newspapers never mentioned him. Nevertheless, the story circulated on the streets about the curious immunity of foreigners.

Newspapers reported that Karim el Har had been killed by

a rival faction, though no one claimed responsibility. Editorials speculated that the government had many enemies who often fell out with each other. The CIA wasn't publicly implicated, but everyone suspected their involvement, rumors often verified only after the operatives had left the country and the regime had changed hands. Six people in all were killed, and thirteen injured.

Kalid and Hamid were brought unharmed but stupefied to a shelter where they fell that night under the watchful eye of missionaries from Bethlehem, Pennsylvania. The missionaries had learned of the explosion and had gone immediately to the hospital where they found the two desert boys who had lost their father. All their belongings, even their camel, had been destroyed in the blast.

The two boys touched no food, nor did they seem to have interest in the confection gumming their sweaty palms, squeezed beyond recognition. Their eyes were glazed when they learned that their father was dead. It was remarked that the boys, who had no known relatives, might even owe money for the expense of disposing of their camel's remains.

The missionaries whispered about finding a new life for the boys who soon recovered their appetites, though a pall curtained their eyelids when questioned about the bombing, and their sleep remained uneasy. The roofs now over their heads precluded observation of stars and the reassuring sounds of nocturnal life on the desert.

✻

There must be a key to why the philanthropist left the orphanage all his money. His biographer reported that he was "shy with boys," and "seldom talked much" even when he visited once a month. He'd remain in the corner and let the houseparent or second help attend to them. Maybe it was the powerful appeal of the penny candy that drew him to them, but then put him off for the cavities all those sweet tooths developed. Maybe it was the monotony of the nights wrapping candies with his mother and Aunt Mattie, then taking basketfuls to sell on the streets of Philadelphia and Lancaster.

The philanthropist was the Pied Piper who had whole communities of children trailing after him. It was the unfair appeal to their appetites when they were at their most vulnerable and couldn't afford dentists and had to live with the pain in their little mouths as the sticky sugars ate into the dentine, maybe that made him shy with children. Some didn't even suck, just chewed the candy outright, champing down to establish dominance over the sweet. Maybe the candy man had guilt over that. When we have anyone so firmly in the palm of our hands we withdraw from them to stand in the shadows, ashamed of the control we have over their frailties.

When someone says I want to go into the food business, immediately bells go off. You imagine a Pharaoh's giant storage bins, biblical control during the seven lean years, an absolute power over people.

Children are so easily seduced with sweets and the philanthropist recognized early on that the addition of milk could give consistency even to caramel. He found that secret out in Denver where he had followed his shiftless father before relocating back East.

A philanthropist is motivated by an array of impulses too vast to catalogue, the basest we won't even consider. The simplest is that Fanny couldn't have children. It's surprising with such a broad-bottomed name to fall back on. Anyway, that was the reason given for deciding to start a school for orphan boys.

The vats of chocolate deeper than the waists of grown men and more capacious than even the roundest body size were daunting. The giant hydraulic sweep of the spatula mixing the thick brown waves of chocolate back and forth made for a powerful impression on the appetite. How could anyone escape, like the pot that would not stop boiling, the spilling out the factory doors and windows, down Main street, the milk chocolate traveling around the lampposts topped with candy kisses, down to the amusement park and the zoo where caged animals already slept on cocoa bean mulch, all the way down to the Swatara River outside town, chocolate coating everything in sight?

The confection informed the night dreams of almost every citizen in the town, connected as they all were with the chocolate factory. Chocolate coating peanuts, almonds, blown rice, and little boys and girls as they slept, wrapping stickily around their white teeth, eating into the hardest substance of their bodies. It was chocolate dreams out of hand churning back and forth in those giant vats of bittersweet and milk chocolate.

During the Great Depression the philanthropist employed the whole town when the rest of the country was out of work. He built a giant hotel and country club, a large indoor ice hockey arena, an independent rail line to the chocolate factory, a sports stadium, and an amusement park with one of the largest roller coasters in the world.

Still the cold sweats of the factory workers were legendary. They went home after each shift jittery from the machines, from the constant movement of the shiny hydraulic like a giant reproductive unit with its lubricated precision that interfered with the pleasures of their sex life.

The little droplets of kisses overwhelmed onlookers even in factory tours. Some fainted from a visible chocolate reaction. There was something threatening about all the kisses ending up being dropped so uniformly without any of the messiness of human beings applying their mouths to each other. The warm brown globules adhering to white paper were a model of sanitation and self-sufficiency. The aluminum foil wrapped the kiss like a preserved memory so precisely that children squealed, "Mommy, can we come back again!"

Row after row of bars were boxed like legions of chocolate soldiers and sent around the world, expressions of the free enterprise system that seduced the appetites of everyone. The chocolate in K rations during World War II transformed every sweet tooth to a life sustaining food rallying for democracy. Today chocolate is classified as a food, not a candy, and historians credit it for helping to win the war. Few admit chocolate is habit-forming, a narcotic, little different from that terrible melodic lure of the Pied Piper where children are led through the nose by the confectionery success.

Little wonder the philanthropist wanted to give back, have the orphanage end up controlling the factory lock, stock, and barrel, as a kind of poetic justice for the confection so thoroughly manipulating the sensibilities of children.

Every seduction always has its comeuppance. Seduce kids then kill them with kindness. Give them three square meals a day and put a roof over their heads, give them a suitcase of clothes and one hundred dollars to make their way in the world and something will spring back into place. We get repaid.

The philanthropist knew that the complete control he exercised over the children's appetite was unfair, and so he vowed to take care of the neediest. It was a gesture almost without parallel, tying up your stock in the neediest, like Jesus suffering only the children to come to him, after seducing them with sweets.

The philanthropist became an institution, the town a part of the culture that never questioned his motives of bringing pleasure to so many, appealing to their tastes, narcotizing them with a gift the Aztecs thought came from the gods, a divine food, till the very air of the town that bore his name was redolent with the rich smell of the confection every time it rained. Cocoa beans were the mulch of record and the streets were named Chocolate and Cocoa avenues, like the town in the highlands of Cuba where the Founder owned sugar cane mills. Even cocoa butter became the soap of choice for most of the town's citizenry.

✤

The school was waiting for just such boys like George Brent. When his mother came and picked George up he was only eight, legally an orphan since his father had died when he was eleven months old. He was taken away from an old woman and her daughter whom he loved for their kindness. The day he was supposed to leave he hoped his invariably tardy mother would never come, but this time she was on time.

George was watching a jungle movie that afternoon and he prayed it would never end. It was the saddest day of his life. His mother wouldn't tell the old woman where she was taking George, only that he was being placed in a school somewhere in Pennsylvania.

On the way to the bus stop, his mother told the teary-eyed, unwed thirty-five-year-old daughter that she should have children of her own.

George never forgot the long ride to Pennsylvania, the Pez candy gun, or the two clear plastic inserts full of ammunition. Numbers comfort us against the vagaries of fate. The ammunition was not to shoot anyone, but to protect his feelings nevertheless, something he could store up and count to employ against the unfamiliarity of his new home.

George should have been overwhelmed by the chocolate, but while children are easily seduced, even sweets quickly eat through to the loneliness exposing aching nerves that often cannot be appeased by a mouthful of candy as easily as adults think. Children always have a nose for blackmail.

At first George consoled himself with the thought that he was going to run away, but the thought gradually dissipated around the twenty-one boys. He lived on various farms at the Home as the orphanage was called. George had an unremarkable school career, outside a certain facility with foreign languages nurtured by the constant drilling of his German teacher, Herr Schwarz, who was fascinated that one of his graduates collected Nazi memorabilia. George developed an ease of recall that became second nature and quickly enabled him to excel.

The life of the boys was remote from the events of the world. They milked the cows every morning and evening, huddled up against their warm bodies in the coldest weather, and sent the milk to the nearby chocolate factory. The more athletic of the boys milked by hand to build up their muscles.

George was assigned to housework too, doing dishes,

cleaning silverware with silver polish and the baseboards with toothbrushes, shining the linoleum floors with shiners, moving back and forth on cut-off pant legs. George took his turn as cook, making oatmeal, eggs, toast, and pancakes for twenty-one boys.

When George left the Home he went into the Army and was sent to a special school because of his aptitude for languages, and later attended a major university for an advanced degree before being recruited by the CIA for covert operations training.

It was the cold war era and so everyone was on edge after the Korean conflict, and more than willing to do their patriotic duty rooting out communists who would upset the most prosperous period in the history of man. Men like George fanned out around the world infiltrating foreign governments to protect the interests of democracy against the contagion of communism, socialism, or whatever threatened our way of life.

George, like most CIA operatives, served his country in an organization whose methods, destabilizing foreign governments, rigging elections, fomenting riots, assassinating undesirables, never clouded his loyalty. Even dictators and military juntas were supported if their interests were compatible with ours, while many a populist opposition leader became our enemy and had to be eliminated. If anyone had any qualms about the crimes they committed, or broke the code of silence, they were "reeducated" in special training centers in Silver Springs, Maryland. Targets were often kept from operatives until the last moment, or they were privy to only a portion of the operation not to directly link their own actions to any atrocity.

As funding improved so did the technology, and the killing became routine. The horrors were rationalized by learned white papers produced by think tanks that called for the expunging of certain individuals, or the toppling of governments unfriendly to our interests. The weaponry guided by miniature components became indescribably sophisticated, with plastic explosives so portable they could be detonated from a shirt pocket or by a ballpoint pen or camera. The ability to blend with the population or simulate tourists became a science; indeed, the CIA became a secretly funded shadow government with its own fleet of airplanes to make sure that the values of democracy and free enterprise flourished in every country whose resources were in our national and business interests.

George became proficient in Arabic and was posted throughout the Middle East. He was quickly reassigned when a country became too hot, or after an exceptionally dangerous mission, whether it be bombings in marketplaces, taking out a Senator standing at a vendor on the very steps of a capitol building, assassinations inside Presidential chambers, the pot shot to intimidate a labor leader at a rally, contact with rebel leaders sympathetic with the West who were then betrayed, the sinking of socialists by pinning atrocities on them, or attacking journalists, breaking their legs or blinding them for writing articles counter to the interests of democracy and free trade. Even local terrorists were enlisted and trained; groups later when our interests changed that we'd eliminate. The workings of the agency became so notorious that Congress passed legislation in the seventies, during the high point of George's activities, making foreign assassinations illegal. But this was easily circumvented by outsourcing to third parties.

✳

It came as a complete surprise when George Brent received a phone call from the Home informing him that he had been chosen "Alumnus of the Year," as the one individual who best demonstrated the humanitarian ideals of the Founder. His vision in starting a school for orphan boys was carried on by its graduates, inspired by the motto "His Deeds Are His Monument, His Life Our Inspiration."

"*This year's winner,*" the President of the School announced at the banquet honoring George, "*has exemplified that venerable tradition by making the world safe for democracy, liberating the children and giving them a better life.*

And as the Home has now reached out to all races around the world, we are honored to recognize men like George Brent for carrying our Founder's legacy beyond our shores.

"*Little did anyone ever imagine a confection as having so much influence, sweetening the lives of so many. Graduates like George Brent have brought democracy to the most unlikely places so zealously that George has even been asked to leave countries that could not grasp the vision of our Founder in opening up markets worldwide in order to afford everyone a more prosperous and democratic life.*

"*That George Brent was declared persona non grata in the Middle East only attests to the zeal of his commitment. Of course, his operations are classified, so we will never entirely know the full extent of the good that George did emulating our Founder's vision for orphans worldwide. So, let's all give a round of applause for this year's Alumnus of the Year recipient.*"

One can only speculate if George, sitting in that auditorium having his deeds extolled, saw through the bright faces of 1,200 boys dressed in their shiny Sunday Best shoes and pressed suits and ties, Salvador Allende slumped over his desk after taking a bullet to the head, or Manuel Noriega, on the payroll of his own CIA for twenty-five years, hounded in the convent in Panama all night by rock music, or the countless bloody revolutions instigated in African countries. He must have seen the misery destabilized governments brought to one indigenous population after another so our sugar mills, our copper and oil companies, could operate unmolested. Did he think of the genocide against the natives in Guatemala, the torture chambers of the military junta, or our hand in the disappearances in Argentina? Did he think of all the families' lives disrupted by our destroying populist movements unfriendly to our multinational companies?

The sheer number of assassinations, the screaming, stunned shoppers in markets and bazaars around the world, the disoriented old men and women, fetuses ripped from wombs, the merciless machetes terrorizing the countryside because our covert operations tipped the scales of what might be resolved peacefully by local people, all the bloodbaths our espionage caused meddling in the affairs of foreign governments, employing their own language and our sophisticated gadgetry, all this must have occurred to George as he sat there.

Countless civilians were caught in the crossfire, peasants riding their donkeys, traveling to market with their chickens or goats, carrying their produce on exploding buses, babies in their mothers' arms trapped inside burning buildings, ambassadors' children killed or an opposition leader's daughter crippled at a disco. Did anyone on the committee think of the tens of thousands of CIA assassinations in Operation Phoenix? George, the brochure admitted, was "persona non grata" in the Middle East, and his top secret activities couldn't be spoken about, but it went on to say that "he made the world a better place to bring up our children."

Did the irreparably damaged eye of a seven-year-old boy pop into the Selection Committee's mind, or the facial disfigurement of a fifteen-year-old girl, the shortened life of the pregnant mother, or even the well-meaning activist whose assassination stopped land reform for another generation and the return of resources to the people, so they could continue to be exploited by foreigners at dirt cheap prices?

Kalid and Hamid sat in the audience looking at George Brent with their shiny dark eyes. Did they recognize the Alumnus of the Year as the man in khakis or his proxy, who ten years before passed in Basra just prior to the explosion that killed their father? Was he the one who walked away from the bazaar after placing the plastic explosives that took the life of Karim el Har and led the two boys on a journey that would end in an orphanage halfway around the world? Could anyone grasp the enormity of awarding a humanitarian prize to someone who could have been that very operative who blew up their father? Of course, we will never know for sure if George was the one, since his actions as the brochure said are classified.

Is childhood not a long line of confection? The sweets we vacuum in our little mouths at a tender age, suck up to dissolve every available crystal, every creamy atom of chocolate. Don't our eyes lose focus when our mouths are so preoccupied and our brains engaged in those peculiar sugar highs that cause us to whack our playmates out of the blue when the teacher's head is turned? Then we'll go on to get the award for good behavior in recess even though we were the aggressor, the ball of candy that we pilfered still in our pocket or bulging from our cheek.

Had the sweet tooth worn off in Kalid and Hamid as they sat in the audience? Did they put two and two together? Obviously the board that made such a decision safely inside the US had lost no loved ones. That George was persona non grata apparently didn't faze them outside serving almost as a merit badge proclaiming that George, formerly an Eagle Scout, had done his job well. In the heady flush that comes with being beneficiaries themselves, the Committee bestowed their reward.

The School had given Kalid and Hamid a home, had taken in these two orphans from Iraq who may otherwise have been wandering around the Al-Hijarah desert gathering dates for the rest of their lives. Who would want that to happen when they could come to America, to the town with the largest chocolate factory in the world?

The nagging question is, had George himself created two of the very orphans that the Home so desperately needed? Social welfare rendered the Home obsolete for the last twenty years, so the school had to alter the Deed of Trust and look abroad. Today single parents can get generous amounts of State money outright rather than place their children in an orphanage. So it was incumbent upon alumni like George to unwittingly create orphans to supply the Home's dwindling population and continue the Founder's vision since the endowment had grown so large that total operating expenses were covered by only a fraction of the interest earned.

One could picture the Founder in his late seventies looking down on the town pool, from the mansion he had turned into a country club, at the youths in their bathing suits, as his official biography noted, imagining that there would always be orphans to continue his philanthropic vision, and that there would always be alumni to promote the shining ideals of his legacy, willing to carry on that vision at whatever cost, even if it meant conferring an honor on a man representing an agency that had created the very orphans that he gave asylum too. For it was crucial at all costs to perpetuate the benevolence.

Did only I detect a wry smile, or was it a brief moment of compunction, on George Brent's face as he shook hands with the President to receive his prize as "Alumnus of the Year"?

Out of State Plates, or Decapitation 101

Why did he come to me? It would just involve all of us. No one would be free, everyone would be implicated even if you were not born yet. That doesn't stop the guilt leaping generations. In fact, it is in everyone deep down. The least suspecting don't get a free pass. I impressed upon him that he didn't, and he admitted it. Yes, he was part of it. So was I. We all are as distant and heinous and unthinkable as it was, they all were. He had touched something in me, that is why I endured the two hours, didn't cut him off when it got too gruesome. In fact, it must have entertained me, well, that's not the word, absorbed is closer. It soaked into me like a spreading stain, like body fluids that include everybody, carefully drained, wiped up, or left spilled carelessly. There were thirty-two to be exact, he said, and there may be more.

He was sent to me because I was recommended by two people. They said I was the one he needed to see about the structure, about shaping the material, his seven years of research. He said he took to it like he was involved, then he stopped talking and mused. It was over a half century ago that they took place.

He admitted he didn't know why exactly he was drawn to it. It could have been the Black Dahlia, but he didn't want to get involved with Mickey McCarthy, or his family, he said. He knows Mickey's dead, but still his family is alive. No, he said. This seemed cleaner and the horror deeper. Or was I thinking that after he described his research?

He had wanted to be a State trooper, or in the medical profession, he said. But then his cousin after a few weeks on the job got into a gunfight and almost got killed and that changed his mind, and so he said this is the closest thing.

"I enjoy digging into old records, police files, FBI reports, newspapers, True Detective magazines reconstructing these crimes. They happened in one area, he said, well two, in a straight line between Cleveland and east of Pittsburgh in New Castle."

"And you did the background checks, the leg work?"

"Yes, I searched the railroad records, many are destroyed or incomplete, or stored in different locations, I hunted them all down. I've been at it for seven years."

"There were all these murders," he said.

"Of whom?" I asked.

"Transients. They had no names, except for two, or maybe three we have names for."

"There must have been many more," I said.

"Yes, but the way they were killed. That's the thing. Their heads were all cut off," he said.

"Decapitated!"

"Yes and disarticulated."

"What else? The genitals?"

"Yes," he said, "and they'd take off arms and legs, and use a red chemical on some, burned off their fingerprints. They'd be placed in separate bags or thrown in the river. That was his profile."

"And this is between 1921 and 1950," he said.

"Thirty years is the vital part of a man's life. When he does his life's work."

"Yes," he said.

"Were there women?"

"About a quarter were women. Jane Does."

"Were there any signs of sexuality, semen?"

"No," he said.

"But it must have been sexual, too."

"The genitalia were removed on the males. Sometimes they were just tossed nearby."

"Any breasts on the women."

"No, they were intact."

"And these were all transients?"

"Yes, drifters. I tracked down the death certificates. They

were unknown except for like I said two, or three. One was a prostitute, the other a pimp. The third she was black, but other than the one there is no evidence it was racial."

"And it happened all along the railway line?"

"Yes, between Cleveland, Ohio and Newcastle, outside Pittsburgh. The trains ran between the two cities twice a day. Thirteen were found in New Castle and twelve in Cleveland.

"The twelve murders between 1935 and 1938 were credited to the Cleveland Torso Murderer, also called the Mad Butcher of Kingsbury Run, an area of overgrown weeds, piles of garbage, abandoned cars and makeshift frame houses. Kingsbury Run was called prime real estate for hobos, and one area was famous for whorehouses and gambling. The victims were drifters from the lower class found in the Jackass Hill area.

"The first one Edward Andressy was a known drunk who procured young girls for prostitution and admitted having male lovers. He died from decapitation. He was alive at the time, bound hand and foot and struggled violently. The second was a John Doe, and the third victim Florence Polillo was called a local drunk and prostitute. Her head was never found but a hand in a bundle made identity possible. The fourth and fifth were John and Jane Does decapitated alive, their heads were never recovered. Neither was the sixth victim's head found. One Jane Doe called Lady of the Lake was discovered on the shores of Lake Erie, but her head was missing. Some dubbed her victim zero. The next Jane Doe was the only black victim. She was found under the Lorain-Carnegie bridge. A rib was missing but the head was recovered. She was later identified as Rose Wallace from dental records.

"John Doe VII and Jane Doe VIII were pulled out of the Cuyahoga River but their heads were never found. A Jane and John Doe were found in the Lake Shore Dump. The latter's head was found in a can. One of the John Does was called the "Tattoo man." He had six tattoos on his body, the names "Helen and Paul" on one tattoo, and initials W. C. G. in another. On his undershorts were the initials J. D. His morgue and death mask were seen by over a hundred thousand people at the Great Lakes Exposition in Cleveland in 1936, but nobody ever identified him.

"The murders in New Castle, Pennsylvania and in boxcars near McKees Rocks took place in 1936 and 1940. Bodies were also found in nearby swamps between 1921 and 1934 and 1936 and 1942. The so-called Murder Swamp Killer was credited by the *New Castle News* with 17 murders, almost identical with the Cleveland, Ohio murders. All appeared connected with the Baltimore and Ohio Railroad line. A decapitated body was found in Cleveland as late as 1950, he was a man living on the fringe of society with a drinking problem.

"The New Castle junction where the homeless squatted in cardboard boxes and shacks was a swampy nightmare called Hell's Half Acre by the locals. There were murky pools, tangled underbrush and slime covered bogs. Officials believed the New Castle killings were planned, not crimes of opportunity. The killer was thought to be strong and skilled with a knife or a saw who knew the swamp and didn't worry about the discovery of the bodies. Like in Cleveland the skilled decapitation indicated medical training. Authorities thought there was one killer. None of the New Castle victims were identified. In one boxcar where a headless corpse was found there were two newspapers from the *Pittsburgh Press* and *Cleveland Plain Dealer* linking the two areas. That the victims were often mutilated and the males usually were castrated made police think the killer was bisexual.

"The police often went undercover into hobo jungles and into the rail yards of New Castle where vagrants had tents and wood shacks. In 1940 when the three men in boxcars were found, on the chest of one of them 'NAZI' was scrawled.

"They all fit the same profiles, and the others I discovered along the rail lines. I found information about those not previously linked. I made another discovery of my own that was overlooked. The boxcars had numbers with white lines drawn through them. No one ever questioned that. These were cars destined for McKees Rocks to be destroyed. Here's a photograph of one of them, detectives taking out the body parts wrapped in burlap bags.

"Oh, and something else," he paused and said, "The women were treated differently. There were no signs of sexual mutilation but the women were bisected," he said, "and later there were some males that were."

"How?"

"They were cut in half at the waist."

"It must have been someone skilled, a physician," I said.

"Maybe," he said, "at least someone with medical training."

"Couldn't this be sexual?"

He didn't know, he said. One of the victims was mentioned as being homosexual.

"It could have been the sexuality gone awry, someone who doesn't accept themselves killing someone like himself."

"It seems it was territorial," he said. "That was the way with transients. Food and space were jealously protected."

"Yes, the times were difficult in the Great Depression. But that the crimes were similar is fascinating."

"Yes, there seems to be a progression, the bisecting didn't come until later."

"This is the worst kind of crime, physically. You can destroy someone emotionally, psychologically, but physically it doesn't get any worse than cutting off their head and genitals."

"Yes," he said, "and erasing the fingerprints."

"There must have been tremendous anger, or else breathtaking detachment, the absence of any feeling, to do this over thirty years, assuming it is the same person, and the profile of the killings appears to be. Why are you interested in this?"

He was a tall, strong man, exceedingly polite. He had a beard that didn't disguise his relative youth, yet he seemed burdened by the crimes, but his broad shoulders looked more than capable of carrying all the bad news.

"I can't understand it myself, but I can't get my mind off of it. All the victims, the secrecy, the questions, they haunt me like a mystery that I have to deal with."

"The injustice of never finding the killer?"

"Yes, that's it, but at the same time I seem to know him intimately, though I wasn't even born yet, but it is as if I carry him around with me, so that every movement could at any moment reveal something, when I am eating breakfast, or with my girlfriend, or right before I fall asleep, then it is sometimes the worst, even when I'm sitting in a restaurant alone someone will look suspicious and I imagine there's a clue there. No matter where I am I'm thinking about it. It's a relief even to talk about it. I can't tell you how many nights I just lay there staring at the ceiling imagining different scenarios. My girlfriend thinks I'm lucky that I found something I love."

"You are," I said, but thought how odd that she accepted such a bizarre passion, an alternate love interest. I almost wanted to say "mistress."

"Do you feel somehow responsible uncovering all of this?" I suddenly asked.

He looked at me, steadying his gaze.

"Yes," he said. "I want to identify the person responsible."

"And the transients," I said. "Are you interested in them?"

"Yes," he said. "I need some justice, to find who did this to them. Tell their story, who ended their lives so disgracefully, and why that haunts me I don't entirely know. Detective Merlyo wrote a book. He was Eliot Ness's hire. He was on the case for eight years, but he never quite came up with anyone. He rode the trains between Cleveland and Pittsburgh disguised for years obsessing over the killer. I can understand him. The case almost drove him crazy, spending every free moment to track him down. He wrote that he began to see the killer everywhere, in every inadvertent gesture, half-feint, in the least inappropriate smile or packed in someone's look of disgust. There were two people of interest at the time, one was charged.

"The prime suspect for the murder was an Irish doctor, Francis E. Sweeney. His family was poor, and he lost his father and mother at a young age. In World War I he received a severe head injury and worked as a medic learning about amputations. He received a partial disability pension when he returned to the

States and worked his way through medical school in St. Louis. He became a surgical resident at St. Alexis hospital close to the Kingsbury Run area in Cleveland. He married in 1927 but was estranged by 1933. His wife filed for divorce in 1936. Sweeney had a drinking problem and he was alleged to have been abusive towards his wife and two children. Rumor had it that he was also bisexual. Sweeney was a large, strong man, some say powerful enough to carry the body of Edward Andrassy down the steep embankment of Jackass Hill in Kingsbury Run. Others said he was too soft to ride the rails between Cleveland and New Castle. In fact, he was briefly associated with the Raus Funeral Home that had a laboratory where such things might have taken place. I even went there, but all I found was a vacant lot.

"When Cleveland Mayor Harold Burton put Eliot Ness on the Kingsbury Run case, Ness confined Sweeney for more than ten days in the old Cleveland Hotel. It took three days for Sweeney to dry out, and then two polygraph tests were administered in secret and Sweeney failed twice. The inventor of the polygraph Leonard Keeler gave the tests and told Ness, 'That's your man.' But Ness had no hard evidence to hold him. Sweeney's brother Congressman Martin Sweeney was Mayor Burton's political enemy. He objected to the Ness investigation. Martin Sweeney was also friends with Cuyahoga County Sheriff Martin O'Donnell who then engineered the arrest of Frank Dolezal, a Bohemian bricklayer, for the murder of Flo Polillo. Dolezal had lived with Polillo for a time. He knew Andrassy and the third identified victim, the petite black woman named Rose Wallace whose torso was washed up on Lake Erie.

"Frank Dolezal confessed giving precise details as if he were coached. Before the trial he was found hanged in his cell. The autopsy revealed six broken ribs while he was in custody. Before his apparent suicide he recanted his statements and said he had been beaten until he confessed. The police wanted to close the case and Congressman Sweeney wanted the attention off his family name.

"Francis Sweeney, some said, lived precariously, riding the rails as he saw fit and checking himself periodically into mental hospitals. The Cleveland killings stopped once he committed himself just a few days after Ness's interrogation. But Sweeney would voluntarily leave for days and months at a time. He was known to venture off to other parts of Ohio and Pennsylvania as well. By 1955 Sweeney was committed to Dayton Veterans hospital.

"Even in the Dayton Hospital Sweeney was free to wander around the neighborhood writing prescriptions for himself and friends until the hospital campaigned with the local pharmacists and cut off his drug supply. He finally died there in 1964. Ness had believed until the end he'd identified the Kingsbury Run Butcher and that he'd got away with murder because of his family and political connections. The man who had brought down Al Capone could not bring down the Butcher of Kingsbury Run.

"Something I found that was not reported. It seems like a new piece of evidence. Sweeney's house was not far from one of the burial sites outside Cleveland. When he returned from World War I his wife, who was divorcing him for heavy drinking, got a lawyer to stop his veteran benefits. Soon after a woman was found mutilated. I don't know if there is a connection.

"Even Eliot Ness couldn't solve the case. It destroyed him."

"That's where you come in," I said.

"Yes, Eliot Ness, famous for taking down bootlegger gangs in Chicago, was made Cleveland's Director of Public Safety in 1934 after Prohibition was repealed. He was in charge of both the city's police and fire departments. In 1938 two mutilated bodies were discovered in a ravine plainly visible from Ness's office. It seemed Ness was being purposely taunted. Two days later police raided the shantytown of Kingsbury Run arresting hundreds of vagrants and, on Ness's orders, burned the shacks to the ground. Ness received a lot of criticism for that. The murders stopped, but the Cleveland Torso murders were never solved, though many speculated who the Mad Butcher was.

"Frank Dolezal, by the way, who carried knives and often threatened people when drunk, and who had lived with Flo Polillo, was arrested after a search of his home turned up dried blood. The papers claimed The Butcher was captured. But later the dried blood was determined not to be blood, and his confession was riddled with holes. The Butcher was also loosely linked to Elizabeth Short, or the Black Dahlia murder in LA. Her body also had been cut in two.

"Eliot Ness's career plummeted because he never got over the taint of the unsolved murders on his reputation. The last decade of his life was full of poverty. He who had destroyed the bootlegging gangs ironically became a heavy drinker himself and suffered from poor health. He resigned as Cleveland's Public Safety Director after a scandal. In 1947 he ran for Cleveland Mayor and was badly defeated. A year later he was turned down for a $60 a week job.

"Sweeney wrote rambling letters and sent post cards to Eliot Ness into the 1950s which seemed to implicate him in the Cleveland murders. Ness in his memoirs thought Sweeney's cousin the US Congressman reached a deal to accept incarceration in a mental hospital.

"Ness met Oscar Farley towards the end of his life and collaborated on *The Untouchables*, but its success never reached him as he died at 54 a broken man the same the year the book came out in 1957.

"The last torso was found in a Cleveland lumber yard in 1950 with head and genitals removed and was said to resemble exactly the torso murders. I forgot to mention at least three decapitated bodies were discovered in 1925, all had their hands removed, two were male and one female. One journalist commented that the killer simply slipped away and vanished into the mists of time. Some believe that some of the victims still walk the area, and the specter of the Butcher himself may walk there as well, perhaps he never left."

He then pulled out the seventy pages he had already completed to show me. He was going to write on 22 of the cases, he said. I suggested that he chart where each body was

98

found, the time and the exact type of mutilation to see if he could establish a pattern. He had black and white aerial photos of the places the bodies were found, white dots along the rail lines from Cleveland to Pittsburgh, and additional photos of the police removing bags from the boxcars and the police reports.

"What do you hope for in your research?" I asked.

"Justice," he repeated, "and to be able to sleep at night. These seven years have been rough. I want to give faces to the unknowns, to those insignificant lives cut so brutally short. Just ordinary people, even if I don't know their names, or never find them out."

"But if you could identify the perpetrator?"

"Yes, that would go far towards naming them, if I could identify the killer who disarticulated them, who disgracefully removed their heads or cut their torso in two, methodically removing limbs, and their manhood, depriving them of the two pieces of identification, their fingerprints and face. Who'd cut a woman in half, and why?"

It was as if he, Jack Jackson, were probing himself sitting in my office, with scalpel and clamp, each bit of evidence, cutting away tissue, removing layer after layer of skin, fat, teasing the mesentery free, the muscles snapping from their attachment to bone, the bone ready for the hacksaw, or a simple osteotome. My office was suddenly a laboratory, as if he had already entered the medical profession, his eyes concentrating, beady, even in my office chair telling his story, and his hands I noticed since he came in always moving as if he were somehow reenacting the thirty-two murders, trying to trace back the gestures of the gruesome perpetrator. Nothing he said could slow his hands down. In fact, talking only accelerated his hand movements. I couldn't tell if he was taking them to heart. His own sympathetic beats joining with the perpetrator's reenacting the scene, as if he with the victims is frozen in time like Dr. Gross's medical team in Eakins' Philadelphia painting over a hundred years ago, but this time with each individual head, limbs, removed, then him standing up, arms akimbo, hovering over his work, looking over himself, his hands covered in blood, his looks pierce his own motivation to follow the path of each and every crime. He unmerges himself, his face, from the murky recesses of old paint. How carefully it not be totally his own fabrication is testified to by painstakingly following the evidence. But he can't help following himself, the same impulses every human being possesses buried inside a simple murder investigation that unsolved leads back to the investigator. How otherwise can he enter the head of the perpetrator? What must he be party to to disregard all the lost time? He had to be there, by sheer will place himself at each scene with the awful responsibility of bringing everything back into focus. He went to Raus Funeral Home next to Dr. Peterka's office, a practice he briefly shared with Sweeney, to try and reconstruct the lab Sweeney may have had access to but found only thin air.

When we look too deeply into anything we follow, we can't help it. We find ourselves, not sitting, thinking, absently observing, but an outright participant sucked into the murderer's heart muscle, beating frantically out of control; we are deep inside his brain for the adrenaline rush of what we have not yet discovered about ourselves, recreating our worst nightmares, our most private moments, attributing to ourselves those substitutes just so we can find out. Yes, it was his own humiliation too following so many heinous murders that he internalized, following what had happened to him so that he too unwittingly took part. He probably didn't even know it, but it was reflected in his inability to sleep, to sit still, to stop moving even sitting in my office telling his story, to even stop investigating so many outrages to the human body, multiplied, that was unprecedented, how could someone fifty years later internalize them and then carry on even the semblance of a normal life these past seven years? Lucky! No, he was cursed. How could the girlfriend not be affected? I mused. She must have known she was short-changed, must have glimpsed the stranger in him popping up, what he was turning into, and that in the end she must have known she too was dead meat. These were not simple murders he was investigating, but the most profound outrages to the human body on record.

They involved her, as an innocent victim, partner to lucubrations she gave the impression of admiring. How could one person possibly endure them without reliving each disarticulation, feeling a twinge in his own bicep, or forearm? How could he look at his woman on the other side of the bed intact, all in one piece? The word "disarticulation" he pronounces with such precision it seemed eerie. It distanced what he thought only brought him closer, the horror of so many profoundly senseless removals of body parts. Not even thinking about the heads! Anyone would wait for the blood to flow after the so-called disarticulation. It blindsided every cut that we are equipped ourselves to avoid. Like unexpected paper cuts. But the blood still comes as if out of nowhere intent on its own ferocity.

"Some of the victims were drained elsewhere," he suddenly said.

It reminds us of what's inside everyone, ready and poised, begging to surface, to bead or spurt. He must have felt distanced from the actual cutting, but perhaps sought relief talking about it in my office. But I knew otherwise, we all do, intimately. There is little access until someone like this gentleman, what's his name, yes, Jack Jackson, walks into your life, your office, whose very name almost begs you to overlook the incest. After all this is Kentucky where an unspoken admission of bloodline is always one remove from polite conversation.

These are not simple murders, they are violations of all men and women, the sanctity of bodies we live with and struggle with daily. These violations were so stupendous that the mouth dropped like we were only a cut or two away from chunks of ham, what one person thought she identified when she discovered body parts in a burlap sack—the same ham on platters we carve up at Thanksgiving or Christmas. What sharp tools mercilessly cut off the heads, arms, legs, and penises, plied through the resistant muscle, to bone with osteotome and hacksaw in a hidden laboratory where some concluded he performed his gruesome rituals, then dumped the bodies off. Bodies he was strong enough to carry. Could it all be in this gentleman's brain, this Jack Jackson? Is that the reason for his investigation? And why am I listening to him, for what I find in myself?

His hands are still moving fast, and I notice too shaky leg syndrome. He doesn't even know it. He has to be up to something. I slide the truckles of my chair noiselessly back, just a hair. I don't want him to notice. I am ready for something. I don't know what he is after with this avalanche of information. Maybe to be buried myself in accusations. His politeness is suspicious as if he is hiding something else. Is he really only coming to seek advice? Can it be as simple as that?

I know that he must tell someone, get it off his chest, seven years of it. I know too the mild boastfulness that accompanies his narrative. But what remains is who could have cut those women's bodies in half, and men's too. What centaur dreams dominated the perpetrator? It'd be mythical were it not so gruesome. But everyone knows mythology is sanitized, has to be cleaned up to be passed on. Just where do those distorted shapes in Satanic books come from? Is it something universal that now struts so pedestrian, crossing cultures, entire oceans, springing up out of the earth centuries, millennia later, walking the streets of Cleveland, of New Castle, tucked in the most ordinary houses, down basements, or does it spring right out of the cellars, or shantytowns, on the banks of the Cuyahoga River or the shores of Lake Erie? Erie yes, what a wonderful sounding name! Has he made that connection? Is it in the vegetables, the local fruit eaten, the minerals and trace elements that enter the brain, certainly it is in the animals we kill, entangled with all those complex strands of protein. And the cuts were so surprisingly precise, everyone claimed he was no amateur. The limbs weren't just hacked off, they were surgically removed. You couldn't tell if anger was involved, molten rage, or the iciest demeanor. The latter is more frightening, making it infinitely harder to detect the trail gone cold.

It is as if Jack Jackson sitting there were probing himself so doggedly that there was not enough room in my office between us; that I was drawn into murders I knew so little about is undeniable. Oddly I found space there, while he was a font of holy water sprinkling what I was trying to bottle so I could feel something proper, a restoration to my own dignity, a defensive sanctity, hearing of all the victims while at the same time something vile still loomed, that I felt contaminated sitting in my own office and that he already was contaminated, or why would he be here polluting my mind with these stories, why would he be so interested in such disgusting treatment of other human beings? Something then whispered in my ear, Justice is not enough. There was something absolutely ghoulish in this string of murders, unified by the B&O Railroad, by the inexorable repetition of the sound of the wheels on train tracks, a rhythm found in our own blood highlighted by his seven-year investigation. It stained red any Monopoly board I'd ever play on with my kids. Certainly the four railroads I rarely was interested in anyway.

I moved back even further despite his relative calmness when all at once he stood straight up and his voice grew, deepened remarkably; there was a kind of chill that echoed the imminence of attack, so much stronger than my just sitting there, a willing auditor, soaking up all the gruesome details, the multiple body parts, the severed heads, all seemed to tumble inside me that I strained in my mind stumbling to my feet as if I had a bag over my shoulder. It was all I could do to sit there preserving my demeanor when he stood so precipitously hovering over me that I thought something was going to fall from my bookshelves in response, my mother's book on witchcraft or Christian Science or her *History of Orgies*. It was almost as if I were taken unawares and his fervor did not one whit diminish the horror.

It was as if my listening so intently stoked the very flames that brought added detail to each victim, stoked the fervor of his investigation, fueled it, and tapped into the anonymous killer and on into each of his victims, as if something in myself wanted to rise up and challenge him for exactly what I didn't know, but it had the nature of an assault I couldn't quite identify but knew it was happening, though I sat there cowardly, timidly, and unmolested. I didn't go on the attack. I was beaten down by the thirty-two victims, by the overwhelming description, the sharp instances of cutting remarks, even the simple mention of his word "disarticulation" not aimed at me, but it threatened, pointed, brandished itself nevertheless, as if each missing body part had touched me. I recalled how I never liked leaving a knife lying around the kitchen, out in the open, and always felt something in my past might have provoked such an irrational fear.

The unknown perpetrator of these crimes was present, even if only in the pile of research, in the black and white photos of the victims, but that he and I were too somehow part of it. My evening meals I knew would never be the same. No matter what I told my wife and son that night, I could never convey what I felt when a platter of meat was on the table. Who would have thought looking at the two of us in that office that what was unidentified fifty years ago was still present in all its horror, manifested by the most unspeakable crimes before either of us were born, well him anyway, but yet that had found a need inside him to seek justice that he hoped would emerge from this dogged scratching away at the past? Who would have thought he'd stumble onto something in himself, through me! Or that I'd discover something in myself! He was like a pig nosing around the very worst offal, the long-decayed remains of his own species. His raised voice made me afraid for his girlfriend and that he had gotten so far inside the head of Sweeney or Dolezal, or whomever he'd come up with, that he didn't know he'd resurrected inside himself a copy cat. That's what he didn't see, but I did when he stood up, the force of personality to commit such horrors himself was there in his voice, in the pertinacity of his exhaustive labors.

Believe me, this is the last thought I want to have. It was a horror that stayed with me since I lived alone in Vermont, sometimes not speaking to a single soul for two or three weeks. You wouldn't know it from just looking at me. Then I would travel to visit my mother in New York City, Washington Heights, close to Columbia-Presbyterian Hospital and all those medical facilities reaching over the Hudson and the broad expanse of land under the George Washington Bridge not just for picnics, but where anything could happen, not just to get lost in, more underbrush than anyone needed even in a city, and those intoxicatingly tall buildings jutting high up where you couldn't see inside or out clearly enough, they were so high, labs full of perfect instruments, and here I'd walk right in unmolested with my license plate under my arm, my imagined pass. I must be on official business for one of the top surgeons, his runner maybe, or my roommate's father in college I would tell the security guard. I'm here to see Chief Surgeon Crikelair. See I wanted to be identified and stopped so I could tell my story.

In Massachusetts I'd stop and change the license plate from Vermont to New York plates, so my car wouldn't be a target of vandals in New York City. Washington Heights was after all the crack capital of the US.

The nagging vision that license plate left in the darkest recesses of my brain when I was bent down screwing one off and the other in, more than once someone's look interrupted me, gave pause as if they wanted to report me to the police. Little did they know! I was often unable to sleep with those rectangular license plates in my mind. I remember one person looking at me at one rest stop so hard that he inspired a spasm of anger that right then and there I wanted to commit some crime that I knew required secret preparation, but I only threw the license plate hastily into the trunk of my Escort and drove away. The gall of him looking at me like that!

Little did anyone imagine the calm calculation that went into who I was or realize what was not behind removing that license plate but built up from the loose metal in my hand. I couldn't get out of my mind its convenient sharpness of what didn't even look dangerous, but still it frightened even me, a weapon in disguise unlike the knife left on the counter in my own home. There was something in my past, dreams of dark

105

fields of meat where Goya's "Colossus" sits and those tiny covered wagons pass, dreams crowded with vivid chunks of fresh meat, purportedly animal but actual chunks, torsos, of human beings; I had had that dream often throughout my life, and the license plate played right into it. It frightened me, its faux sharpness that in fact could easily, surgically, cut flesh, and not only flesh but a head clean off. That's what gave me comfort, it was something I could get away with, that nobody would suspect. *With a license plate! No way.* Until that is you looked carefully at it, or had the experience of a paper cut.

He did what? Not me, but the imagined perp, the Mad Butcher of Kingsbury, the Cleveland Torso Murderer. I know I am nobody, but it is just that that accumulates inside anyone and can with little effort identify Jack Jackson. Would he ever find the killer? It would be like finding himself. And I sensed he knew that. If he could get out of the way, he would have the killer cold after all these years. It is in every investigator, every sheriff, policeman, detective, amateur sleuth. They themselves point the way if they only let themselves. It is themselves they are hunting but removed when they admit that they find the killer. It's true even if you think this license plate story is a lot of hokum, it is not, it just translates the violence to the civilian population behind all that police brutality, behind all the guns drawn, the knives, hacksaws wielded, the license given even to soldiers in foreign lands, the infinite hours of boredom to kill inside the devil's workshop, the horrors are there and in the civilians they fight for, in the idle minds in their local communities, only it bursts out, periodically, in places like Cleveland and New Castle.

Of course, I am somebody with a fertile imagination and a past of soiled yellow underwear rubbed in my nose by the old woman who took care of me when I'd be bathed sitting at the kitchen sink. I am one who has endured the pinches of my mother who visited so infrequently, or all the humiliations by those bigger, stronger, smarter boys in the orphanage, the beatings at night, the sacking in the balls, the constant flagging of my self-esteem, the later humiliation of all those rejections by women, all turned into my bare, white-knuckled grip on the license plate that belied even the screwdriver in hand. It was too crude. The license plate with its large-lettered identification, and there I was incognito, only effecting a simple exchange. I scoffed at the identification being associated with me and the blood I could wash off afterwards. The deed would be done already before the conscience would kick in. In fact, I was proud of the license plate, living in the Green Mountains of Vermont, and New York, the Empire state of mind. I straddled them both. And besides no one would be alive to register it. Fifty years hence I too would not be discovered. All I needed was to get started. The first two I imagined would be the most difficult.

I didn't imagine myself a bad person, maybe it'd be an internet contact, a transient not along a railroad track, someone I picked up in town or on the highway traveling to New York City or Rutland, Vermont, someone whose head I'd remove with the out-of-state plate. In some vague way I understood why Jack Jackson came to me and why too I indulged him; something similar in both of us must have already been identified by the idea of nameless transients, an inexhaustible well of violence that we could get away with, the unidentified swamp life poking through a mouth full of teeth, for the harm stirring in each of us, even if we are required to cover it up for seven years or suppress it a lifetime sitting passively in an office surrounded by books, when suddenly it breaks through a gesture, an inadvertent moment hovering over you with raised voice, recognized by someone who has already found himself but hasn't admitted it, who has discovered criminals everywhere, in fact hiding thinly veiled in the past along a railroad line. The wild goose chase ends in identifying one perpetrator to tell our own story to to postpone finding it in ourselves. Putting off the assault as long as we can, the urge to go out with a bang. Yes, we all want attention. You'd think more people would do something. Through all the research to dredge up too in myself thoughts about the suitability of an otherwise harmless license plate from New York or even

Vermont that needed changed just so I or my car would not be the target of crime in New York City. We all need protected.

Spoons

The event I am about to recount happened in Lebanon, Pennsylvania. Lebanon is up the road from Palmyra on Route 422. Maybe there is some relation to the desolation of Middle East sand where there is not a grain to be found, or the stark irony of the total absence of palm trees. Maybe there is some exotic date palm that invades the psyche with oases and girls with veils doing belly dances that merge with the stationary camels on neon signs, or with the heat that blends the concrete into the unreality of a name. Maybe it is the cargo on the camel's back of silver spoons being transported East to West that provides the connection.

It is definitely something pre-Christian that these towns had to offer, a passion that Christianity has lost sight of beyond saints having already been canonized, some underground spring in this oasis in rural Pennsylvania where the mind rests from a culture that makes so many demands on youth. The morality of sand burns every desire away, mocking even the walk over hot coals. And the absence of cedars in Lebanon is another reason to conclude a skewed desire could flourish with reflective gleams not found elsewhere, along with the lack of a desert and the absence of camels and girls dancing with veils.

But something is always substituted and always will be, rich veins that nourish the eyeball, for example, enabling it to feed deeply on the reflection in spoons. Was it at one fell swoop that the eye fell on the spoon, or did the so-called spoonlight embellish the eye with its own reflections? And did the reflections mature over the years when Mark had to polish the silverware on Saturday mornings with the other boys, or later in private when he polished his mother's collection. Did his own reflection in the bowl of the spoon enchant him? Or did the image of the houseparent's daughter early on set the stage?

There were twenty-one boys living together in an orphanage where Mark had been sent after his mother died. For so serenely arduous were those mornings, and so never-ending the task of buffing the gray and pink silver polish off the tarnished spoons as it dried, then washing them thoroughly in hot soapy water to remove the last residue, that the whole process must have inspired him with personal reflections that later in life he could draw on, if only for admiring his own face.

He was a student at the college like the others. Despite the Middle Eastern name of the town, there wasn't anything especially odd about him that didn't fit into rural America, for the bologna factory took care of that. Lebanon bologna was famous all the way to Harrisburg, the state capital.

Dark red meat dotted with tiny circles of fat normalized things; the tang of spices and the nitrites and nitrates quickly dispelled the taste of dates, figs, and halva, while the camels' humps were absorbed level with the sand, and the palm trees too melted into the heat and left only the town in Pennsylvania with a small college adjacent to Palmyra where not one palm tree grew, outside the neon sign on the old Palm Motel.

Classes began that year like any other. The college was almost a hundred years old, and nothing unusual had ever taken place, once you were reconciled with the name. In fact, it was so normal that an astute observer of human nature knew something was bound to happen.

The Lebanon Cedars kept winning at basketball year after year, fielding the tallest teams in Central Pennsylvania. There was a conscious effort of the coaches to recruit the tallest players in the State. And the school newspaper again garnered its yearly allotment of awards.

The school always had its share of odd faculty caught in the college bookstore shoplifting, involved in petty scandals; its share too of the occasionally pregnant students who had to drop out, of the hazing resulting in late night arrests for drinking and indecent exposure in the town square, but that was about all.

And so this one year in the mid-sixties was like any other, a year when the clash between the solid values of the decade before and the moral uncertainties of the current generation had not yet reached the college.

Those who grew up in the fifties still placed pretty women up on a pedestal, plated it with gold foil, gave them tiaras that sparkled like bright stars in the night.

Even today personal appearance is everything. We believe, despite chapter and verse to the contrary, that all virtues can be summarized by what we look like. And sometimes when we are young we can barely look at beauty, but instead must catch reflections in store windows, in the chrome of automobile bumpers, in highly polished silverware.

We named him Mark for the Biblical antecedent, and because some would say that he was indeed marked; that within him was to be found a conjunction of time and place in this oasis of a whole childhood of reflective values.

Mark was inward looking and kept to himself; some were fond of saying that he picked up his brilliance from shining his mother's spoons; and given all the angles of his desire, the infinite possibilities mirrored there, those desires were always somehow out of reach, captured only on bright surfaces, elongated as he tilted the shaft, and let the bowl completely submerge a person into the hot soup he was eating, or had them floating on the round oval like some gelatinous dessert he couldn't control.

Mark described Melissa as floating on air. The way she'd walk across the room, or take a seat in the auditorium, made a deep impression on him. Perhaps she was mostly in his imagination, for it was remembered afterwards that he never had any real contact with her outside of asking her out once or twice and writing her a long rambling letter that she never took seriously.

In the letter he told her she had beautiful eyes, that she didn't walk but glided across the room, down hallways, over the most expensive carpets that were not good enough for her. He worshipped the ground she walked on, energized as it was by her passing. There was a magnetic field from the trailing energy of her suspension above it, he once explained to disbelieving listeners in his physics class. He claimed like Dante's Beatrice that he could barely look at Melissa directly. He even told her

111

in the letter that he constantly caught her reflection in the dining room in his spoons, adding that he would like to sweep her off to a desert oasis like Lawrence of Arabia.

Classmates joked that he was thinking instead of the Palm Motel with the blue neon palm tree out front.

It was in his sophomore year that everything seemed to focus on Melissa, though she paid Mark less attention than ever. This seemed only to fire his imagination.

One afternoon Melissa was sitting in the cafeteria across from him with two girlfriends, and another boy. Mark was sitting alone with his back to her as usual, separated by a small aisle, when he again caught her reflection in the spoon he was using. In fact there were two spoons that afternoon, like some sort of physics experiment. He held them at right angles with the convex ovals facing Melissa to catch her reflection.

Some students thought he was trying to direct light beams into her eyes and blind her. Then he'd suddenly switch the spoons around to reflect Melissa seated upside down on her head. Maybe it was this inversion, like the Middle East named town in the heart of Pennsylvania Dutch country, that intimated that he would never be able to get closer to Melissa than this light show in the bowls of the two spoons that he moved in unison.

The next moment he placed the spoons on the depressions of both his eyes, as if he were taking some sort of measurement. The depressions seemed uniquely made for the spoons, so uncannily did they fit.

Perhaps he had a sunscreen in mind under the hot cafeteria sun, that his imagination must have visualized more than once? Had he been transformed out of the temperate Central Pennsylvania climate into the blinding hot desert of the Middle East? Were the displaced names, Lebanon or Palmyra, to blame? For some this was the only explanation, as his antics were mild compared to the bullets that would soon be whizzing overhead in war torn Beirut to the screams of children, goats, women with bundles running for cover from submachine gun fire and pipe bombs placed in vehicles, or plastic explosives under the stands of merchandise in huge bazaars. Perhaps this was a prelude to that horror thousands of miles away a decade later.

Was the searing sun a backdrop which fired the brains of Mark, like in a skillet where the brains of a pig were fried out of spite over longtime Middle Eastern rivalries?

Some testified later that they saw him smile. Others said it was the twisted scream of Melissa.

For Mark stood up and dug the spoons with all his might, as if they still contained Melissa's image, into the two sockets of his eyes. He buried her reflection there forever, and then scooped both eyes out onto the cafeteria floor amidst screams and confusion. Blood streamed down his cheeks, as he stood there in shock.

Though some students reported him smiling, most were horrified and surprised. Melissa jumped up and headed for the entrance, trying to stem the tide of blood coming after her. Other girls threw up or screamed to stop what Mark had done with their high-pitched voices.

Despite all these years, whenever I sit down to a table, and in an unguarded moment, the gleam of a spoon catches my attention and my own eyes begin to ache. I can hardly keep my hand from reaching for the spoon until the thought has passed. And the horror was brought back recently when last weekend I heard over the radio an inmate at the mental hospital for the criminally insane on Wards Island recounting what he did to his own mother. He told how he took both her eyes out, one with a fork and the other with his finger.

Mark returns with a shining purity that makes vulnerable my own looks at women. He has developed within me a relationship with spoons that has never been quite the same; and now that it is connected with forks, it curiously leaves only the knife as the most harmless piece of cutlery.

Glasses

I forbade her to wear her glasses, saying it disfigured her face. Impressing upon her that it was how she looked to me that was more important than how everything looked to her. She couldn't see herself like I saw her, I said, so how could she possibly have expected me to approve of that metal apparatus that hides the beauty of her eyes, that made her nose and the little plastic pieces like transparent fiberglass lifeboats a vessel to contend with. I didn't want her face mechanicalized.

"Nature didn't give you such beautiful irises," I said, "just to be magnified to death, all out of earthly proportion."

Swimming, that's what they were. The brown green flecked marsh of color I didn't want floating double over her face, catching each reflection like white aquatic birds, egrets landing in the rice paddies of her eyes all the time.

"I could look at all the Far Eastern paintings I wanted for that," I said.

They should be drained dry of glasses and their illusion of a transparent depth, I told her, even if it did make her eyes a little watery for a time.

And she closed her eyes from the strain of what seemed to be brighter light from not having the glasses on her face. She looked naked, more alluring, more helpless.

"And the greasy temples," I said, "always against your skin. The salts of your body are trying to get at them too, capsizing the plastic like the nose pieces into a fretting ocean of body fluid. The body doesn't like mechanical structures any more than I do, and revolts against their floating on the face, even if they be the excuse to see with."

And she blinked at me, looking into my desk lamp, as if its blinding illumination somehow accounted for the forfeiture of eyesight. She sat there pitifully small and helpless.

"You look more beautiful than ever," I said, as she reached out for my hand to wrap her fingers firmly around it.

"I'll be your seeing eye dog," and barked, amusing her that

she broke into a childish laughter.

"I'll be the eyes for you. See I don't wear any glasses, only when I'm driving and watching a movie."

"But your eyes are stronger than mine," she hazarded an objection.

"That's just the point," I rumbled back all out of proportion to the meekness of her comment. "That's just the point! They are stronger! Yes, yes."

And she sighed and laid her head on my shoulder sideways.

"I'll look at what needs to be seen. I'll interpret things for you. You always said you trusted my opinions, didn't you? Moles, do you know about them, they can get along on less light. You attend to the burrow and I'll make the sallies into the daylight. I'll risk my eyesight for both of us. You keep your eyes protected, weak for me."

And she reached out to drape her body in mine, as if the will had completely gone out of it. Almost determined as she was now not to see for herself.

"I know, I know," I fondled her.

Her eyes were sad, as when I always took her glasses off so she could be more intimate with me. I was again amazed at how like a child she was, so trusting, how completely she gave herself over to me.

At first it started as a joke. I would hide her glasses before she got up, or was to do the dishes, or before she read the evening newspaper, finally saying, "I'll interpret it for you. What do you want to know?"

I wanted her to give herself to me without having to look at anyone else. And how dependent she was astonished, even frightened, me. Never had I had so much power over a person, or such devotion. Her helplessness kindled my deepest protective instincts. They went far beyond the mere sexual now. Like a Great Wall of China they ringed her and built up day by day and brick by brick her confidence in me, in the gradual and painstaking civilizing process of keeping everyone else outside our lives. Labeling them as barbarians. That was our secret name for them.

115

Not to take advantage of her, no, I wouldn't think of that, but simply to nurse and care for her and have her under my extended wing, so to speak, sweeping the countryside like the spanning of a great wall that kept people out.

At first I took pleasure in her groping as I labored tirelessly over her body, up and down its curves, around bends and slopes surveying what I took to be my kingdom, and sure she got angry sometimes, that too pleased me like a mock invasion or outside threat that I felt we both had to practice for, engage in these simple maneuvers, an insurrection that my quelling each time brought her closer.

Gradually I accustomed her altogether to going without her glasses, to being the mole burrowing deep in my life, displacing soil that would have at other times buried me for living alone as I did. Her not wearing them was the structure that kept others away, until she depended upon me both night and day, until physically I became the eyes for her, that she came to rely on me for absolutely everything.

Even undressing she claimed to feel my eyes on her unfastening the clasps of her skirt, loosening the buttons on her blouse with soft looks. Ever so gently I removed one article of clothing after another. She responded almost on cue to my looks.

In fact, to live with my conscience, I even had her do palming, and long swings, and sunning of her eyes, all to improve them without really trusting in their efficacy myself. Reading books upside down, I had her do that too. Everything I tried just because of my vanity, because I wanted her face free. I wanted to be seen with a woman without glasses. Even though it was really those with weak eyes, with glasses at first, that always attracted me, for what I perceived as their helplessness.

The challenge of glasses on a woman always aroused me. The thicker the better. I'd fantasize taking them off for the first time. Their dependence on me after I removed the lenses from the face, that virgin moment when I could observe them in all their innocence, and I'd find a whole new person there. My own secret discovery. But never before had I found someone who could submit so thoroughly, so totally to my program for improvement.

Meanwhile I would be the crutch that she relied on. The stiff wooden structure that when need be she could rest her whole weight on and take the next unsteady step down to the basement, for example, for potatoes, or up to our bedroom where her faulty eyesight gave her a sense of touch that only kings dream about!

Ijime

Children are perhaps the most sensitive of all creatures, and the cruelest. The force of one can so sink into the other creating multiples of itself that the child becomes obsessed by the constant pressure of the other. It is the same pressure adults exert daily on each other, but rarely with the calm, uncomplicated strokes of childhood. Every meeting, every insult is like another blow that the weaker child cannot escape, so thoroughly oppressed is he. If pounds per square inch could be measured by insult, Jiro Watanabe would be a walking example of its effect.

The place where our story takes place is fittingly called Daikumachi, or Carpenter's Village. Years ago, tradesmen gathered there to ply their trade all over the prefecture. Maybe it was no accident that Jiro and Hiroyuki Hirata lived in that village. Maybe the very tools bound them. Tools after all are domesticated weapons. Perhaps their story goes back to the first instance of feuding craftsmen and the implements they wielded to defend themselves. Such childhood dramas are played out regularly throughout Japan, so it isn't surprising that they capture the public imagination. They magnify by news coverage all the problems that arise among children who try to assert themselves over their smaller, more timid peers.

Hiroyuki was a big-boned boy, like those inflated figures on top of restaurants by the same name in the United States, figures that loom larger than life dominating the horizon, informing the dreams of smaller victims, then magically appearing with a friendly grin the next morning.

Jiro and Hiroyuki were both junior high school students. Hiroyuki was in the last year, and Jiro was just starting out. On the first day of school a subtle connection between the two boys was established. Maybe it was the white-skinned delicacy of Jiro, and the extraordinary dark brown moles that dotted his milky complexion, as if his face represented the first twilight of a brilliantly clear night where the stars are dark and the background white.

Jiro had a feminine beauty that Hiroyuki was drawn to just before he'd make the jump to high school to find girls the object of his attention. It was an unacknowledged sexual attraction that boys in the absence of female companionship develop. As for Jiro, he was repulsed by the budding pubescence of Hiroyuki, the facial hair, the deep voice, the manly movements. All represented expectations that he couldn't dream of realizing. The revulsion was visceral. He felt contempt for Hiroyuki at first sight. It was as if before him stood the horror of all he was to become. Someone manly, yes, but possessed of bullying instincts and anger at everyone smaller for not yet having found the courage to approach a woman, though he had already taken to crudely joking about them.

When the two caught each other's eye Jiro dropped his out of shame, but Hiroyuki bore into the younger boy with an intensity that terrorized him, as if he were already tearing through soft walls of resistance.

It started on the bus with Hiroyuki taking Jiro's pencil one day, his eraser the next, then flinging his cap out of the bus window. Every day there was something different, as the bigger boy bore down on the smaller one. He made him give up part of his lunch, first a rice ball, then a piece of fruit, finally on some days his whole box lunch. He took to cuffing him in the back of the head despite the cultural prohibition against it. He referred to Jiro's head as his "cuffing dome" and called him "piss ant," spreading the rumor that he still wet his bed at night. He made Jiro give him protection money so other boys would not beat him up, though it was Hiroyuki alone who sent him home with black and blue marks that Jiro carefully hid from his mother, frightened that Hiroyuki would retaliate against his whole family if she found out and made a fuss.

Once Hiroyuki made the diminutive Jiro wear a sign that said, "*Watashi wa baka desu*," or "I am a fool." And he was laughed at by everyone on the bus to the immense delight of Hiroyuki. Another time Jiro pretended to be an epileptic sticking his head out the bus window just as it passed through the center of town; it was not to mock spastics so much as an effort to amuse Hiroyuki and divert him from using the little boy as a punching bag, but Jiro only received a more perverse beating after that for making everyone laugh. Once Hiroyuki tore up Jiro's math homework, and the younger boy, though a diligent student, just accepted the teacher's reprimand in silence.

One day Hiroyuki was with a group of classmates and they spotted Jiro and motioned the reluctant boy over to them. When he came they restrained him and Hiroyuki digging his fingers into Jiro's cheeks forced open his mouth as another boy produced an earthworm and dropped it inside. Jiro gagged and threw up in the tall grasses as the boys left him with their laughter in the distance.

Jiro was tripped, kicked, cuffed by Hiroyuki routinely, and though he was punished at home for his constantly dirty school uniform, he remained silent. His parents grew suspicious, but since Jiro produced not even a scrap of explanation they didn't pursue the matter, assuming it was a stage their son was passing through. Had Jiro a brother or sister who took his side, perhaps his situation might have come to light sooner. But, being an only child, he seemed to be all alone. What friends he did have were themselves in mortal fear of Hiroyuki and anxious not to be the target of bullying, all except Taro who took pity on Jiro.

Once the group of older boys led by Hiroyuki cut Jiro's hair crooked—it was the day of the school pictures. As Jiro sat there, large tears welled up in his eyes catching the photographer's light as tiny streaks glittered down his cheek.

"Come on son, it's only a flash, and not so bright to hurt you," the photographer had said.

Jiro left school early that day saying that he was ill and stayed home for a whole week with a malady Dr. Kato diagnosed as the growing pains of a child that simply needed more time to adjust to his new school setting.

When Jiro's homeroom teacher came on his annual visit to the house he had nothing to reveal to Jiro's mother, except to say that Jiro was the only student to object to his smoking.

Students were asked confidentially for their opinions, but after the teacher found out that it was Jiro who had written the only protest he approached his mother.

Jiro remembered clear as a frosty silver bell his mother's response as she sympathized with the teacher, "Oh, I am sorry, I have such an inconsiderate boy!"

Hiroyuki once forced Jiro to steal a watermelon, and another time forced him to set a match to the tail of a cat they had dipped in kerosene. Jiro was forced by Hiroyuki to smoke, and once to put the live cigarette into the eyes of a dead sparrow whose pink body didn't even have feathers yet. All these horrors Jiro catalogued, and with each one he grew more remote, and there appeared a fixed look in his eyes as if he were keeping count.

One day in the summer Hiroyuki knocked Jiro down on impulse and plumes of dust trapped by his blue uniform with gold buttons rose on each side of the fallen boy, and Hiroyuki heard a stubborn "forty-three" from Jiro.

"What's 'forty-three' mean? Tell me!" Hiroyuki screamed as Jiro turned stubbornly away. Hiroyuki grabbed his arm at the wrist and twisted it, "Tell me, piss ant, tell me!"

But Jiro clenched his jaws. So Hiroyuki twisted until Jiro finally burst into tears.

"It's my father's age, today's his birthday."

"You better be careful, or he'll never reach forty-four! Ha, ha, ha!" Hiroyuki laughed.

By fall Hiroyuki would not let Jiro out of his sight. In fact, the torment seemed to create a rather odd infatuation with the smaller boy. And his classmates began to invest Jiro with a certain respect over the constant abuse by Hiroyuki. Jiro sensed that he too was feared by the other younger boys. He felt how the slightest movement of his eyebrows, for instance, had the power to inspire confusion and doubt in them. And sometimes he took advantage of this by requiring them to run errands. They too had such a profound fear of Hiroyuki that they felt intuitively nothing could happen to them if they obeyed Jiro. Though mostly they looked on in silence like children do when another child is being punished.

In Christian terminology, Jiro was their martyr, sacrificed to the relief of the rest. And though Jiro's sacrifice was not willing, it seemed fated, as if Jiro were destined by the larger, stronger boy to play that role.

Oh, he objected at first, even on occasion fought back, but that only intensified the beatings. Gradually, however, he grew resigned, at least on the surface, neglected his studies, had in fact broken his glasses so often that now he wore them taped. And he never gave away when he couldn't read the numbers on the blackboard whenever a lens was missing, and so his math scores dropped even though he kept count in his head.

Jiro was going to keep a journal but was afraid Hiroyuki would read it, would appear in the night and open his small desk, just like he routinely invaded his dreams, so that he woke even in cold weather sweating all over.

Jiro's white skin gradually lost its luster, grew sallow, though the color too could have been from the countless tangerines his family ate sitting round the kotatsu.

From the money that Jiro received from his relatives just after New Year's, Jiro's parents bought him a red bicycle.

One day after school Hiroyuki saw Jiro with his new bicycle and asked for a ride. Jiro said no, and Hiroyuki kicked the bicycle bending the spokes.

"Here, let me take it for a ride," he said, pushing Jiro to the ground and grabbing the handlebars. But as he got on and tried to peddle, the bike wobbled left and right and Hiroyuki in disgust shouted, "This is a piece of junk," and picked the bike up and threw it against a cinder block wall.

The shiny front fender collapsed like a paper lantern, and Hiroyuki walked away in disgust as Jiro lay there stunned. He explained later to his family that he had an accident.

It is hard to tell if that was the turning point, or just what event broke the camel's back. All we know is that it was not a straw that Jiro had to deal with, but a list of carefully recorded insults an arm long that one day would be clearly enumerated to everyone. And the beatings, they were so numerous that Jiro treated them as one category unless they were exceptional, like the twisting of his wrist till it was near breaking, that he couldn't lift his arm for days to copy his Chinese characters into his notebook. The stealing of the watermelon was one, the bike was another, the tearing up of the math homework and setting fire to the cat's tail perhaps were two or three, the forced smoking was one, as was the putting out of the baby bird's eyes with a cigarette, the worm dropped into the mouth was another, the "red hot" salve that was rubbed between his legs was another, the unwanted hair cut, the broken glasses, the stealing of his pencils and erasers, his compasses, all figured into Jiro's calculations.

Remember, Jiro was good at math. There is a certain willfulness that stubbornly doesn't lose track, no matter how many times it gets derailed. You'd not expect milk-white skin and such silent moles like constellations to be mathematically proficient, but rather to be the object of distant worship, not attack close up with the kind of perturbations his heavenly countenance experienced until his face twisted ugly and purple as Hiroyuki got him in another headlock.

One day Jiro was behind Hiroyuki and he made a remark slightly critical of him and the older boy sprang at him and knocked him to the ground and placed his fist squarely in his face, as he twisted his tongue in the customary fold between his clenched teeth and raised his arm as if to smash the little boy once and for all. It was all so fast that even Hiroyuki's friends were surprised. That too figured into the calculations.

Perhaps it was the younger boy's beauty that Hiroyuki pounced on in order to embolden his own interest in girls. Or maybe it was a genuine, deep-seated attraction for Jiro and that was the only way he knew to show it unashamedly. Whatever the reason, it was destined to reach a climax before the school year ended in March.

It was a bitter cold January when Jiro hatched a plan while observing the patterns of frost on the window panes, how so many interdependent crystals came together to form such hardness. It was a plan that only the deeply humiliated could hatch in their psyche to combat all the ignominy that threatened to ruin even the capacity for limited reprisal. Under such conditions the mind always works best, broods longest, and despite the degree of terror calculates with the coolness of an adding machine. So dispassionate was the plan that perhaps such responses are endemic in society and will appear even in the bloodstream of a pale, beautiful, and, it could be argued, no count boy. For everyone is capable of some mathematics, so much more a boy gifted.

Jiro's friend Taro agreed to accompany him to a little copse not far from Daikumachi that was fed by an unidentified stream, but now in the winter was only a tangle of brush and trees. They went there in late February and found a culvert between a large yew tree and a small oak. There the two boys dug a shallow hole and Jiro took out of his satchel a colorfully embroidered box in which were stuffed bills that he had taken secretly from his parents. There was about twenty-five thousand yen in all.

One day just before school ended, Jiro told Hiroyuki that he knew of a place where there was money buried. Hiroyuki glanced suspiciously at the younger boy, then leered with the same smile as on the day when he first saw Jiro at the opening ceremonies of school.

"Show me," he said.

"After school today," Jiro said. "Taro is going to come."

As the three boys walked towards the copse the sun disappeared and it grew prematurely dark. By four-thirty they could barely see each other.

"How far is it?" Hiroyuki asked.

"Just ahead," Jiro said.

Soon they came to the culvert beneath the yew tree, next to the small oak.

"In there," Jiro pointed.

"Are you kidding me?" Hiroyuki snapped back and grabbed Jiro by the collar, then by the neck and squeezed with his powerful grip. Taro dropped to his knees and took a thin branch and poked in the dirt until a brightness of material showed through the gloom. Hiroyuki immediately released Jiro and jumped down pushing Taro aside and started scratching with his hands.

At this Jiro groped in his school bag and moved towards Hiroyuki as Taro said, "That must be it."

"Yeah," Hiroyuki said greedily, his hands digging like two powerful talons through the debris. The next moment something crashed into Hiroyuki's skull and he fell over, struggled with one arm, "*Nani* . . . ? What . . . ?" and groaned, but a second blow came before he could complete his question, and a third till his eyes twitched wildly, and his mouth twisted permanently open, but the blows kept coming in the dark as if Jiro were counting.

The forensic experts counted fifty-eight blows to the skull from a hammer that was later found in a winter rice field not far away from Hiroyuki's body.

The Coat

The trap was set at the bottom of their run, in shallow water. You could tell where their bellies went all slippery in the grass and mud, and you could imagine they'd be traveling so fast that they'd hit the pan with both hind legs, or even their two forepaws, and the steel jaws of the number two trap would close on them in an instant. This happened time and again, so you had to make sure that the stake was pounded in firmly enough, or they'd pull it out and drag your trap into someone else's line.

On dry land you'd sift fine soil over the trap then scatter leaves hiding it, preferably by the bank of a creek so the running water would divert the animal. Maybe too you'd put some bait around. Sometimes they'd get only one paw caught, and if it was the forepaw it'd be gnawed off if you didn't check your traps early enough.

It took twenty-four animals to produce Gretchen's muskrat coat. Half the animals were caught in the runs, the other half on relatively dry land. About half of those on dry land gnawed their paws off, or the coat would have been sewn together sooner. Though maybe she wouldn't have bought that particular coat, for it was a matter of the woman and the trapped animals and the anticipation of an exceptionally cold winter that brought its manufacture together and conspired in the purchase.

Gretchen, despite her inordinate compassion, most probably never heard the animals squealing, the broods left behind in their dens, or even in their own bodies. She only felt the fur, its deep luxuriant pile, its rich golden brown that ill-suited her own wig of artificial orange fibers. The coat gave the impression that there was something feral in her nature, something in the Pennsylvania wilds that was transposed to her. It gave the impression of runs slid down, animals browsing in the moonlight following the scent of their desires.

When she wore the coat, it seemed like countless families

of shimmering animals were on the move, or huddled in the dark silhouette of some underbrush, or in the tangle of blackberry bushes or tall grasses. Their tails had for sure disappeared along with their paws, and the black noses and beady eyes on their little faces, but the animals still seemed to be huddled in fear before being skinned, when in truth they were only tossed on careless mounds to be put on stretchers to dry.

The fur looked so exhausted like the remains of mutilated bodies—desire stopped in its tracks by the shrewdness of strategically placed steel jaws. Matted fur mixed with mesentery and visceral fluids, stained with flecks of blood and yellow clots of fat. But after it was treated and brushed it transformed into a deep, rich lustrous pile, as if it were still on the animal's back.

All of Gretchen's friends wanted to dig their fingers into the fur. Though Gretchen didn't really have many friends, only one or two associates at work who'd visit the house once every two or three years to have dinner with her mother.

Gretchen took care of her mother who was in her seventies saying her rosary beads all day while lying on the living room sofa till she returned. And for the little boy that they raised she'd bring home sweets: halva, Baby Ruth bars, Almond Joy, or sometimes for herself big snowballs of sponge cake topped with pink or white icing and shredded coconut. The artificial ingredients didn't go well with the muskrat fur, the red dyes, or the list of additives longer than some of the letters she typed at the Red Cross.

Gretchen herself didn't need help, for there was no urgency, no one lying bleeding on a battlefield, or needing to contact family members to arrange for a hardship leave. There was in fact the calm assurance that things were going as they should, that the economy was prospering so that in the Fifties a fur coat could be purchased just like the alligator handbags and shoes a few years before when the reptile was all the rage. But now they were all at the bottom of closets, in the dry swamp of dusty discarded fashions. At the time muskrat coats appeared, Gretchen took an immediate fancy to them; in fact, she surprised everyone by the boldness of her purchase.

That Gretchen's humdrum life went on as before probably need not be mentioned. She was a hit at work, but everyone soon grew accustomed to the coat. It was for warmth, even if it did stir up brief excitement at the office. Gretchen didn't once push up the collar with both hands around her cheeks, tilt her head to one side, bat her eyelashes and kick up her heels like Betty Grable. Had she done that she'd quickly have sat down flushed and embarrassed. No, the coat just draped her body. It seemed in fact too big for her, so that twenty-four is a conservative number of animals considering that the paws and heads were missing.

The coat, however, grew to be part of her. The chestnut browns that were crisp and clear turned yellowish and lost their gloss, from cleaning, storage, from the underpile of shorter hairs showing through, that the coat soon started to match Gretchen's orange hair.

The animals were permanently buried in the coat to provide warmth, to bring excitement to Gretchen's life. Their desires of course were in the missing paws and heads, the nose, the eyes that were no more, the ears that would never again hear the call of a mate. Not even the tiny beads of glass that replaced the organs of sight in fox stoles were evident in the rather nondescript fur. All the sensory organs were gone entirely, and only the fur that had warmed was left. Gretchen herself had poor eyesight, but her sense of touch grew exceptional, typing from a Dictaphone for eight hours a day. So she never missed the absent organs of the animals.

The one man in Gretchen's life had stopped courting one summer. Philly would come over on Thursday nights and sit with Gretchen and her mother and watch TV, but finally nothing ever came of it when Philly died unexpectedly. Gretchen was obviously grieved and seemed to take it pretty hard. It was shortly after that that she purchased the fur coat for herself, to the surprise even of her mother who usually had a say in everything Gretchen bought. Soon all interest in Gretchen and the coat subsided.

In fact the animal rights people made Gretchen finally put the coat away, stop wearing it prematurely, so she had it dry-cleaned one spring and permanently stored. After that Gretchen somehow seemed exposed without the heavy fur on her body. Where before the coat revealed at least an intent to identify with the two dozen or so muskrats that roamed the woods of Pennsylvania finding mates, reproducing at will, till they were stretched and stitched together for a coat, now there was no such suggestion as the following fall Gretchen went out and bought a wool coat.

The curly hairs fit her wig of artificial fibers. When a parakeet one day got loose at work, Gretchen panicked fearing that the bird would get tangled in her hair and she would be exposed. For that reason too she seemed to pull the material more tightly around her body. In any event the wool coat suited Gretchen after the muskrat coat. And anyway Philly was long dead and the new coat gave evidence that she was entering another phase of her life.

Though the dead animals she wore, it could be argued, fit her, the fact that she and Philly just sat on those Thursdays still as cream cheese watching TV with Gretchen's mother, and then had cake and coffee, suggested that no animals had slid through those Thursdays either, splashed into no creeks even though Philly, Gretchen, and her mother swallowed tall glasses of ice water. The fact that anyone was trapped was not even visible, for when Philly came over the coat was not yet hanging in the closet.

The wool coat looked sleek, even though Gretchen's body now in her late thirties was filling out, plump and pink like the snowball cakes she devoured weekly. In fact the coat and the impression it made with its beautiful black lamb's wool was the opposite of Gretchen, unless of course you had the imagination to see the sheered sheep or consider what it was that made Gretchen take to wearing a wig. A weak gene in the family? For her mother too wore a wig.

In fact the coat was serviceable, and Gretchen wore it well and at the beginning even got a few compliments. Privately many co-workers were glad that Gretchen had gotten rid of the ratty muskrat. For some attributed their allergies to the dander they said was on the coat. At times the wool coat looked almost elegant, though it did draw attention to the lusterless orange hair that was always done exactly the same.

I have tried to fathom Gretchen's private life and thought that the muskrat and sheep could provide access. I even thought the polyester fibers in the coat she bought in her mid-fifties could do it. But no, I found out that the coats only threw one off the track. There was a meadow that the bounding sheep would lead you too, a simple clover field that told of a life of simplicity, standing there clipped, all pink, vulnerable, exposed. She had not been manipulated, not even instinctively out of filial duty. That's not what forced her to live at home all her life.

The dead muskrats were not a conscious comment on her desires that had been caught and throttled. The men never came calling outside of Philly, not because there was some family secret or religion that associated every desire with impure acts. The reproducing muskrat population you could argue belied that. For thousands and thousands of such coats were thoughtlessly made and they only made women more attractive, so they too would be caught. No, it was something that didn't end with polyester, those artificial fibers that are bound to work their way into anyone's life eventually even if they are not wearing a wig.

And it wasn't entirely the loyalty to the Red Cross, other people's problems, though that could easily devour a lifetime of desire, so you give to others leaving yourself a hollow garment synthetically spun from the oil in the ground.

No, circumstance didn't entirely do it, though dutifulness to her mother and the early death of Philly contributed. But just what staved off all the men, just what was it that buried the desires in leather handbags, high heel shoes, and coats that were fashionable? Regularly Gretchen and her mother would make the trip down to 149th Street for a new hat. Does fashion drain just what it is meant to elevate into the commercial? It can't be only religion either, though that contributes, along with the tug of the mother. Everyone said she had been too strict, and maybe that accounted for Gretchen's poor eyesight, and not only the fact that she was so small at birth that she fit into a shoebox and had to be placed in an incubator. It must have been, too, in the body beneath all that clothing. What was it that made me ascribe a larger than life character to Gretchen? The curious elevation that always comes of denial? True, she followed fashion, but finally only to the extent that one had to be clad. The dress finally didn't do what it was supposed to, attract men.

The time my fiancée came over should have told me, but I didn't see it then. I could see the radiant glow in Gretchen's cheeks as she circled the living room with the exquisitely beautiful Ildiko and the stiffness in her limbs, and how she trembled as their fingers intertwined. For years later she referred to her dancing that day as heavenly. Since Ildiko taught dance at Arthur Murray's, I had just credited her comments to Ildiko's light-footedness and grace.

Finally after Gretchen retired and her mother had long since died, I discovered what placed her in the social limbo of a muskrat coat between desires and the garments we wear to assure their fulfillment. I had known she wrote poetry when she was younger, and one afternoon she showed the poems to me. The verse was to a young woman, a love poem. I read more, and immediately the poems told of a passion that all her life and considering her strict Catholic upbringing was buried in alligator shoes, closed up in fancy leather handbags, hidden under hats, wigs, inside a muskrat, then wool, and finally a polyester coat. Garments abetted by every shade of pocketbook to hide the unorthodoxy of a desire whose time would not come for another thirty or forty years, and only then in big cities. I wondered how many other lives were tucked away in the mad scramble for fashion.

Gretchen today lives in a nursing home, where the aids I have heard have to struggle nightly to get her into her nightgown.

The Tension of Suspenders

The tension of suspenders stretches far beyond their elasticity and the pants they hold up. It reaches all the way back to the old country and involves body size, those external pads of flesh that hide what is within by crossing oceans and leaping back in time the more body weight becomes a matter of gravity.

He studies his genealogy, his and his wife's ancestors. He gives papers at the Historical Society in Ephrata. He is trying to get in contact with the original strain, identify where it all started. He has to overleap the suicide of both his parents and return to a time that only history can recapture.

Once in Holland he bought a large heavy wool coat trying to get at the heart of Europe through its fabric. He sent letters to friends commiserating when the Queen Mother of the Netherlands died. Everything that took place on the continent involved him. Anything Swiss German, any related people had an effect on him; his Amish roots were quickened by contact with the past.

Perhaps he could find the original plant, the scion off which he developed. Just what was it that made him what he was? He overlooked the suicides and thought it was something larger on the continent, in the historical records of the German immigrants. Who was it that first strayed? Was it something that they had magically subdued, or a fabric they became enamored of suddenly unraveling, was it learned from animals? For that reason, he kept a dog and cat to learn their secrets, but as usual they gave only obtuse leads based mostly on their sense of smell.

He sought in mathematics when he was younger for the world to add up, and he was the first to balance equations in chemistry class. He thought Oskar's childhood might hold the secret in his tin drum, or Steinbeck in the crushing gentleness of his characters, but finally he was thrown on his own resources.

Could it have been biology pure and simple, a gene that

was passed on in the turbid pool of molecules? He was the blatant recipient of one and to mollify it geared his whole life towards the past, towards the discovery that would uncover just who he was.

He ate through it daily and gained inordinate weight. In fact every meal was motivated by an astounding gluttony, despite his religious nature, to devour huge portions of food. He'd be nervous and trembling almost beforehand that the food became visibly crucial. A dessert not on time would have him anxious and salivating. For the next moment there was the fear that he'd miss the dessert altogether, that the waitress had forgotten, and who knows what that might lead to; low blood sugar, an appetite revealed before a whole roomful of diners, or even a close friend.

"I didn't really know Cecil," they'd say, and the game would be up.

But not if he could have his toothsome desserts, his mash potatoes and gravy, his giblets, his meat, and his puddings and dumplings for dessert at lunch. Once the heavy German midday meal was dispatched he could rest easy that that day at least he wouldn't reveal himself.

And his pants when I saw him shocked me. So large they were and suspended. He was round like an Easter egg, curiously balanced by his tiny arms and legs, like an insect on its back at the mercy of his body so that only with breathless difficulty could he reach his shoelaces. His hair was matted but at the back a cowlick stood up in defiance of a premature decrepitude. He was round-cheeked and red-faced as if there was always something embarrassing about to take place.

For every day he woke up he asked himself the question. Is this the day that I am going to be found out? Will it be shouted from the rooftops by this afternoon, will it be in the morning headlines, or on the evening news?

Maybe that is one reason why he moved so often and to the city, to be among the deafening and impersonal roar of traffic, to drown out such publication. All that bustle makes for an uncanny cleverness at dealing with people.

But still there was always the sacrificial animal look in his eyes, as if the slaughterhouse was just around the corner. Could that be why he devoured so many legs of lamb with mint sauce, so much pork with apple sauce, turkey with stuffing, or ham baked with sliced pineapples and cloves, and braised beef on rice, for where could be the complaint if the abattoirs were in business? Nobody would come for him. And the veal, the young animals too he dug into their bodies with added gusto, into the cutlets, the regular Thursday specials.

And he was as polite as could be to everyone after demolishing another meal, staving off another day, staunching leaking queries with a full stomach, and even his own conscience was dulled by another day of indigestion, when the blood drains from the brain down to the agitated demands of the stomach. And by the time it returned, he was safely buried in research, digging unwittingly in the past, remaining late into the evening at the library, tracing once again the history from Europe in another family's lineage, another sea journey, through another ship's logbook that had tangential references to his own ancestors whose genes fanned out into Central Pennsylvania, looking for the missing gene that got lost, or though nobody knew buried in him.

He took courses at Penn and went to watering holes in downtown Philadelphia to find out but turned away in disgust. He even romanticized about his own gene, through religion and a belief in his own spirituality felt the purity of it, but his interest was stained by a hysterical society ignorant of the good he did.

But something must have struck him, something fallen, that when he looked at himself in the mirror expressed itself in those unrelated rages when he lost his temper in the too long intervals between meals and flailed and swung in the emptiness of the air.

He took refuge in Franz Kline and Van Gogh, in the Lancaster artist Demuth, himself trapped by so many watercolors of flowers and silos. Something inside him was doubly bound for not having that creative outlet. Instead, he uncovered every aspect of the artists' lives with a fine-toothed comb and cherished them as if they held the secret of himself.

And so when I saw him at the banquet, the meal was Chicken Cordon Bleu, with apologies on the menu for not having beef, I thought of his dilemma. He looked like a nineteen-twenties news reporter, a Mencken, a Clarence Darrow in suspenders, without their brilliance, but with a plodding kind of portly dignity in metal-rimmed glasses that in a moment could be excoriated by the community, beaten by the chairs everyone was politely sitting on.

I saw the almost mechanical movements his weight and secret had placed on him. His cherub-red face, his beady eyes— he always had them, unsympathetic looking under his eyeglasses—for the lifetime of hiding even from his wife and almost all his friends.

The toll was taken, and I thought he wrestled with more demons than the whole roomful of people combined. Demons that any day threatened to mobilize into a telling knock on the door. Demons of the past who were now adults, but whom he had entertained in the privacy of his apartment as angels that he would cherish a lifetime with strokes as deft and graceful as any of the great Renaissance painters like Botticelli, or Michelangelo.

Another Zoo Story

How he delighted the crowds with a Havana cigar in one hand and a can of beer in the other. He wore a Lincolnesque top hat and a gold-braided purple vest that went with the creamy brown of his skin. His antics had everyone rollicking at seeing their vices aped before their eyes.

He'd chug the beer and drum on his belly, inhale on the cigar, then roll over backwards without spilling a drop or losing his top hat and come up puffing smoke rings. It was a performance that delighted his handlers who never knew what he would do next, and so found themselves clapping along with the crowd.

Alfonse was jealous of Julie and Romeo who were always together, and he'd quickly step in when they had fights. Alfonse had given up Lily to Jocko, who was drawn to the pink tutu she wore when Alfonse would let her perform with him.

All the while Phillip bowed to everyone with his massive gray weight, and his trunk always raised for travel, though he never went anywhere. He was a living example of how bulk could be left behind. The most precious part of him had been sawed off and now he stood around all day resigned, unaffected by Alfonse's performance. For years he had acknowledged Charles only by moving backwards in his presence, hiding all emotion.

Ray was king of them all, whose tan ruff had forgotten about his proud walk. Instead he stalked shadows rolling over on his back, as lunatics do, growling at rainstorms or a full moon, imagining an affinity with thunder and lightning.

Babs, Lila, and Sara were always displaying the purplest rumps to each other, a permanently streaked dress that changed colors with their moods. Only they could read the delicate shades on their backsides, the exact degree of wiggle. Sam was the Mormon of the population, lording over the three females.

Slip left the herd to dote on Sandy who could go for days without water; so regal was he that he seemed to give Ray competition, though everyone knew despite his tawny hue he was only a humpbacked, spindly-legged impersonator. Slip gazed starry-eyed at Sandy, felt the shifting dune between them, as Jack and Billy, little more than harmless two-year-olds, sharpened their claws on the palm tree as if it were balsa, surveying the two love birds with bemused lynx eyes.

Lulu wanted to fly before she grew pregnant with Rosie by Henry who groaned for two straight nights with a constant toothache, as if it were he who was giving birth. She would have settled for bathing in the Tshopo River that ran by their compound, but it was fenced off, so she lay in the mud looking at the inviting current that bore her along like the smoothest fingers of a masseuse.

And there was Sherman who was fond of Lulu, and her soft skin, probably because of his prominent nose that some already coveted as an aphrodisiac. Sherman was as light-footed as the idea of war was absent from his armor-plated bulk.

Stripes who stood by incarcerated always had an eye out for Slip who was more graceful than Stripes despite his reputation for running. Maybe Stripes could imagine, despite shivers through his prison garb, his pink snout already buried in her soft coat.

Savannah towered above everyone with her exaggerated neck and always seemed to have a sore throat. Some wondered that she must have had the biggest heart of all for the blood to climb so high.

"How's the weather up there?" someone would inevitably ask. When she sneezed, tiny droplets of water would land on Stripes and Slip and everybody.

And then there was Chip, who ate so heartily that he could supply whole villages with fuel to burn. Also there was Jewel, more colorfully bedecked than any royalty. She seemed to fan herself and pirouette every time she was looked at. Jack and Billy had dreams of her, but never seemed to get past the idea of feathers already in their mouth and eyes accusatorily trained on them.

People came in busloads, herds of them from Brussels,

Antwerp, London, Paris, and from far away as New York and Tokyo. And with every paid admission the lawns were better tended, the tropical flowers more astonishingly colorful, the population healthier and better fed, and the Tshopo River more sparkling than ever threading its way through the most luxuriant vegetation.

Since 1954 the Gardens had been the Jewel of the Congo, the most prominent setting in the tiara of perhaps the richest continent in the world.

And the visitors grimaced, grew delighted, barked, squirmed, snorted, worked their jaws endlessly with mouths agape, pointing and marveling at the diversity of the life—redheads with freckles, with green, blue, gray eyes, and hair styles that shot out of their heads like beehives, pony tails, pig tails, flat tops, crew cuts, layered, spiked, crimped, wavy, yellowed, straightened and curled, kinky-black, flaxen, and lately fluorescent pink, green, and orange. The visitors looked on in amazement and belched in contentment at seeing themselves mirrored.

They wore black habits with white wimples, uniforms decorated with the most colorful insignia, hemp, silk, cotton, and polyester dresses, garb the likes of which the creatures they came to see were sometimes a poor imitation of. Even the toucan. They sported platform shoes, high heels, heavy boots, leather and straw sandals, sneakers, tennis shoes, clogs, and thongs.

But still the wildlife set the standard for the visitors, gave them ideas beyond adorning themselves with boas and skins, spots and stripes, with armor and crests, they taught them about living in close quarters, about boredom and abstinence, about mating rituals, parenting, aggression and peacefulness, about hunting and stalking, about every aspect of life imaginable.

The keepers too marveled at the visitors, how odd their dress, their habits, how they stopped to kiss and caress each other in all seasons, chewed gum and smoked tobacco, how boisterous they were, and shameless. And the copulation they came to see only warranted a bored glance from the participants, little different than what occurs everyday on the stages in Amsterdam.

All except Alfonse and his ilk, compelled as they were to entertain the tourists with their own habits. Some think that is why they came all the way from Europe, to see their behavior mimicked in Central Africa. The local population thought this a strange payback for all the years of colonialism. For despite the live imports to Europe, it wasn't the same as coming to the Congo and seeing these creatures in their natural habitat, with weather conducive to behavior that was unknown up North.

But one night there was an explosion and the sky lit up with the groan of shells and an orange tracery of bullets. The residents hunkered down and just looked on in amazement at the bursts of red flame, tried to protect their ears from the deafening roar, felt the vibrations race up their hooves. Alfonse groaned, Romeo and Julie hugged each other. Charles and Phillip lay mute like large gray boulders, immovable but sensitive to every tremor. They both had endured the grating sounds of hacksaws on their tusks, but still grew frightened at the periodic bursts of light.

Even Ray hunched closer to the ground as if his kingdom was now smaller than ever. Jack and Billy after fighting all day pretended to sleep balled up in each other's fur. They were young but not oblivious to the successive concussions that assumed a kind of rhythm, like the hum of an old hotel air conditioner whose wheezing and mechanical readjustments are required for the comfort of the human race.

Babs, Lila, and Sara quickly had patched up their differences and were huddled together around Sam, as their accelerated pulse now seemed one circulatory system.

Slip had rejoined the herd that stood still as if grazing, for the antelopes had no place to hide—maybe they thought Kenny the kudu, or Giles the impala, with their magnificent horns, might yet protect them. Slip kept her eyes on the camel tent all night to make sure Sandy was all right.

Lulu lay in mud with Rosie curled up in her belly, believing the bath of wet earth would amply hide her offspring. Sherman

139

couldn't see behind a solid metal door, but could smell Lulu's fear, and periodically between concussions would scratch the ground for her to hear.

Stripes was skittish and would have liked to break out from the enclosure and run to the savannas twenty kilometers away, lead the herd from the gunfire—and bring Savannah with her long neck along for reconnaissance. Maybe Chip and the rest could lead the way, stampede through the city for the open savannas. Jewel and her ilk would probably stay behind preening themselves, their feathers bound to be used for dusters or to amuse house cats.

The next day the keepers came to work, despite the stench of gunpowder still in the air, and the pockmarked earth. The stunned population was up looking out of their enclosures. The keepers were nervous, like the animals tentative, and seemed to have lost their appetites and focus on their surroundings. The residents picked up on the keepers' whispering, their hesitancy, their fears.

When the gates opened at nine there were no visitors, and for the next few weeks nobody but a few local families came. Civil war had broken out and the city was divided in two camps. After two weeks the rebels took over the city and the government had to flee to the countryside.

The workers' loyalties were divided, some fled with the government troops, others joined the rebels. Most of the senior staff stayed on to take care of the residents; however, since government functions were interrupted, they were paid out of petty cash, three days one week, two the next, finally they were reduced to getting a day's wages for a week's work.

The rebels were not disorganized, but their resources went into essential services. They could barely feed the people, so black markets sprang up overnight and the economy neared collapse. The influx of tourists stopped altogether, and even mediators from abroad canceled flights to Kisangani.

The keepers had to cut the rations of the residents in half, then quarter them. The enormous caloric requirements could no longer be met. The animals lost weight, grew lethargic, lost the sparkle in their eyes and the luster of their coats. The keepers at first brought food from their homes, some even stinting with their own families, but were overwhelmed by the metabolism of even smaller-sized animals.

The laughter, the joviality, the good spirits that existed before between the keepers and animals disappeared. Disgruntled, starved, accusatorial looks replaced them as the animals looked at their keepers in bewilderment, and the keepers dropped their eyes. The chimps pleaded with their yellowed eyeballs, the tiny red threads and rheum telling of a hunger that kept them awake at night. They no longer swung from chains or climbed on tires.

Alfonse took off his purple vest in protest, and of course the cigars and beer stopped. The top hat lay crushed in the corner of the cage, soiled with dry excrement, and nobody bothered to pick it up. Romeo and Julie lay in opposite sides of the cage among stiff brown banana skins. Phillip and Charles grew gaunt and their wrinkles multiplied massively as their loose skin lengthened even their sawed-off tusks.

Ray's ruff was matted with clots of filthy debris, as his long purple tongue tried lazily to catch the rows of flies lining the wet mucus of his eyelids. The youngsters Jack and Billy seemed fluffier now that they grew emaciated. They no longer played except to push each other feebly away. There was water from the Tshopo River, but it was infested with typhus from the dead bodies. The keepers hadn't the fuel to boil the water, not even from Chip.

Babs, Lila, and Sara were red-rumped as their sexuality had lost its purple and withered the rest of their bodies with hunger. Slip was just that, a slip of an antelope whose legs were rickety as a newborn an hour after birth. Sandy sat all day and stared, that the keepers wondered if he'd ever have the strength to get up. Lulu seemed to have lost all her flesh except the bulge that was Rosie. And Sherman seemed only armor and horn. Stripes seemed totally black now as his white stripes were collapsing into one absence of color. Savannah too lost her reach and could barely feed herself. Chip and his kind were lying in their own dry droppings so long they became a permanent part of their bodies.

Then one day a shell fell into the elephant house. Neither Phillip nor Charles was hit, though the ground shook wildly. But the next morning Charles crossed his buckling knees and crashed to the ground. It shook as if another shell had struck the compound. The palm trees trembled and dropped their last two coconuts. But the flesh was rotten inside as one of the workers opened them in vain. The keepers went up to Charles who was breathing heavily. Some remembered the rides he dutifully gave tourists, how majestically he bent down, rose and swayed back and forth as his tail kept a kind of rhythm to his ears flapping gently fanning himself. They noted how especially gentle he was with children on board.

The veterinarian was called, but by that time Charles's heart gave out and he died of a massive hemorrhage. Phillip stood in the corner and didn't move, but then for the first time in years came out of his stall head first. Inside a week he too was dead, and mysteriously that is when the disappearances started. It was as if nobody had gotten the idea until Charles died.

The remaining workers had not been paid for months and were living from hand to mouth, coming to work every day hoping for a change. Soon the cages started to empty one by one and lost the odor of life and the bracing stench of ammonia. Each night another animal disappeared, and by day a curious eeriness filled the zoo.

The workers went about their duties cleaning the cages of dust and bird droppings, for the animals now rarely fouled them with anything more than little greenish brown puddles, or the tiniest balls of excrement. Some looked sadder than before, others healthier. The antelope, zebras, giraffes, and buffalo were first to go after the elephants. But though they were starving by the time of Charles's collapse and had little flesh on their bones, it is certainly to the keepers' credit that they waited so long.

When Professor Samuel Ndomba's article appeared in the newspaper that too signaled the beginning of the end.

"How can people feed the animals when they are hungry themselves, when our children are malnourished. It's a crime!" he wrote.

That's when the disappearances accelerated. One night the two chimps disappeared, Romeo and Julie, then Alfonse himself. Some of the keepers were in tears the next morning remembering Alfonse's antics, how he mimicked their behavior chugging beer and blowing smoke rings, how he brought smiles to countless tourists over the years. His handler went into a deep depression and said he didn't want Alfonse's vest. And his crushed top hat remained in the corner even after the cage was cleaned.

Only Ray's ruff was left scattered around the cage one morning when the keepers arrived, though fresh blood was still on the bars. Jack and Billy disappeared the same night. Babs, Lila, and Sara were missed on successive days, soon after Sam, though people in that part of Africa had never been heard to eat baboon.

The hippo and the rhino were last to go, all except for Roc the crocodile. He was the only survivor and stayed alive for more than three months after his last meal of fish in January. He lived until April. It was rumored that Julie was fed to Roc, but nobody believed it. Still some keepers had an especial respect for the longevity of the crocodile, for its cold-blooded tenacity. It was a survivor, like they were, and so a pall of gloom settled over the facility when Roc died. They had tried to feed him snakes, but he wouldn't take them.

"He was one tough guy," a worker said.

The workers still show up promptly every morning because the zoo is officially open. They go about their duties cleaning the empty cages, tidying up for the animals' return. Maybe they don't admit to themselves they are really gone, such ponderously massive presences, such graceful dignified creatures, so in possession of themselves, and with whom they formed such intimacy. Chimps and baboons, so like them that they gave audiences and keepers alike endless pleasure. Even Roc in his element floated into their psyches, all nostrils and eyes, with a dental heritage they too denied, refusing to admit openly the animals they had eaten.

"They were like relatives!" one keeper said bursting into tears.

Alfonse's handler refused to speak to journalists, he was too broken up. Everyone now had grave expressions on their faces going through the motions of a normal day, carrying inside them the huge deception that there were still animals to care for. Though there was no smell of excrement, or urine that kept their airways free of colds and respiratory infections. Their blood pressures even rose now that there were no animals to pet or care for. In fact a curious malaise overtook the workers.

Pierre Bambalayo, a senior worker, insists the zoo isn't closed, that it is open.

"There just aren't any animals," he says.

Ramazan Bekanda still claims "they died of hunger."

The skull in Joseph Okoko's office nobody will say for sure is Alfonse, but everyone knows it contains a spirit that some believe at night blows smoke rings.

The civil war still rages, but the remaining zookeepers are curiously pacific— perhaps from their charges safely in their bellies, contributing to the remaining luster in their eye, the gloss of their hair, their own body movements and animal strength, as they go about the business of now caring more meticulously for their absence.

But a closer look reveals that they are less healthy than before. Maybe they have simply been aged by all the turmoil, by the betrayal, and loss of their reason for living—the absent antics of their charges, their missing love affairs or attachments, by Charles and Phillip not getting along for years without coming to blows, by Ray who would lie in the sunshine and not want anymore to pounce on Slip or any member of her herd, by the antics of the jaguars Billy and Jack, little more than cubs who lost the habit of playing only when they grew emaciated, by the love triangle of Lila, Babs, and Sara for Sam, by the distance always in Sandy's eyes, or the gravid beauty of Lulu with tiny Rosie inside her belly, by Sherman always standing before the metal door of his concrete cage, or Stripes permanently wearing the emblem of his incarceration with dignity, and by Chip who may already be sewn together for someone's shoes, or Roc who surely is a handbag, or last but not least Jewel and her feathers for dusting or decorations.

Unoka now has gout worse than ever. Maybe it is from the purines in the meat he ate when the rest of the city was starving that he can hardly get around the grounds anymore. Okoye has heart disease; his cholesterol got out of hand a few weeks before, and the doctor advises a diet of legumes and grains. Okonokwo is having dizzy spells from, his wife says, "moping all the time and not eating—he doesn't even know a civil war is raging."

Tombo is forever lying in the doorway of the tiger cage he used to take care of. Some whisper the spirits of Ben and Louise pass him by and flies collect on his body like they did on Louise when she didn't have the strength to brush them off. Babo has constant eye infections since he puts his hands in them, for he no longer washes them after petting Stripes. Samba's liver is bothering him since, his brother says, he drinks all the time. Nobody knows where he gets the money. They say he constantly talks to Stripes about Savannah and tells him she is all right. Alfonse's handler they say is losing his mind, talking to himself more and more these days, swatting at flies not even on him. They say sometimes he sits in his office and stares at Alphonse's skull for hours.

Still they all turn up each morning to clean cages whose occupants in a moment of hunger filled their empty bellies.

The Lifesaver

The round white candy gives the impression of a life preserver, something to reach out with the tongue for the sweet to dissolve in the mouth much like the sea that when we cease fighting will pleasantly absorb us. The old woman who took care of him liked them, as if when her daughter who worked for the Red Cross brought them back after work they somehow prolonged her existence.

There was also the idea with the mint's replication that the sweet experience could drown the aches and pains of old age, sibling rivalry, the teasing and torment, the inexactitude of love shown to each, for sheer numbers alone preserve, much like the Pez candy the man remembered as a boy when he was being placed in the orphanage that he could pop into his mouth on the long bus ride to Pennsylvania as a reminder of the love he experienced in his former home. The sadness was so palpable when he was being taken away that he hoped that long afternoon that his mother would never show up. He remembered the jungle film he was watching just before she arrived and the walk to the bus stop on Castle Hill Avenue. Only sugars could cut through that, a sweetness that was an antidote to the bitterness of being taken away.

And he had a little gun into which balls of candy went, and a refill, not to shoot anyone of course, but as ammunition against them nevertheless. The remarkable thing is that the boy didn't eat the candy but saved it, was comforted by those balls of candy in reserve, by the Pez, and the Life Savers the old woman who had taken care of him liked, and that reminded him of his current predicament. For numbers count just like the waves that kept coming, just like successive generations piling on top of each other until the old are crushed by the weight of the times, by every new discovery and invention that leaves them feeling unneeded and barely able to keep up. Wave after wave of youths keep coming incentivized by the need to make money, by the bottom line, by ever more personalized electronic gadgets, by marginalizing those left behind.

In the ocean the same man swam years later with his two children. He was seventy, his boy fifteen and girl eighteen. The boy's manhood was coming into his own, his voice deepening, his assertive powers growing daily. The man was irritated by that and by his not wearing a shirt in the house, showing off his muscles at mealtimes. His sister had bullied him all his childhood, but not any more. Now it was his turn, but to balance that the father ganged up on him just before high noon. He kept the boy's kickboard he had brought to the beach away from him, passing it to his daughter so the boy couldn't get it. The boy dove, lunged, angrily splashed water on the father and daughter, but they were successful keeping the board from him, frustrating him, the father even letting the board drift close to him then with its nylon cord yanking it back at the last moment, teasing the boy.

No one was mindful of the waves. A big one comes and smacks the boy from behind and he goes under, tumbles around, then comes up wiping the seawater from his eyes. He locates his father and sister and imagining they are responsible goes after them resuming his efforts to get the board. Finally he grabs the board from his sister, punches her and turns around and splashes water in his father's face. He does to the father and his sister what the two did to him, teasing them with the board, letting it float in front of them, then quickly yanking it back. But the father ignores the board until the boy loses interest, then he turns to his sister. She taunts him. He gets angry and tries to hit her with the board. The father yells at him then suddenly grabs the board.

The boy turns and swims toward the father who backs up pulling the board. He can touch bottom, so he lets the board float up to the boy and just as he grabs for it pulls it out of his reach, then lets it go again, but close enough to keep the boy's interest. He then passes the board around to his daughter. She gets it and swims away from her brother kicking, madly splashing him, then just before he catches up she circles and throws the board to the father. The son swims madly after the

147

father who is backing up pulling the board away. But the boy gets it, then turns again and attacks his sister. They struggle with the board until it is released, and the boy screams to his father, and sister, to "go get it" as a crashing wave sends the board sailing towards the shore. Nobody goes after it on the principle that the boy touched it last.

The waves crash and flow and spin the board around carrying it further away from everyone then towards them, but finally further away. The board is bobbing independently as if glad to be out of the internecine struggle, free of the family feud, merrily riding the waves, being in fact a board made of the most buoyant material.

The son yells, "Get it!" to the father.

Still the father doesn't move after it, while the boy continues to attack his sister. He yells out again, "Get the board!"

The ocean has other ideas and leaves the board to the whim of each crashing wave. It is as if a relief from the taunting play and rough handling by the family, a relief from their grudges, from the powerful sibling rivalry, the jealousies, from the father's authority and the son's challenge to it. Each wave, one after another, crashes clearly but at erratic intervals, though sometimes in synchronous patterns relieving associations the board has with the fight. Yet the board is symbolic of the struggle, now bobbing freely. The ocean itself is playing with the board, demonstrating an autonomy the family doesn't have. Their playing is urgent, teasing almost beyond endurance, even mean-spirited. The son gets so angry that the daughter gloats over the state she's brought her brother to, but the father is conflicted.

The ocean tosses the board up and down, turns it every which way around, lets it float freely beyond all consideration that it will be retrieved, allows it to sail away on its own.

The father finally swims after it. It is as elusive as if one of them were still holding it, as the waves continue crashing. He finally catches up with it.

The brother and sister are far out now still fighting,

splashing each other. He's chasing her, she is out-swimming him.

The father yells to them not to go far. But the crashing waves mute his warnings, and their power makes him ineffectual. They are both thoroughly absorbed with each other. The hostility is enough to give them a peculiar buoyancy, unmindful of the ocean's depth and danger. The boy is not a strong swimmer, and the girl always swims too far for comfort. The father swims towards them, but the waves thrust him back. He can't reach them carrying the board. Finally he holds the board in front of him and kicks. Still he can't reach them. The waves are higher now, separating him. He is thrown back time and again. The board is bright blue and has a grinning shark on it with a fearsome mouth full of yellow teeth, a grin, but threatening. Earlier the father said taking his daughter's side that that's his son pictured on the board. Finally expending all his efforts swimming, despite the board pulling him back, the father gets close to his son and manages to thrust the board to him.

For a moment his son thinks he is taunting him and backs up, but then takes the board in surprise. The water is deeper, he can't touch bottom.

"Are you okay?" the father asks.

"Yes," the boy says.

Then to his daughter the man yells.

She is far out and so he doesn't know if she has heard him. He's told her to be careful all week. He imagines she can't hear him for the crashing waves that seem more relentless, determined, now that he is fatigued. He is worried she might be caught like both were three summers ago. An undercurrent trapped them and didn't let them return to shore. He could do nothing to help her. He calmed her down, and himself, saying, "Don't fight it. We'll drift out of it. Don't panic."

To be so near to her and not be able to help her was unimaginable, the worst feeling in the world. The father never forgot it. The ocean worked against their strokes, caught them in the undertow, like his conflicting feelings for each child trapped him, the constant weighing. He absolutely couldn't do anything, so close to her, yet separated. The sea wouldn't let them in. He was afraid they'd both drown. Afterwards, they never went back to that beach.

Now the waves have gotten bigger, were crashing and pulling him out but he was still yelling to her if she was all right.

Yes, she seemed to say, but he realized he was caught. He could not touch bottom and the waves were crashing relentlessly one after another and pulling him back and wouldn't let him go ashore. He'd lost his footing long ago and was tired. His boy on the left seemed okay on the board. His girl was out further still swimming. Worried, he yelled more than once for her to go in, but he himself felt he couldn't. He was thrown back by each wave, unable to swim a clean stroke, the water was so rough and he was exhausted. He who had permitted himself the luxury of taunting was now tossed by successive waves in a cachinnation of crashing that he couldn't tell apart from machine gun fire, so rapid was it. He hoped they would slacken, swimming against their giant troughs that drew him down and further out to sea, not letting him touch bottom or gain headway closer to the shore.

He thought, Oh, no, what an undignified way to die. He struggled fatigued, then thought, Will it just overpower him? Is this the end? He'd run out of energy and that would be that. His fatigue would get the better of him and he'd sink down. The feeling for a second was almost pleasant. His body was so fatigued physically and mentally. What a relief! All the lifelong work, the pressure of daily exercise, all those calisthenics, just to keep on top of things, all the hours spent at his desk, the terrible tension of producing something worthwhile, the exhausting choice of food to maintain his health, the burden of the mind to daily fortify his self-esteem, to please people, his ever-dwindling ego. Just let all that go and succumb. What a relief! He'd lose inevitably in the end. Why not now, give in finally and be released. It's not so bad, cradled by the sea. He'd lived enough of life. They wouldn't miss him, the way he took sides, tried to balance their rivalry for years, stop their pitiless crushing each other, in the end alienating both of them. The girl hated him for years whenever he took her smaller brother's side. Now it was the boy's turn, and so he tried to protect the girl from his physical strength. Something gave way, relaxed for a moment, consoled him, the struggle of a whole lifetime, finally to be over with a much-deserved rest in saltwater.

But the irony. Only that he suddenly pulled himself together from, a brief second or two of thoughts, and fought the ignominious drowning. What an embarrassment to end like this! It was for all its appeal too simple. Drowned at the ocean one summer day. While on vacation! Of course, the force pulling him under was greater than the inevitable gravity on land, the tall scythed reaper had become one with its watery extension. He was not to enter the ocean. The father wouldn't let him so his kids would be safe, but he'd drown himself, get caught without their knowing it. He who was so certain about things, they could hardly imagine it. He felt humiliated fighting another crashing wave, ever more exhausted, but then realized what he already knew. Don't fight it. Just let the waves take you out, conserve your energy. They will bring you back. Be smart. His heart was pounding so that he thought his sternum would crack.

He looked towards his daughter, yelled again for her to "swim in."

"I'm telling you to!" and he finally saw her drift closer to shore.

He was thoroughly exhausted, let himself catch wave after wave, tried not to panic, or fight against them. They pulled him back so much he'd borne the brunt of their assault and little by little he rode them and was ushered forward when finally his feet touched bottom. His chest was about to split open in pain. His girl on the other side also seemed to have found the bottom. The boy was okay too, already walking down the beach, his board trailing.

The father realized that he'd almost drowned. Neither child came towards him. The boy was angry at the taunting, at the father taking sides; the girl realized just like him that she

151

was alone.

He remembered one night visiting her when she was very young to tuck her into bed and she was so distant, unresponsive to anything he said, and he realized for the first time she knew the solitude of being alone. He was shocked by her discovery so young, but it was something even hugs or kisses could not overcome. He was alone all his life, even with his family. So was she.

He could barely breathe ashamed and exhausted as he walked on the beach, free of the ocean that had pulled them so far out. The children barely talked when they reached their towels.

"I almost drowned," the father said to his wife, but the children were silent.

The boy vaguely referred to being taunted. The daughter said she was all right.

It was only him.

His wife said people in Japan drowned all the time. Especially parents trying to save their children.

"No," the son said, "nobody drowns in South Carolina."

"Yes," they do she says.

"You don't realize it's happening," the father said and dropped on his knees trying to cross two pieces of straw to make a man walking over the bridge his son had so carefully constructed out of sand and materials he found on the beach. The boy was always eclipsed by what his father did in the sand. Yesterday the father buried a glob of seaweed that distinctly resembled a hand and made a circular pattern around it and placed a ball the size of a baseball to one side, then added another. Then he placed pieces of rush at the top and side of the balls, so their shadows united everything into an abstract design that connected the hand and the balls. In a few simple moves he had conveyed so much. More than once his son had destroyed his own constructions that week, and even occasionally what his father made.

It drove the boy that morning to make an elaborate bridge of hundreds of pieces of straw and sand, and to finally give the

152

boy room to breathe the father made nothing, but now looked around for material. He just wanted to give the bridge focus, the reality of someone passing over it. But the crossed rush wasn't firm enough to make a man. He continued to look in the piles of debris but couldn't find anything durable that would crisscross to sustain arms. Not even seaweed for hair or a hat did he find, or anything to bulk out a body, but then he spied a large dried black beetle. He put it on the bridge, readjusted it after trying to affix straws through it, in order to make an upright passenger, but finally decided the beetle looked like a vehicle itself. In placing it the father knocked the overhead supports.

"Dad's destroying my bridge," the boy quickly said, while the father tried to repair the damage he had done, not unlike the boy breaking the father's sand sculptures the last few days, not giving his son's creative energies a chance to flourish.

The father tried to make love that night. The night before his wife had rebuffed him. He came inside her this time, but suddenly lost all feeling and desire. Even though her womb was moving in waves. It was as if he already had gone limp in the ocean, was drowned inside her. His wife tried to please him afterwards, but he knew it wouldn't work. He was just lucky to be there, having escaped with enough power to exit the ocean.

The Child Molester

Just as a diver will visualize a dive he himself is about to make, he likewise sees the whole scene in graphic detail. The walk to the end of the board, the tiny pirouette, the arms horizontal, the back to the pool, the spring, the back flip, twist, the entry into the water, clean like a knife leaving almost no splash. It is a perfectly executed dive.

He too sees it all. The candy, shiny through the wrapping, the multicolored presents, the actual couch in the apartment where the man lives alone, the brown stains on it. He doesn't need forensics, magnifying glasses, hair samples, lab analyses. He's visualized everything himself. He imagines a thicket of curly pubic hair, fingers entwining it, the softest down on the cheek, the little boy trapped, the moans, screams, finally a whimper. The man pudgy, doughy-fingered, red-cheeked, like a cherub himself, middle-aged, puffing, having difficulty moving, breathing, but prodded by his desires that light up his whole body until he positively glows. The cajoling, the wheedling, the games to undress each other, the police officer has cataloged all of it, every move in his mind. He has children of his own. So he is horrified by what he envisions, but the visualizations persist against his will. The thoughts crowd his brain and torment him. He gets hotter under the collar. His clothes are ill-fitting lately, an inconvenience, a line of sweat trickles from his underarms, down his back to the elastic of his briefs. He pushes his spouse away when she is solicitous about what's wrong. He can't shake the pictures in his mind. They upset him too much. He is rough with her at times, then retreats further into silence.

"Just leave me alone," he says to her. He lives his job.

"Round them all up! Get them off the streets!"

"Hey Jack, take two," someone at the station house says.

It is his personal crusade. He loves children, is bound to their safety and welfare, can't accept anyone taking advantage of them, gets ill over even the thought of it, the visualizations.

They disturb his sleep, his relationship with his own children. He's stopped spending time with them, doesn't tuck them into bed anymore, and they've stopped calling out to him to come. He's an absentee father scouring the streets for their protection.

His job has become a mission, a one-man crusade. He works overtime collaring what he calls the scum of the earth "to make the streets safe," he says, "for our children."

He lapses into gloomy reverie even at parties. Has to be snapped out of it. Friends comment that he's not himself, has taken his job too much to heart. He needs a vacation.

But he's afraid the street population of criminals will multiply with him gone, infest the whole city by the time he's back. He's needed to stop "the plague, the infestation," as he calls it.

He's sitting at the house of friends, at the precinct, in his car staking out an apartment on the outskirts of town that he is ready to bust into on a neighbor's tip.

"Let's wait for backup this time, Jack," his partner says.

Jack imagines the pudgy fingers at the last button on the little boy's clothes. The boy is down to his underpants. The man is slipping his index finger around back and working the elastic down over the little round buttocks. Just then there is a flurry of activity in the police car, a 1045 call on a robbery in progress. And the police car speeds away to a convenience store on Hardwick. A man is running up the street, cash in hand. The cruiser pulls up beside him. Jack rolls down his window and takes out his service revolver.

"Freeze," he says, "or I'll blow your head off!"

The man stops dead. Crouches on the pavement and covers his head with the cash.

"Take it, take it. Don't shoot!" he whimpers.

Jack jumps out of the vehicle and grabs the man.

"Stand up, hands behind your back!" They handcuff him and book him.

In a couple of hours Jack and his partner are back staking out the apartment. Jack's mind continues the narrative. There is blood on the buttocks this time, a torn sphincter muscle, like a balled-up leech trying to protect itself. The multiple corrugations pulled tight to prevent opening. The globes of the white bottom are streaked red. The little boy is crying. Jack holds his fist to his forehead. There is a static sound against the roots of his hair where he turns his head in disgust at what's happening out there.

He gets out of the cruiser.

"Jack, where're you goin'?"

He walks aimlessly, then returns more silent.

He's visualized it all, a hundred times before. He can barely look at his own kids. It torments him, but the rare arrest also bothers him. He wants to get them all. Round them all up like sheep, pigs for slaughter, every last one of them, use a Gatling gun or something. Then burn down the whole smelly stockyard. Or erect his own crematoria to burn their genes out of the human race forever, stop the bloodlines of pederasts once and for all.

Jack imagines himself goose-stepping through the city, searching every last house, with the authority of swastikas on each collar, and on the streets rounding up suspect men with young boys, every last one of them!

"Taking the kid to a movie, the park, a ball game. Yeah, sure. Tell me another one!" as he pushes their heads into the police car, crowds them inside the paddy wagon.

"Sweep the streets clean!" He imagines himself a Pied Piper. That's what that tale was all about. Saving the children from molesters! He'll boxcar every last one in the city.

They'll not know what hit'em, or where they're going. They'll be taken to camps all over the country that'll be operated in secret to stamp out the gene once and for all, eradicate the vermin, an inferior strain of people, to remove the plague on all our families!

"Greek love!" he laughs to himself, shaking his head, and has visions of marble statuary, lewd nymphs, young goddesses, boys with delicately translucent bodies where the light almost goes through their slender limbs, and the giant phalluses all broken off, smashed to bits, powdered like the Acropolis by the Turks.

Jack imagines a simon-pure society, the removal of every sick obsession with body parts, and the preoccupation with youth. Sometimes he imagines everyone has designs on prepubescence, lowers his eyes and buries his head in his hands at the discouraging thought of just what he is up against.

"You OK, Jack?" his partner asks.

"Yeah, I was just thinking."

"About what?"

"Nothing, nothing."

He can't stand the mental picture, sees bloody leeches everywhere, dripping from billboards, the reddest lips holding cigarettes on the dry mouths of even coworkers he talks too. They must be saved even from themselves. He wants to do the cleansing himself, with sulfuric acid, something! But it is beyond him. It's all over the city, and he can't seem to stop it. The streets need hosed down, and he's only one man on the force.

Then they get a call, over on Gunhill Road they have word of a molester. A charge has been filed. The police car speeds crosstown. Sirens blaring, the blue light revolving. On the way Jack once again visualizes it all, relives the seduction. He's seen it a hundred times in gross movements that make him almost shy away from his own children, suspecting molesters everywhere, sniffing out body fluids, their behavior on their clothes, on furniture fabrics, not making eye contact anymore.

They get to 521 and are out of the patrol car in a flash. Jack is the first to the entrance, pounding on the door.

"Police, open up! Police!"

He knocks, turns the knob, pushes at the door with his shoulder.

The door is opened by a large pudgy man with red cherubic cheeks and gold metal-rimmed glasses. The shock of hair over his forehead gives him a middle-aged boyish look. He's just like Jack visualized. He knows the man already, every feint, gesture,

157

blink, the camouflage of abundant pink flesh. Jack is wiry, gaunt, and pushes the man inside his apartment, muscles him across the room.

"We got a call on you, man," he says. "You've been seen with a young boy? Taking him places, entertaining him here! In your apartment? Huh?"

"Oh, Johnny?"

"What'd you do to him? Where is he? Someone's filed a complaint."

"I don't know."

Jack pokes him in the chest with his forefinger, pushes him down on the couch. Jack is spitting epithets at the man, frothing at the mouth.

"You scum, low life! Turn over, turn over! What I'd like to do to you!"

"Jack, take it easy!" his partner yells, as Jack unhooks his handcuffs, grabs the man's hands, and clicks them on his wrists.

"What am I being charged with?" the man asks.

"Molesting a minor!"

"We just want to take you downtown for questioning," the second officer says.

The man is silent. He no longer bothers to defend himself. He remembers the times he had with Johnny. It seemed too good to be true. Taking him to the amusement park, the gifts, buying his favorite toys, food, their holding hands. His mother was rarely at home, and his father was always working, so Johnny spent more and more time with him. Many an afternoon they sat on the same couch and watched TV, talked, played games, the man read to the boy, helped him with his homework. On Saturdays he took him to the park. Occasionally the boy brought friends over, but mostly seemed to want the man all to himself.

No, the man had no wife, and even met Johnny's mother once or twice at the supermarket or somewhere, but she was unimpressed with the man and was just glad Johnny was out of her hair and behaving better lately. She didn't question the money Johnny got, or didn't seem to mind the time he spent away from home.

The little boy was the light of the man's life. He just enjoyed being around him, enjoyed his innocence, purity, grew in fact to love the little boy, his freshness, his quick responsiveness to the world, to the man's tutoring, to the simple pleasure they took in each other's company.

And was the man attracted to the boy in the way the officer had so often visualized? The man didn't know himself. His desire was piqued by the anticipation of the boy coming over, by seeing the boy, by being with him, sharing sweets, holding hands at the amusement park. That was the extent of their physical involvement. Had the man wanted to touch the boy further, and had he, both the boy and the man would have been confused.

You might say that the man's sexuality was at ground level, never plumbed or visualized taking a dive beneath that. There was no pool behind him, or acrobatic back flip, no seamless entry into the water, no bloody sphincter leeches like Jack envisioned, no bottom breached.

The man was the kind bemused by sexuality, for it seemed not to pertain to him, or be an issue in his life. What was kept alive and visualized by the man's neighbor, by Jack, had never occurred to the pudgy, pink man with a cherub face and gold-rimmed glasses.

The man did speak of the boy to friends, describing the beauty of the boy, but to them it was almost marmoreal, for his limbs had the smooth polish of remote Greek statuary. His friends even joked that the little boy must have wings.

But visions of statues can break, be smashed by the most unexpected violence, so too the man found himself on the floor of his apartment. Jack's rage got the better of him. He couldn't wait to book the man, for the trial, for court proceedings, the verdict, the incarceration, couldn't wait for the boxcar, the gas chamber, the crematoria in his own mind burning with anger at the man. Couldn't wait to reduce the pink flesh to ashes as his fist collided with the man's jaw and sent him reeling backwards, crashing amidst not only the statuary of his own mind, but Jack's preoccupation with every stain he already spied on the couch, around which he had sniffed like a police dog with the most sensitive snout you could imagine on one human being who can visualize every last detail of another man's crime.

The Watchband

She lost interest in me soon after I bought an alligator watchband. She said it was not me. That there had been nothing about it that even remotely suggested that I should have that strip of leather on my arm, even to tell time.

She knew I didn't even like Florida, the clammy warmth of its climate, the almost year-round humidity, the heat and swampiness. She said she knew I wasn't made for everglades, that there was something deciduous in my personality, that the air I needed was brisk, bracing, and seasonal, that a part of me had to be shed periodically, not cut away in strips, torn from for profit. And too she knew that there wasn't anything stubbornly hidebound about me, that nothing in me could be flayed and dried in the sun and stitched together into a handbag, shoes, much less a simple watchband.

Yes, she did admit that I had rather large bumps on my head, that my cranium had certain prominent orbits that heightened the roundness and protuberance of my eyes. And, yes, too there was a certain underbite, a certain prognathous jutting of the jaw that until I had the watchband on she had never noticed before. And my arms, they had never seemed so short, and the froglike fingers now that she noticed them were webby, and stumpy, that's what she said, and when I smiled at her she seemed to notice my teeth for the first time, the incisors elongated into a silly grin that nothing could wipe off.

But it wasn't until I suggested that we go for a swim, even though it was at a lake and admittedly a temperate climate up in New England, that she hesitated and for the first time I read fear on her face.

Never before had I seen such an emotion on a woman. My awkwardness on land had always been a joke between us. She always took it as a kind of embellishment to her own grace. And though she knew I was a good swimmer—at least I told her I had represented my high school on the swimming team—she never put the two together, my talent in the water and my awkwardness on land with the alligator band I was now wearing. But she only repeated, "It's not you," as if to assure herself.

She looked at me as I grinned at her and I could sense how she lengthened further my already large nose into a snout, how the nares floated up in her mind long before we were to enter the water and already became large breathing vents that alone were enough to give also the impression that my eyes were lidlessly drifting up the side of my head depriving me of bifocal vision. And not even I could see how she then imagined a thick tail, and the convulsion of disgust that rippled through her body as my skin grew more reticulated, swelling my midriff so that someone could ride me in the water, and tame me, that too she turned away from, as from my white underbelly.

She wanted power in a man, but not the kind that would at one swift and unexpected stroke snap its head with the strength of ten men and dismember the person on top—even if it were someone holding onto my neck for a joke. She turned away from that as if wreathes of blood were already garlanding a lost limb in the water that was hanging onto the body only by the whitest pretext of a solitary tendon.

She sat there on the beach, me with my robe still on, and smiled at my two legs deceptively exiting from the hem and said, "Don't you think you better take your watch off—looking at the alligator band—before you go in the water?"

"Oh," I said looking at her with a train of thought as long as the body the rest of the band had been cut from. "No, it's waterproof."

Food: A Brief Family History

The Old Man

The trunk of food was kept under the bed. Only he had the key.

Food is not easy, and it can make life more difficult than it is. His wife had just died of consumption, and the family, except for what the old man doled out, was always hungry. That makes an impression on you that doesn't go away no matter how many meals eaten in compensation, or banquets attended. The specter of the wolf at the door is always there. Food becomes the short-lived passion hiding the most ravenous appetite, though we bag it, jar it, can it, and freeze it, our stomachs are never full enough even after we are sated.

His control was almost biblical, like Joseph's. He determined the lean periods, those times of dearth, and plenty though they never quite came. He knew which of the six children felt hungry, who went without lunch or to bed without supper, or, when they moved to Blackrock Avenue, who lived in the attic. They naturally got less. The rest never minded the trunk.

"Pop never did that!" exclaimed the youngest boy who'd grow up to be a doctor. "Not Pop!"

But Mary knew better and said her father beat her and called her "Cockroach" because of her red hair. In her seventies she said her son was just like her father. She never got over his calling her not Carrot Top, but the very insect that ravaged the food supply.

No wonder her father saw himself as Joseph doling out food. The Great Depression dictated that. There were, after all, dust bowls, bank failures, and food shortages everywhere, so why not in the cold water flat in New York City where the Irish immigrants had come to a land of plenty. Mike who boarded the boat in Dublin was that old man who snapped the lid on the trunk down, but not before the children caught sight of biscuits, raisins, and sugar.

Often Mary and Sarah conspired in the attic to break into the trunk at night, but Mary ended up moving out early on, abandoning the family so her father claimed. She never got over the old man. He was all men depriving her of if not food outright, then her dignity. She was always on the alert to the loss of self-esteem, and bought stacks of books to bolster it, *The Power of Positive Thinking, How to Win Friends and Influence People, The Knack of Selling Yourself, The Science of Successful Living.*

What possessed the old man to lock up the food can be traced to potato famines in Ireland, the blight that had people grubbing in the soil for roots. Hunger pervaded Ireland for hundreds of years. It must have been imprinted in his genes and the idea of a lock and key answered that privation with his rationing of the food supply to his own children. His favorites Aggie, Kathleen, and Joe got more being younger. That was never lost on Mary and Sarah. The least inequality is measured more than we know; it adds a metabolism of resentment that weighs on the mind and loses flesh. None of the girls ever got fat; the memories were too vivid, the hunger ever present. Later they ate voraciously, burning off what they ate with memories of the trunk with thick brass bands that crossed an ocean. The trunk was too imposing to break into. It was the extra room in the house, emblem of a new life across the sea, but where blissful visions of sweets were kept under lock and key. What was inside like all goodness was only barely glimpsed, until a cold hard look destroys the dreams that made the children's mouths water at the thought of eating the imagined delicacies within.

The children's stomachs growled as if they were animals sniffing to appease their appetites. But fear of their father kept them out. The youngest had the confidence of being favored. But Mary and Sarah living in the attic away from the trunk were objects of his peculiar austerity.

Maybe Mike imagined himself an archangel and his bright key the sharp sword protecting the food supply, for every man's home is his castle.

What was passed on in the old man runs deep in the Irish personality, inspires jigs on an empty stomach until the dancers fall down exhausted at their hunger and lose consciousness.

The trick was to keep moving for as long as you can, hoping the trunk will open, a crock of gold will turn up, or the generosity of strangers will bring relief, a wealthy relative, or the kindness of a classmate's mother who recognizes again that you have no lunch. The senselessness of hunger inspires music and dance to remove the blight on the population, when landowners close their doors and the house food supply is kept under lock and key. It causes the most lyrical songs and frenzied movements to dispel the white saliva on lips that crack and ooze blood. It rouses the instincts to song and dance that define a people whose superficially happy jigs have them dropping from exhaustion in triumph over hunger.

"Why they *are* a lively people! Let's bring'em to the mainland. Do jigs at our meals! Boy, the Irish can dance. Is your name Danny boy? Kick'em high, that's right, and I know you can sing for your supper! Katie, I've heard you."

"Amuse us and we'll fill your stomach with potato bread, potato pancakes, potato soup, spuds for the poor souls who can't feed themselves."

"What's wrong with them anyway? They seem lively enough! And their island is green as an emerald, it must be full of riches!"

"Then why are our landowners losing money?"

"Let them dance, instead of always rooting around in our garbage, yelling potato famine. Why can't they feed themselves like everyone else?"

"I guess we have to take care of them. Still it is the Christian thing to do! Though it's exhausting even collecting taxes. Why don't we cut them off altogether?"

"But then who'll amuse us at our banquets? They do tell a jolly tale and do a mighty fine jig!"

"I know they think their poets are more musical! Their jigs are what amuses us! We own the stage but can use their stomping and background music. And the grain bins are under our lock and key. We determine who shall eat. We dole out the food. We are the masters, the stewards, ungrateful Micks! Give them a potato pancake and they're in seventh heaven, and they think they have a right to our larders, give them the key and they always want more, more flour, more sugar! It'll upset their digestion! They can wait! How about another dance? Sean, get the company in here!"

"But they haven't eaten, milord."

"Afterwards! Afterwards!"

The old man fiddled in the cold water flat and his children danced for him and sang for their supper. The youngest girls had the most beautiful and willing voices and so they pleased the old man and got the most food and became his favorites.

Mary felt so clumsy, criticized by her father, that years after she left home she took ballet lessons, art classes, anything to win his praise.

The personality traits that hunger buries may skip a generation or take decades to emerge; only then can the deprivation be stood up to, when the circumstances have changed. They may surface as a gluttonous craving for attention or punishment, or even as an eccentric pattern of storage.

Her father remarked on Mary's artwork from her courses at the Fashion Institute of Technology, "Mary, did you do that?"

The Old Woman

A child never forgets going to bed on an empty stomach, no matter how old she gets. Age means nothing to the memories of the food locked in a trunk. Privation is countered the rest of our lives despite what other people observe as only eccentricity. The cans of food stacked in Mary's small apartment made certain she'd never go hungry again. They lined the kitchen floor close to the refrigerator, and underneath her small table. The jars and plastic containers were kept in the bedroom.

166

Everything that the cockroaches could get at was sealed and ribbons of soda bicarbonate were sprinkled on the floor. She kept a nonworking refrigerator for sealed food and her medications. No insect dared enter its enclosure of powerful smells.

Getting her own small apartment answered the food locked up in her father's trunk. Now she was the steward. She lived alone to make sure she could eat without interference and be the final arbiter of when and what she ate, and how much. No one was going to deprive her again. No man would get in her way. With her store of cans, jars, and sealed packets, she styled herself a regular Joseph whose eye favored those bright colors of the Spanish who recently moved to the city. Her small working refrigerator was jam packed so that each time it was opened it was a chore to close the door. It was so stuffed that only she knew how to arrange its contents. She had positive contempt for her boyfriend who claimed it was too cluttered, like all her small apartment with boxes stacked to the ceiling, full of dolls, books, clothes, that you had to move sideways to get into her bedroom where the boxes like the tall tenement buildings outside surrounded even her small bed and little nightstand where she kept her notebooks to write down all her dreams. She described her bed to her brother, the doctor who lived on Long Island, as Danish Provincial beside what she called her Princess phone whose dial lit up at night.

The clutter of the boxes reaching to the ceiling gave her a sense of security, despite being overwhelmed by the task of sorting through an endless accumulation of newspaper and magazine clippings, but her food she knew the whereabouts of every jar, can, package, and sweet. Her mind had a precision leavened by memories of an empty stomach.

Few people visited her small apartment. When they did she'd serve coffee at a small table with biscuits, or cookies, or a small piece of fruit. She gave her boyfriend half of what she gave her son which gave him fits. Food should be plentiful, spilling over, an orgy of pleasure, he thought, even though he himself could tell the exact depth of the honey used, knew how many crackers were missing, and had an uncanny ability to weigh herbs or tea to the ounce. He always switched plates to give Giuseppe larger portions than his mother had given him.

His mother claimed a banana was a whole meal and cleaned the inside of the banana skin right in front of him. Her teeth scraped the peels until all that was left was an unrecognized transparency. A banana when she was growing up was as good as gold. Maybe her father only shared the skins with her and that developed her taste for their tartness. She kept ripe fruit on saucers on her small table long after her son thought it was edible, and bananas were sometimes eaten black. She rarely threw anything away, and chopped meat she ate handfuls raw before cooking the rest.

Her cat she doled out food to in such niggardly portions that when her son visited he got large porcelain cereal bowls out of the cupboard instead of the small aluminum cream cheese containers she used for water or food.

It wasn't only her father, but something primitive inside her with regard to food. We are more bound than we know to an elusive spirituality governed by our appetite. The body and blood of Jesus involves a need for food, to avoid waste that damages the spirit just as parsimony does. Maybe it is a head for calculations that draws us to storage, whether it be rice or oil. Maybe there is some ancestral anger in the dim reaches of our psyche, hunger pangs from having to forage day and night to stay alive. The daily indignity of tracking down what runs so nimbly away from us must have been infinitely discouraging. Even though today we've mastered that by fattening our stall-fed animals, allowing limited pasture time, still we are pumped full of just as many instincts to manage our larders.

Mary was fascinated by what would grow in the little pots in the limited sunlight that slanted into her apartment thirty minutes a day. There must have been something of the farmer in her; and the artist, too, in the way she'd pick up a leaf and comment on the delicate venation, but an appreciation of beauty was trumped by the compelling needs of a full stomach. Her favorite meal was chicken wings. Her son joked about so little meat on the bones, but she savored them and the chicken fat dripping onto the rice, potatoes, carrots, onions, and green peppers she placed underneath.

The high points of Mary's life were the holidays Thanksgiving and Christmas, when she was invited to her brother and sister's houses. Somehow the plenty compensated for the dearth of her childhood. Her brother was well off, and his whole family treated food casually. His wife prepared sumptuous holiday meals that were eaten indifferently by all but Aunt Mary.

"The children have too much," Mary later remarked. One Christmas she gave her oldest niece Dickens's *Hard Times*.

Mary would stop eating a day or two before going out to her brother's house where she never refused anything offered, eating long after everyone had finished.

"Here, Mary, take more," her sister-in-law would say.

"Yes, I can have more potatoes, and meat, and the green beans are delicious."

You could see it'd never be enough. It was her childhood emptiness she was filling, a decades old hunger that never went away. Her brother who had no such vivid memories of Pop again scoffed at her narrative about the trunk of food underneath the bed.

"Pop didn't do that!"

"Mary, have you had enough? Aunt Mary has a good appetite!" he'd quip and smile with a gleam in his eye at his children, amused by what failed to embarrass her.

"Joe, stop!" his wife would say.

Her son's cardinal rule was always to refuse what was offered. That constituted the politeness of the middle class to his mind. No matter how hungry he was, he took seconds only if he was asked twice. He had no memory of hunger, attics, of the famous trunk of food, despite his keen eye for what everyone ate.

And when Mary took her son out to restaurants, the tension started from the moment they were seated. The bread was always sent back as stale, the meat wasn't cooked enough.

"Look, it's raw inside!"

"You gave us yesterday's bread!"

Everything made her son sink lower into his chair.

But Mary did enjoy making coffee and prided herself on the cup she served, the blends from Colombia and Brazil. And blackberry brandy or Kahlua, she reserved for just before bedtime. She had the makings of a bon vivant, sampling tastes that had their genesis in poverty. Her son called her a peasant, which for all her ballet, jazz, art lessons, acting classes, Bible study, and scientology, bothered her.

Something always ate into her with its lifelong appetite. What we want is almost secondary to the look and smell of food; its color, texture, the insinuating odors and bouquet, the shocking spoilage, the absolute reproach at being wasted. Whenever that happened Mary almost took it personally.

The potatoes, how she loved them, buried in her psyche as a life sustaining food that got her ancestors through many a freezing winter until the blights had them huddled for warmth nibbling on each other's earlobes dreaming of the New World. The unthinkable closeness later chilled the Irish emotionally, but spawned an inimitable personality and attendant humor. They knew well the shame of huddling for simple warmth on an empty stomach and so developed a gift for language that set them apart, made famine tolerable, created the distance of wit, dance, and gaiety. There is a thirst even today quenched by brimming good spirits that confounds the silence with heel clicking jigs. Mary would grow quiet when she didn't have center stage in leotards with her castanets, or ballet dancing, or performing at Actor's Studio. The Irish on ships packed like sardines escaped the dampness of the bogs, the disagreements of relatives pitched into them lifeless over a contested bushel basket of potatoes that would get a family through the winter.

Mike wasn't an anomaly protecting the food supply. He practiced a frugality that served his family well despite the older children Sarah and Mary skipping meals and sent to bed hungry. He had to skimp somewhere. It kept the family together through the cold weather, reminiscent of the shortages back in Ireland.

One brother named Frank was written off. The vagaries of food distribution were too much for him. The story of his father's anger at him tipping over the bucket of paint on the ladder was the last straw. He was sent away, suffering from hallucinations it was later rumored, though food wasn't mentioned but that he simply read too much.

You can't lock food up and expect normal growth. Not every mind remains balanced by mornings without a bowl of porridge, or lunches not packed, or skipped suppers.

Food takes on a life of its own in the thoughts we have. It is the extra helping for the mouth not at the table. Eaten or not food grows on us, spoils with our thoughts, blights our memories; scarcity develops a cold logic like frost on a window tracing inevitable connecting patterns. Our temperature may be normal, but something freezes in us. Its flow is blocked by the unfair doling out of food, by a painful expectation, by the murderous hatred that comes from watching others eat while we are denied, by the piece of meat we didn't get, by the pat of butter or roll larger than our own. Every plateful of food is in the way, so is a dinner snatched away, unprepared, or spoiled. Food leaves gaping wounds from its absence, just as overabundance lowers our defenses for gluttonous servings that we can barely move. The weight attaches to our bodies until we end up on a feeding tube. Mary observing the consumption of her mother knew how a body wastes away.

I'd like to say hunger is confined to the genes, but experience is crucial. The monkey flinging the banana peel is a model of indifference. He has no need to scrape the skin with his teeth, or worry about where the next meal is coming from.

Mary's son too enjoyed food, grew dizzy tasting fruit from all around the world, persimmon in Korea, rambutan in the Philippines, figs in Greece, Monukka raisins in Portugal. Early on he recognized it as one of the pleasures of living, unmindful of famine, the trunk under lock and key. It wasn't until Myra reached adolescence that food consumption took a novel turn, emerged from the dark recesses of a past that made the food kept in a trunk a mere stepping stone.

The Young Girl

It's hard to know where she came from, but it's almost certain she skipped generations and was directly linked to the old man, but hugely modified. Clearly she possessed the attention to detail of her grandmother along with an astonishing prodigality. There was something spontaneous in her, spawned like on riverbanks from mud and sunlight, something almost new in nature. Her tastes swept everyone from consideration. It was the appetite of all her ancestors rolled into one that left a trail of cleaned bones that led to her as their crowning achievement.

When you think of all the animals you've eaten in your lifetime, the bones stacked to the ceiling, totally obliterating the animal's slow walk to pasture, gamboling freely in meadows, and then the overpowering smells of fear on the way to the slaughter, the moans, the din alone wipes out your humanity. We stop the animal's sex life in its tracks to appease our appetite. Imagine the fields of refuse from fruit or vegetables. Landfills would mount to the sky if it weren't for decomposition, and in our own bodies too there is a breathless acceleration of acids, enzymes, food trapped in airless cavities in the long transit through us. We are a factory of gasses sealed at both ends that we squeeze back to prevent outbursts.

It may be difficult to compare the inside of Myra's body to her as a picture of health, but she became a devourer of the first order. Her family knew instinctively that one day she would turn on them.

We might as well have kept her caged down the basement, locked up as we were by her appetite. She was a force of nature, a constant birth that daily signaled the reproduction of itself, her changing face on everything. Our appetites needed protected around her. Her need for food altered fields just like those weather conditions that flatten every stalk of wheat. The house was always under siege. She plagued the doorways of every room, even when she was out of the house. She had the best room in the house; still she took over the kitchen with all its windows and skylight, the living room, and moved into her father's study, and haunted their bedroom to be closer to her mother's jewelry and clothes. Her brother's room she periodically raided just for meanness. The household food supply served only her whims. No one approached the force of her personality. Her parents tried but capitulated, especially her mother who tried to purchase her love with multiple gifts. You might as well deny an approaching storm, the tumbling mass of gray clouds, when she got angry. Her brows would darken into a disapproving crevice that swallowed you in her displeasure. She'd interrupt her brother in mid-forkful and took the food right out of his mouth.

There was no denying her.

"Give me that!"

It was like the trunk crowbarred open to expose its contents with one swift movement, but years later. Nothing was secret from her. She had access denied two generations. Mike couldn't have stored the food under the bed without her appearance at the other end.

Two half gallons of ice cream were nothing to her in one night.

Cherries, she swiped them before anyone else and laughing spit the seeds in her brother's face.

Fortunately the apricots were too hard, but had to be eaten before they were ripe to get any yourself. The granola bars, only she ate them, so her energy level surpassed everyone as she zoomed around the house eating everything in sight.

Fortunately she doesn't eat tomatoes, mushrooms, eggs, pickles, soup or sandwiches, or meat, or anything her father made. Mostly her mother's rice balls are all she likes wrapped in seaweed, and chicken, and salads drenched with salad oil. She'll stuff her mouth with leafy vegetables like a swarm of grasshoppers or locusts has just stripped a field. You imagine

173

there are not enough migrants to keep up with her appetite for greens.

Everything in the house is up for grabs. We are supposed to be a family, but she is always watching with her large eyes. Her face is so well-defined that if it weren't for her beauty you'd see a giant insect. The ears, the mouth, the beetling brows are all enlarged.

Meals are for sharing even though today everyone is on the run, but she inhales what is on her plate in moments and takes your appetite away. Her reach is lightning quick, and the size of her mouth in motion is astonishing. When she sticks out her tongue its length alone reveals an extra limb that provides a bodily advantage over the rest of us. Sometimes just what you want, what you are saving, determines her appetite. She can read your mind. She will take the food out of anyone's mouth, the exact opposite of a bird tending its young. Like spectators our mouths are agape, astonished at her. She grabs what you want before you want it. The shock is discovering that she is the fountain of your own appetite, that the tiny jets of saliva in your mouth are already hers whetting what you barely realize you had a desire for.

Her mother hides the pistachio nuts to eat them in peace, the clementines are in her husband's study, where he stashes the chocolate behind his books, unconcerned about the silverfish he hasn't seen for years. But she has a nose for everything, especially bittersweet chocolate, though milk chocolate too she'll ferret it out as if she hid it there herself just because that is her brother's favorite. You cannot do anything without her tracking it down. Cockroaches have a million-year history but her keen sense of smell seems developed in one lifetime.

Her family fears she'll nibble their feet or earlobes in their sleep, or letting their guard down during naps they'll find part of a finger missing. They joke about it to dispel their fears. They want to say that she is their own flesh and blood, to imagine even the voracity of her appetite is somehow communal. Simple gluttony you could understand, but this is what eats all the peaches for breakfast or a freezer of ice cream bought the day before. It is a strange penchant for devastation heedless of everyone else. It is as if even the factory production of sweets, Skittles or gummy bears for example, couldn't keep up with her once she turns her attention to them. And Junior Mints, forget it; they're history if you ever expect to dissolve the bracing sweetness of even one left on your tongue. You must gobble down the whole box like her hardly tasting them. The important thing is that the contents be already lodged in your belly.

More than once she has barged into her parents' room for something, toying with their fears, sometimes not even knowing what she's come for, valuables or the food hidden. Her parents imagine she hatches plans about food in their sleep, though her notions seem spontaneous. The pantry doors are never closed because she is always there grubbing, foraging, to appease her inexhaustible appetite.

She eats without a thought what her brother is saving for later; in fact, that is an inducement to devour it on the spot, grinning ear to ear from the added pleasure of his anger. She boldly displays what we all hide, the fear of not getting enough, the trunk under the bed, to the hundredth power. She demonstrates not only the obvious gluttony that plagues society, advertisers, but an astonishing metabolism that never slows her desire to devour everything under the sun, confined at present to her own house. Were it made of gingerbread it too would already be gone.

Her svelte body shows the lie of appearances, her smile and large eyes give almost nothing away. Her sociability is on the order of a street angel that thoroughly masks the house devil. Your shoe leather you feel is not safe around her; her mother dreams about her Coach handbags being moistened by her daughter's saliva.

Myra's appearance contradicts what might give others pause. The fat pads on their bodies, buttocks, inside the thighs, around their waists and hanging from their arms, their fleshy jowls on puffed-up faces are all missing from her. Her large healthy white teeth are almost suspended in air like Dali's

Christ on the cross when she smiles. But it is her family up in the air, for Myra is a disappearance act. She makes all substantiality, anything edible, suspect. Here today and gone tomorrow is her motto. Nothing is saved. There are no grain bins. It is worse than the food locked up in her great grandfather's trunk; that at least has a stationary logic all its own, but this, this is an exploding prodigality, an ever-expanding universe that eats for the sheer gusto of it, less for pleasure than for the constant alteration of matter. All that is edible is her prisoner, potentially trapped in the recesses of her alimentary canal, the darkness of her intestine. Light is absent like in the old man's trunk.

All winter she scarfs down frozen blueberries by the bagful. You are lucky to get a handful. Even her mother who tries to please her stops buying them. Nothing is ever enough for her. But the fact that you can't tell it on her face floors you. Like something prehistoric any call for the food to be rationed or equitable distribution falls on deaf ears. The great grandfather's trunk has evolved into multiple smaller hiding places around the house that she methodically uncovers.

Her father is always the last sitting at the table, chewing so methodically with his little rat's teeth, as she calls them. They are stained brown from the tea he drinks every morning, while her teeth are sparkling white, horse teeth with enough extra enamel to distribute to a herd of wild mustangs. The dentine hardens her heart, for she never has a cavity. Her smile is winning, gets her voted President of her class every year at school. Everyone without a clue wants to unwittingly participate in her smile.

Keeping one peach for yourself requires a full-time strategy and dry cereal, forget it. Certainly the contents of the box settles, but she'll leave only a few squares of an unopened box of Life after one sitting, or a few flakes, as if to emphasize her own vitality. It's gotten so her parents only keep Shredded Wheat or Old-Fashioned Quaker Oats in the house. Eggs she'll never eat unless she could break into what something else was incubating.

Cherries, a favorite of her mother's, can't be bought for it's painful to see all the pits lying about the house before you've tasted one.

But dates, she'll not eat them, particularly the Medjool her father likes she doesn't have a taste for, and frozen raspberries she doesn't like either. He can eat them in peace. Myra will eat baby sardines about an inch long with enormous eyes like hers, and she admits to having the longest tongue in her class. It is frightening when she sticks it out, as if she is the perfect antidote to the timidity of her grandmother at her father keeping the food locked up.

Her mother buys power bars when she plays basketball, so her body needs will be met and she'll not turn on her family, and everyone can eat in peace.

The family loses weight because she eats so fast, because of her predilections for what each one likes. It is like she is taking the food out of your mouth, not like a baby bird being lovingly fed, but overnight turning into a giant hooked beak augmented by a huge wingspan whose voracious shadow expresses no sanctity for human life beyond refueling itself. Her appetite robs everyone to feed her caloric intake like a bright furnace. Always on the go her eyes rivet on anything bought, has her rustling through shopping bags, extending her inventory from pantry and refrigerator, for the simple days of pleasing her are past; now it is entirely in her own hands, at the end of her reach, or wherever she turns her salivating gaze, irrespective of any ethical considerations. They are the luxury only of the well-fed, not the hungry with a family history of straitened circumstances and parsimony. Lately her head revolves 360 degrees like a giant predator. She seems to hover around food even in her absence with a perspective that groundlings lack.

She ends wanting just what you do, whatever was hidden from her she has a nose for, and she'll intercept your hand with her viselike grip. In some ways she seems not to have an appetite of her own, beyond what she appropriates from others. It is like the envy that governs everyone simplified to food. There is something pure about it. An answer to simple warehouses, grain bins, or trunks of the past. Of course distribution is the key, but in their own household food could be managed until Myra came along. Her father imagined when he got really old and lacked the strength to remove what he already recognized was her talon. He saw his body torn open by her ravenous appetite; it all adds up to competing appetites in the end. Living is so exhausting because it is a never-ending struggle to feed ourselves concealed behind so many good manners and handbooks of etiquette. With Myra the opposite emerged from a brief family history of being under lock and key. It should have added up to simple distribution; the strong and clever take what they want, then assume the pleasure of doling out to others. It is so simple and yet we complicate it overlooking the savage reach in our own family, scattering doilies, placemats, the best silverware and service available. So much for table settings, and the correct alignment of cutlery torn from each other's grip, so much for even saying grace before meals.

She was stronger than the rest, shamed her father in arm wrestling, and beat up her twelve-year-old brother for fun when no one was around. Once tearing herself away from her mother she sent her flying that she injured her coccyx. Her mother always thought tears could soften her daughter's heart, but she has no respect for weakness. Her mother gains weight to spite her daughter's ravenous appetite. It is a competition she invariably loses as her daughter stays slim.

Food is funny for the bulk it unfairly apportions, collects at the belly, hips, buttocks of some but not others, rounds the face hanging flab but leaves others gaunt as if they have a tapeworm. Myra with her perfectly sculpted profile and slim figure is a nightmare of gusto. She is her grandmother's answer to her great grandfather come to haunt the family, for her grandmother being confined to the attic, for food being allocated and kept under lock and key, and for having to endure the intolerable favoritism that spoils a lifetime. Everything comes round in the end.

Myra had her own room, three large picture windows, two closets, one walk-in, a stepladder to the attic that, ironically, she wanted redone. She was the queen of the house who dispensed with ceremony and devoured at will. It was she who named all the cats. No one else existed besides her. Her father knew she was trapped by food, the sheer mouthwatering, astonishing hold what we eat has on us. What better way to deal with that than by controlling what everyone else eats.

How exhausting to decide on food every day. Better be deprived so we'll value it more, better be put on rations, on bread and water, better to be disgruntled so we can make eating meaningful. The countless choices of fast foods ruin the appetite, all the varieties of ice cream, the pastries, cloying sweets and drinks, fats and oils, make fasting a pleasure. Maybe Myra will plant the seed like the great grandfather, until we eschew food altogether. Maybe Simone Weil was right to turn on eating in disgust and all the anorexics in the world have a point. The pendulum needs to swing back to stop modern day excess. Maybe Myra is a harbinger of something to come, the very controlled excess that teaches us a lesson.

The delight in food is almost a thing of the past, natural tastes are replaced by artificial sweeteners and flavors that make us look for ever new sensations. Maybe Myra is intended to restore something lost, break into that trunk, strike the hinges from attic doors, free the human potential to restore the appetite. But can it be? Won't we all be cut down looking out only for ourselves? Compromised grain bins are no solution to how we will feed ourselves, for even they end in a locked trunk. Still the community returns with a vengeance to break the spine of the lone wolf no matter how she hides in sheep's clothing.

The sheer mouthwatering hold it has on us to control what everyone eats, to manage perishability by freezing or drying, with jars or cans lining our apartment floors, makes sure we never go hungry again. Famine is always just around the corner, the fear alone tramples whole populations not to mention those whom we love, for when there is not enough to eat that love goes out the window. The hoarding begins, and food management becomes a law unto itself. The trunks are out there, the locked refrigerators, the passwords on freezers. We don't realize we are following our ancestral imperative, masking our gluttony and cannibalization eating so daintily, using the right fork, finger bowls, daubing our lips with napkins; the most refined table manners clear elbows off the table. We start with a knife and fork that gets chucked aside, and we quickly train our eyes on only what others eat, taking what is almost in their mouths, or what they keep locked up. Maybe a generation is never skipped, and everyone is trapped in their own family history of food.

"Not now, don't eat until I tell you. Let's bow our heads."

"Wait until everyone is served, Jack."

"You must say grace! Thank the Lord," and pass the beans Jack smiles to himself.

The first time Myra stalks off to eat in her own room, defying her parents about eating only in the kitchen, shocks everyone, but not anymore.

Her father, now a bag of bones, masticates slowly enough to get the nutriment from limited rations. Myra swallows so fast that she waxes healthy, nubile, but the father can't imagine her having children who will not be carved up! He remembers the rosy glow of her own rubbery limbs as a baby and how he had to restrain himself from biting her. He muses until she startles his reverie with another rudeness, "Keep your trunk, you dried-up old man!" as if he is his grandfather and she's allowing him only a few saltines.

Though there is still enough food that the rest can feed on, what she doesn't like, the family loses their appetite over her. No one is sure they will get enough, not go hungry this winter. The father doesn't want to be around her. He pictures an infinite reflection of locked trunks. He sits at the table thirty minutes to her five. She is forever circling them. They never know what she will eat.

When she leaves for a three-day weekend everyone relaxes. There's peace at the meals and the tension over desserts is gone. The family eats at their leisure. But before long she's back. The weekend is too short and the blueberries the family indulged themselves buying are devoured. She's only in the house thirty minutes. The chocolate her father imagines cleverly hidden is quickly sniffed out. She needs only a few minutes for what her mind turns to. The ice cream is history and juices are drunk like water, while unfinished water bottles are scattered all around the house. It is like the family is on a desert island and the food left is subject to the corrosive effects of air, the spoilage of hot sun before they get the least moisture to their lips.

I want to write how the family, the father and mother and son, called Myra down to the basement one night early that winter. The overwrought parents stood there like mere skeletons, the mother unnaturally bloated, her father and brother two sticks. Myra imagined a convocation to sheepishly continue the family history and dub her food administrator. The pretext was to show her how the eggs in cardboard sheets of two dozen at a time could be stacked in the coolness of the basement, and explain other ideas about storage, so Myra would get more. A potato bin and cubicle for the onions could be added. She imagined a surrender to appease her appetite, unaware herself of all the pleasure she took depriving them, the joy she took of what she would do to them in their sleep, their foamy lips white from thirst, bodies unnaturally bloated or wasting away from hunger; she relished the humiliation, their whispering to her. They all had purple rings under their eyes, and yellow brown discolorations from bruises.

Myra went downstairs and bent over the tiers of eggs as if to count them when her brother stepped between his parents, his mother in an apron that she never wore had a chicken on it as if to represent Myra's dislike of eggs, and with an axe handle almost as thin as his own body clubbed her over the head multiple times as she crumpled to the floor. Her parents stood frozen in shock at what they had all done, like a small community stunned now that the menace to the family is removed so they could finally eat in peace. This is how the story should end. But who would have the courage for that? Even as fiction, who could live with it in real life?

Jerusalem Grill

She had a choice. Indian, Chinese, Italian, either one was fine.

"No, you decide," she said.

"I want you to," he said.

"Okay, Chinese," she said, since they often went to King Buffet and Richland was about twenty minutes away from Lexington. But while driving on I-75 she googled restaurants in Richland and found the Jerusalem Grill.

"Do you want to go there?" she asked.

"Whatever you want," he said.

"It's downtown."

"That's okay, we just turn right at the university?"

"Yes," she said.

"Are you sure it's okay."

"It's fine."

It was a grim day, the end of the year, gray and darkening.

"I know you may not want to go to a Jewish restaurant."

"I said it's fine. I buy matzos, don't I? I know about the boycott, but I don't take it that personally," he said.

They spied the restaurant on the corner of West Main Street.

"It's right over there," she said.

Most parking spots on the street were empty, so they parked easily and headed towards the restaurant. Outside it looked blighted, not open, but they entered. Along the left wall was a row of cushioned seats and tables backed with large mirrors. On the right side was a counter and food displayed under glass, and against the wall were large racks of lamb, beef, and chicken.

"Welcome," a man said, a big man with a large oval face and a deep voice. His English wasn't native, and Jack and his wife Emiko immediately sensed that the atmosphere was authentic.

Jack thought, what have we walked into since no one else was in the restaurant.

The man was uncomfortably welcoming, too solicitous, as if the pressure was placed on the patrons not the establishment, and it was called the Jerusalem Grill, occupied territory for someone.

Jack had a history of supporting Palestinians with letters and editorials that he sent to the newspapers over the years, and that was one reason Emiko had quizzed him about coming.

Immediately Jack felt the pressure of the place. He always did in regard to food, was careful about what he allowed into his body. Emiko ate anything, eagerly accepted all ethnic foods, and peoples. Jack was picky as a youngster, but now would characterize himself as discriminating.

The restaurant extended back into a long gloomy recess. The mirrors duplicated more than you wanted and were moderately lit before the back of the restaurant became dark. Jack imagined the place had a history, had served countless customers over the years. Who knew what had occurred there.

The waiter, his size, the roundness of his body, the oval of his face impressed the couple as a presence bearing down on them as he came and gave them the menu.

"What would you like to drink?"

"Water," they both said.

Jack noticed the hummus and Mediterranean food on the menu that he knew Emiko would like. He quickly scanned the servings for what he could eat and decided on the Chicken Shawarma. Emiko selected the Kufta Kabob.

"That's on a stick?" Jack asked.

"Yes," the cook said and pointed to the sticks of limp meat displayed under glass. The meat was oxidized and discolored, but Jack thought maybe it's okay if cooked.

"What kind of salad do you want?" the cook asked. "Jerusalem, Mediterranean, House Salad . . ."

"Just plain," Jack said. "No olive oil, or any kind of dressing, just the vegetables."

"I'll have Mediterranean," Emiko said.

Jack and Emiko looked around after ordering and Emiko said she had to go to the restroom and got up and started to walk to the back of the restaurant.

"No, it's not there," the cook said quickly. "Through that door, up the stairs, then to the right."

So she backtracked through the glass door that was beside their table.

Jack sat and thought how he got himself into such an unappetizingly empty restaurant just before the year's end.

He looked at the cook who seemed to take his job very seriously preparing the food. He thought about the Middle East, his own indignation about the Israeli occupation of the West Bank, and especially Gaza, when Emiko returned.

"You can't imagine what's on the other side. It must have been a hotel," she said. "There are rooms and a giant lobby."

"Was this once a hotel?" Jack asked the cook.

"Yes, it was called The G . . ."

"The Grand?" Jack said.

"No, The Glen," Jack thought he said.

Jack wondered why it would be called The Glen when the location was on a hill that in the distance the landscape sloped downward.

"You have to see it," Emiko repeated. "It is nothing like you'd expect."

The cook then brought the salad. Jack's was on a little dish with finely chopped square vegetables. Emiko's that followed was also chopped but bathed in sauce and also there was a plate of off-white hummus where you could see the yellow oil. The cook then brought a basket of pita bread.

The couple all the while looked around.

"You have to see the other room," Emiko repeated once more to Jack when another customer came in, a young man in short pants, who after looking at the menu ordered takeout in a language the couple did not understand.

There are more of them, Jack thought, and began to review

what had been done to the Palestinians in his mind, feeling self-righteously angry at their treatment, and wondering how their tormentors found themselves in Richland, Kentucky of all places. Who would find their way here, and for what reason, extending their influence where no one suspected what they had done to the poor Palestinian population?

Jack imagined he'd keel over from the salad if the cook read his mind beforehand.

The cook then brought the main dish while Jack observed the waiting customer.

Suddenly in front of Jack were two giant mounds of yellow and orange rice piled so high that Jack immediately lost his appetite thinking how he was going to eat it all, and a larger amount of chicken was spread out, and there were distinct servings of pickles and onions clearly seasoned with flakes of some condiment, and a small dish of white sauce that Jack's wife thought was sour cream, but Jack thought it was something else.

Emiko's plate came next and the servings of rice were similar, the pickles and onions too clearly seasoned, and the three kabobs had lost their transparency being thoroughly cooked.

'What do you think they are?" Emiko asked.

"Probably lamb," Jack said, and reviewed the implications of that for both of them. Was there something sacrificial taking place at the Jerusalem Grill, some extension of the hostilities towards the Palestinians that had found its way to Kentucky and this forced feeding under the aegis of hospitality. These unappetizing mounds of food stood piled in front of them. Would that stave off their criticism, glut them that the blood would abandon their brain and the lightheadedness would create a wobbly critique of the injustices in their homeland? Did the cook think Americans could be so easily overfed and the criticism would disappear with this exemplary hospitality, for the quickest way to a man's heart is through his stomach, people say. Was this cook at the Jerusalem Grill a mind reader as soon as customers passed through the front door? The way his greeting and eyes bore down on the couple suggested some extraordinary abilities. Perhaps he thought food could convince anyone of anything, even contrary to the truth of what was happening in his homeland. The way the eyes bore down was just short of another grilling, an interrogation of where you stand, for Jack met his gaze each time even if he wondered at its intent.

The way the large round cook lorded over the couple even after he delivered the food continued to be disturbing. The two platefuls he left were like two large amounts of earth that the very rice sprang from that fed the desert society, the Golan Heights, lording over with settlements of imported rice, yellow and orange compartments in the sunlight, turmeric and whatever else, rationed out to the native population, but in this case just the opposite of starvation rations to subdue all criticism with overabundance. Outsiders come and take over with their religion with the aid of the British mandate, with their cuisine, with the help of the Americans to run off the native populations from their villages. Their self-righteousness propelled by such a powerful incentive from the Old Testament God who was behind them, Biblical mandates about the restoration of the Holy Land, and the sheer guilt of the West from what it had allowed to happen in Germany. Behind their cuisine, the holocaust was an excuse to terrorize a whole people, the indigestion, the food insufficiency, reaching all the way to Richland, Kentucky, having already seduced our Congress and successive presidents peddling influence and with the powerful incentive of election money so no one spoke against the atrocities. In mid-invasion of Gaza our House and Senate pass resolutions in support of the aggression. Sixty-seven Israelis killed in the last 2012 invasion, only seven were civilians, compared to over 1,400 Palestinians who died.

The man should be ashamed of himself, of his cuisine. But no, he wants to establish his influence, his dominance with food, the brute distracting force of appetite, serving them and pressuring them after they took their first bites and then midway through the meal, he again comes over when Jack is wondering how he is going to finish the disturbing amount of food, where his appetite has to constantly recalibrate exactly how he will do the food on his plate justice. He considers the injustice of the man, or at least his people, of the very name of the restaurant, towards the Palestinians.

His size is enough to indict him, identify him as a bully, his false salutation when he comes again to the table and says to Emiko, "You like?" bearing down on the couple, but especially Emiko with the full force of his personality, his perfectly oval face, his gimlet eyes that Jack sees as small, and the wheedling out of the politeness of not even customers so much as guests trapped.

"Yes," Emiko says.

Jack too smiles apparent approval with the food, though he is racked by the sheer amount, feels buried alive under all the rice still left, the unfinished chicken, the disturbing quantity his appetite has to constantly maneuver, can he make it, do the food justice without getting sick? He considers again the injustice of the man towards the Palestinians, his size, his false salutation when they entered the front door.

"If you don't like, I can change it!" the man coyly says, laying it on to Emiko.

Jack wonders if they will be taken by the scruff of the neck and themselves grilled if they don't like it, or what will be the consequences! He's big enough, and a foreigner, so who knows what he is thinking or will do, if he will even be accountable; he could disappear into the woodwork without even papers to prove he exists in the first place. That Americans are uninformed, only care about a full gut, don't appreciate the holocaust, and the precautions his people must take against the Arabs must not even be apparent.

"No, I like it," Emiko says.

At the first taste of chicken Jack tasted the heavy, but not unpleasant, spices, and said to Emiko that it is good, but the longer he eats the stronger the spices become, the more he thinks too of the injustices towards the Palestinians and that he is no match for the man, but he knows nothing about him Jack thinks, even though he is not entirely convinced the man is not a mind reader. Jack feels vulnerable, more naked, exposed as he is before this basic plate of food, forced-fed as he imagines himself to be. But he knows that he too needs to be a man before his wife and finish the food. He knows how food works on us and can erode our resolve and spread doubt to other areas of our lives. Jack wonders how much the cook knows about them, and just how expert he is on managing people's appetites.

Food Jack knows has a history of being used as a weapon, has always been, mounds of it, silos of it, giant grain bins of it as much as privation, those seven lean years, the enforced famine on a people bottled up in Gaza, but it is used to seduce with spices, with plenty, to kill all opposition so convinced you are of your own cuisine so they'll want to get into your country, but you won't let them. You establish checkpoints all around, 139 for Gaza alone, so women can't get to the hospital and give birth while waiting in line, people with health conditions collapse and die on the spot. The check point lines are so long that people are turned away daily.

And here in Richland, Kentucky is this shower of food, Biblical manna. The yellow and orange rice would be enough without the meat, the chicken, the lamb, the beef. Two mounds of rice that alone has Jack floored at how he is going to finish them; the political concerns about his country almost recede before the tactical problem of high piled multicolored rice, before the savory chicken, the spices getting stronger as he eats, the sheer amount of onions and pickles with visible flakes of condiments; the obligation to try the multiple sauces throws all Jack's thoughts off, but only to finish the meal to please his Israeli master. Jack is resentful at what they've done to his country. Walt and Mearsheimer, the two university scholars, are right; they are bad for the US, our foreign policy should not revolve around such a small country at the expense of a billion Muslims. Who do they think they are dictating the policy of a country of 320 million, so no one can say anything or they'll lose the next Congressional election, or even the Presidency? Who are they to come into our country and open a restaurant on a corner in Richland, Kentucky extending their settlements to America, or as Pat Buchanan said, "Capitol Hill is Israeli occupied territory!" It's wrong, downright wrong. AIPAC has completely moved in and J Street will eventually be nudged out, closed off, and meanwhile there is all this food to finish. It's impossible but Jack bears down, doesn't think of anything for the moment but finishing, pleasing his wife who selected the restaurant in the first place, and the cook.

Why Jack had to please the cook, someone he doesn't even know, an Israeli out of his depth, despite his size, his commanding presence, here in Kentucky where Jack has lived for three decades, is a mystery. What right does he have to come in here with his ethnic food, trailing all that bloodshed, the absolute injustice in the Middle East and feed the locals, stuff them with too much food for them to think or get their bearings? Who is he anyway?

Jack has been blindsided. Okay, okay, he told Emiko it was all right, but little did he realize how he'd be caught by so much food, by his anger at how the Palestinians were treated entangled with his appetite, how it would be balled up with this power show. Force-fed, that was it, the terror of it, of his having a hand in the injustice, the Biblical injunctions regarding lean years or those of plenty, the driblets of food let into Gaza; it was a disgrace to be sitting there, mindful of the rationing to over a million and a half people, and here the way they were served in such abundance seems like an insult with so many hungry. It was reverse psychology to win over the locals, just as effective to glut the body, give it something to do that is beyond them, and watch them squirm bound to finish what's on their plate.

It's only two mounds of rice. What are you bellyaching about, you are not asked to move mountains like we are in our homeland!

It is so far beyond "eat your peas" that Jack heard from Mrs. Layman as a child. It was simply the expectation of gluttony, the Americans at the trough, the most overweight people in the world.

But Jack did it justice and managed to work his way through the food, eliminating for a moment his resentment towards the cook from Israel for all the food he served, for having the food drain his brain down to the agitated demands of his stomach to digest the colorful yellow and orange rice, the pickles, the sharp taste of onion, the spicy chicken. Jack thought he could save the rest in a box partway through the meal and bring it home when Emiko to his surprise said she wanted to order take-out for their son, another order of Chicken Shawarma!

Jack was shocked, again blindsided, but knew intimately food seduces and that his wife was a sucker for ethnic foods. Food is love, or at least an overture of good will, when it doesn't have designs. Its seductiveness only an ascetic like Jack knew, the lean, the suspicious kind that he was. Food opens avenues, charts courses to the heart, starts conversations that when deprived ends in faint whispers. But did she know what was being done? Jack had always taken the lead on the Middle East and Emiko was his reluctant audience. Always concerned about her own stomach Jack didn't know how to tell her that she was being seduced by the cuisine. She didn't know what the cook was doing.

"If you don't like it, I can make you something different!"

Oh, it made Jack want to crawl up the wall. What a trap! Didn't she know what he was doing to her?

But Jack too was caught up pleasing him, stuffing himself like a partridge, something to be taken out in hunting season if it came to that, then plucked, for a glutton can't stand up to injustice, the blood is too intent on rushing from the brain down to the stomach. Who could confront the cook with the injustice towards the Palestinians but on an empty stomach, not someone worried about cleaning his plate?

It was like a concentration camp where just the opposite of starvation rations overtook Jack and Emiko, glutted as they both were in that Richland restaurant on Main Street. Jack felt they had been invaded even in this little nondescript corner of the country by a foreign cuisine and all the expectations that go

190

along with that of agreeing with the cook and therefore with the ruthless policies of his country.

Jack took a certain pleasure when food was still on his plate of asking the cook for another order, such was his need to please that he couldn't help himself. What was he thinking but that it took the pressure off of himself to finish, so the cook would be pleased. Jack was privately ashamed of himself, his capitulation to the secret dealings of the man.

Here this thug, yes, that's what he was, even though Jack had no proof, but his size and the name of the restaurant were convincing enough. His obvious pride in the preparation, in stuffing them, in wanting compliments; it was a forced march of forkful after forkful into their mouths nonstop until both had cleaned their plates.

Food is deadly, masks as love with a woman, the motherly preparation, but this here was clear bullying just like the Israelis were doing to the Palestinians. Starvation is only one side, the other is the nauseating, cloying, deadly way food attaches, piles up, unappetizing amounts of rice like a range of mountains on top of you. You are bound to eat three times a day, seasoned as it was this time, thinking he'd trap you underneath, and the rest of the hotel would be a cinch. There you could be interrogated unknown to anyone else, Mossad would come out of the woodwork, who knew what was going on, the connections made in the dark, in the dim, gloomy recesses of the room you are in, or just behind the glass door, with today's technology, what screams were muffled over the years, or even recently, in this very hotel, who could decipher even the earlier spasms of unintelligible static?

He was probably a colonel, hid his epaulettes, picked the couple out beforehand, knew they'd come, thought he could separate Jack from his Asian wife. Israelis control the narrative; their intelligence is second to none. Americans are only pawns in their own country, ill-informed, but he doesn't know Jack knew of his country's crimes. Such ignorance. He sticks out like a sore thumb. Mossad in Richland, Kentucky! Ha. Did they come for the coal crackers, the poverty, the reputation for incest, the guilt already here that would cancel out their own, the imagined bare feet, lack of indoor plumbing? Just what was it? The take-out customer who spoke his own language had left already. Nobody else was there, only them.

It was in this frame of mind that Jack left for the restroom, behind the glass door right next to their table to see what his wife had wanted him to.

He entered a wide circular room, bigger than he had expected, at least six times the size of the restaurant with a giant round foyer that went up one floor where a visible guard railing circled all around, and there were two more floors after that. The room was menacingly dark. Immediately Jack thought of interrogation, and that the room like all hotels had a past, that there was more to the Jerusalem Grill than anyone realized, more than just the serving of ethnic food, perhaps an actual grilling was taking place periodically, who knows all that had been done to the Palestinians, perfected on them, might not be brought over here, who knows if the force-feeding, the mounds of food were only the start, and what may follow, why Jack and Emiko were not the only two patrons for nothing.

The room felt like it contained the haunting ghosts of a concentration camp, or like up on Pat's Hill at Hotel Hershey where they kept Nazi officers. Jack's German name might figure in, not only his own childhood in Pennsylvania. That too with his Palestinian objections may have made him a target. Perhaps the Grill was divulging itself tucked away in the hinterlands of Kentucky, hidden out in the open on Main Street just like Sinclair Lewis's books that are not read today.

The cook coming over to his wife flirting, "I could make something else for you."

What else? Jack now thinks. Yes, what was he cooking up? What was in this unexpectedly large oblong room next door, what did Israeli intelligence want with him? His schizophrenic uncle had been institutionalized on Long Island for paranoia, and still he thought when Jack visited that the subway was running under the facility. The underground really never goes away once you have been exposed to it. Not only Jack's editorials over the years, there must be something else. Was he being tracked down in this surprisingly large space for other reasons, his early childhood, his German name and some association with the horrors of the holocaust?

The way the cook's large body hovered and his small eyes, the way they riveted, bore into Emiko as if he had territorial rights that he was trying to establish had unsettled Jack, had the opposite effect now when Jack was alone of blue lettering on the skin of camp numbers, of actual starvation, the skeletal bones just around the corner pushing through the emaciated flesh, the numbers collapsing into a blur of blue, piles of bodies, of rotting food, staring out of bunkbeds, then mounds of rice, some reprisal for the holocaust starvation extended now to this land of plenty, force-feeding oversized portions, the unwitting population with their bloated stomachs not quite knowing what was happening to them, this distractingly slow preparation for two. Just next door the answer must be in that nefarious darkness. Who knew what it all meant, what was waiting for these two outside their own past, well, outside Jack's paranoia?

Could it be just a lone proprietor starting his own business, another instance of the American dream in the New World, as innocent as Kafka's Karl Rossmann in *Amerika* and there is no agenda, nothing more to the Jerusalem Grill, to be taken with a grain of salt, no Palestinian children lying on the street limp, rocks still in hand or lying nearby, no imprisoned population, just good business sense here in Kentucky. Is that possible?

Yes, it was a hotel he had to admit, and they were the sole restaurant patrons, guests, victims in the hands of Israeli captors. See Jack can't get away from it, from the big man, making ends meet to escape the horrors of the Twentieth Century. Was it a new day, had the invasion begun with so few knowing about it, Jack and his wife and the cook? The acceptance of ethnic food started it, spices that seduced, the hummus for his wife, and now this in the next room, barely lit enough to get his bearings, to relieve himself, easier than the plate he left on the table. Jack looked up and marveled at all the rooms looking sealed off, hiding all that went on behind them for so long. Were there secret interrogations going on now? No, it was too dark. Was Israeli intelligence installed in this remote town, a foolish thought if Jack hadn't known the history, the infiltration already of both houses of Congress, the shaft they gave the Palestinians time and again, or the big body in the next room, in the Grill. Did he leave him alone now with his wife? Just the name Grill should send shivers down Jack's spine no different than Kafka's penal colony. Kafka was prescient enough to see it all and died in 1924 even before the horrors! It impinged on Jack's consciousness, along with whom he had left his wife with, the cook.

Jack went up the stairs as he was told where to find the bathroom; with the door partially ajar, he hit the switch and noticed immediately the tongue and groove woodwork, the age of the place. Emiko alone he suddenly thought, almost panicked, and couldn't pee fast enough.

Outside the bathroom again he marveled at the hidden expansiveness of the place, what could be a front desk at one time, the eerie feel of the past, and he wondered if the intelligence operatives were on a seasonal break, had they returned to Israel for the holidays, or were they going to jump out at him, through the sheer gloom of the place? Undoubtedly, they'd have the equipment today, or was this just a convenient façade? For the rooms already told of a past beyond the Middle East, cooked up in the next room as the perfect cover.

The hotel was called Glyndon, a haven of rest, it meant, and was built in 1892. Ladies once entered by a separate entrance. Clark Gable, Carol Lombard, and a Vice President stayed there. There was said to be someone's ghost on the stairway, and the hands of the grandfather clock were said to have frozen either when the Lindbergh baby died, or when Hauptmann was executed. A desk clerk too who once gave a guest a ride was found chopped to pieces. The Glyndon Hotel was said to be a hangout for closet homosexuals.

The mural of Daniel Boone added in 1932 was a distraction that minimized the goings on in the hotel as it established a historical context, the Americana that clouded even the activities of the recent immigrant in the next room and his suspected intelligence associates. There was a gold yellow carpet too upstairs said to have been there for decades. The stains alone kept the past alive. All of this didn't affect Jack, only he wondered why there was not more going on in the ill-lit hotel. It looked like no one occupied any of the rooms, but couldn't that be the front for interrogation rooms? Still the abandoned hotel made an impression on Jack when he returned, already anxious about Emiko being left alone with the cook.

"Are you ready?" he said to his wife.

"Well, what did you think?"

"Yes, it is impressive. Who could have imagined what is on the other side?"

Jack went up to the cash register to pay. The cook looked at Jack and read off an apparent check that he never gave him, "Eighty-four dollars," he said.

Jack shot the man a look and was just going to ask to see the bill when he said "thirty-four!" and smiled.

"You thought I said eighty-four!"

Jack thought Jewish humor, and took out his wallet and gave the man his credit card.

"If you want to give a tip."

"Five is okay," and Jack signed the receipt.

He and his wife then left, both stuffed, and Jack running through his mind what exactly the Jerusalem Grill meant. What was the intent of such an imposing, overbearing man; what could they want here in the sticks? Was he truly Jack's nemesis come to get even for all his articles against what was being done to the Palestinians, or to further entrench themselves in the US, get a foothold? Or could it be his German name, a past observing Hotel Hershey on the hill, a re-creation of the horrors of the Forties?

Jack thought of his last editorial that the local newspaper titled "Is Never Again Happening Again?" Had the man found out about it?

It read:

In 1938 Germany, Jews could no longer head businesses, attend university, and they had to surrender their drivers' licenses and car registrations. Already by 1935 they had lost their citizenship and couldn't marry or have sexual relations with Aryans. In 1939 they had to give their radios to the police. In 1940 they could no longer have telephones and they started to be taken to concentration camps for "protective custody." By 1941 they could not leave their residences without police permission. They had to hand in woolen or fur clothing in 1942 and were forbidden to keep dogs, cats, birds, etc. From May 29 they couldn't visit barber shops, and from June 19 they had to turn in all electrical and optical equipment, bicycles, and typewriters. By September they could no longer buy meat, eggs, or milk. The unspeakable horrors of the concentration camps are well-documented so that everyone should support the cry "Never Again!"

Fast forward to Gaza where 1.6 million people are crowded into 139 square miles, what Noam Chomsky calls "the largest open air prison in the world." Israel blockades the sea, air, and land. Palestinians cannot travel or import goods freely, so they have built thousands of tunnels to Egypt. Israel is punishing Gaza for having elected Hamas. Reuters reported a US diplomatic cable released by WikiLeaks in 2011 as saying that Israeli officials want to "keep the Gazan economy on the brink of collapse." The UN Secretary-General said in 2010 that the blockade was causing "unacceptable suffering." The head of the Goldstone report said in 2009 the blockade should be referred to the International Criminal Court as a possible "crime against humanity," if the situation does not improve. Former President Carter spoke of the blockade as "a terrible human rights crime."

Here are some of the goods Israel would not let enter Gaza in 2010 & 2011: wheelchairs, dry food items, canned fruit, fruit juices, chocolate, tomato paste, lentils, crayons, stationery, soccer balls, musical instruments, and steel, cement, and glass, so the infrastructure destroyed during Operation Cast Lead (2009) cannot be rebuilt. A 2009 UN report called the restrictions "draconian" and reported that 61% percent of the population is "food insecure." Over half the infants up to age one had anemia. In November of 2008 Gaza was reported as receiving 28% of goods traded before Hamas was elected. During Operation Cast Lead, when Israel killed 1,400 Palestinians within three weeks and destroyed 3,500 homes, Congress passed resolutions in support of Israel. The Israeli Committee Against Home Demolitions has reported that 27,000 Palestinian houses have been destroyed by Israel since 1967.

The recent eight-day attack by Israel on Gaza killed 162 Palestinians, including 42 children, and injured over a thousand, half were women and children. On November 16 before the cease fire, the House and Senate again passed resolutions in support of the assault. Israel claimed that 1,450 targets were hit. Outside the original assassination of Hamas's senior military leader to start the hostilities, the targets included homes, security units, the minister of the interior's office, the prime minister's office, police stations, roads and bridges connecting refugee camps, journalists' offices and media centers. During the hostilities Secretary of State Clinton reiterated President Obama saying that our support for Israel is "rock solid."

That the unspeakable crimes against the Jewish people should lead to Israel of all countries humiliating and brutalizing 1.6 million people, supported by a US President, who himself conducts assassination meetings every week, and an intimidated Congress, makes a mockery of "Never Again!"

The Jerusalem Grill is a puzzle, the Israeli influence in such an out of the way place, Richland, Kentucky, that not only did Jack look up the enigmatic Glyndon Hotel, but looked at the receipt and saw the name of the cook, Maher Yakev, and out of curiosity he typed in his name just to see what would turn up on the internet. To his surprise a Facebook site appeared and at the beginning a picture of Abu Jihad, or Khalil al-Wizr, popped up, the cofounder of the Palestinian Fatah party,

Arafat's top aide who was assassinated at his home in Tunis by Israeli commandos.

Next was a video that it said had been broadcast continuously on Iraqi television with the translation "Oh Jerusalem" and "Allah Akbar," or "Allah is Great," showing Iraqi sword dances and Saddam Hussein multiple times extending a rifle in the air.

There were many personal pictures of travel, marriage celebrations, and gatherings of friends, and finally Maher Yakev himself, the very cook at the Jerusalem Grill with his nephews and nieces, relatives, and more important looking elders, family photos interspersed with political videos. One video was of an Arab boy with only a torso, an upper body "praying despite his disability," and one of successive Arab women lying dead in the street in their own puddles of blood, and a video of an imam saying, "I swear we don't need only a little bit of dignity."

There was a video of giant tires rolling downhill toward Israeli soldiers backed by a giant armored personnel carrier. The soldiers are trying to stop the tires and one of them is knocked to the ground and the unseen crowd bursts with laughter and cheering at the fallen Israeli soldier.

There are photographs of an unarmed boy stiff arming an Israeli soldier, and a small boy standing up to a soldier twice his size, and a little boy with arms on hips confronting a tank, a small girl with her chin raised defiantly to an Israeli soldier, a young man who thrusts his chest into a soldier's gun pointed at him, and a young girl with fist held up high surrounded by five Israeli soldiers.

There were successive Arafat photos, and pictures of Palestinian life, of Maher Yakev's mother and loving words for her interspersed with red hearts, photos too of dead Palestinians carried through the streets in funeral ceremonies and footage of the many bodies in morgues, of wailing women and bloody bandaged children, young girls, and old men. Pictures too of the opening of the Jerusalem Grill in April and Jack thought how he had been so thoroughly misled by the name of the restaurant not knowing that the holy city of Jerusalem, a holy site for 3,000 years, that even William Blake thought would one day come to the shores of England, had now arrived in Richland, Kentucky.

King David proclaimed Jerusalem his capital and on the Temple of the Mount the Talmud says God gathered the dust to produce the first man, Adam, and it is the site also of the al-Aqsa mosque where Muslims believed Muhammed ascended to heaven. The Christians too saw it as the site of Jesus's Last Supper and of his crucifixion at Golgotha. It was declared the capital of Arab culture even in 2009. The *2000 Statistical Yearbook of Jerusalem* lists 1,204 synagogues, 158 Christian churches, and 73 mosques in the city, sufficient conflation for Jack to be easily confused thinking the Jerusalem Grill could only be Israeli, and the cook Maher Yakev only a Jew, not knowing his name could pass for Arab. He did not realize that ironically the person whom he had thought was an overbearing man who prepared their food and served them was not an Israeli at all, the man who spawned all his resentment. What would Jack have thought if he had known he was Palestinian who had his sympathies, might he have been less overbearing, less a threat to him, the mounds of food not quite so high, the skewers of meat under glass more fresh, the man more moderate in size, warmer, more hospitable, or the food less overly seasoned, the man less of a danger to his wife whom he appeared to charm with the preparation of an amount of food that seemed more like torture than the culinary delight of eating ethnic one evening in Richland, Kentucky?

Coach

It was hard to picture him in a factory, but there he was. Overnight his life had changed. He worked for Crane. It was backbreaking work. They made sinks, toilets, and urinals. The lifting would get to anyone, much less someone who has recently taught biology. How the delicate light blue crane with a trace of green made it onto the porcelain was a mystery. Maybe there was a connection with his teaching biology that brought him to this particular factory, something symbolic of how low he had sunk.

The factory floor was half lit by skylights, but being so high despite the brightness of the white porcelain fixtures the atmosphere below was one of gloom, and when the sunlight did strike for about thirty or forty minutes a day, the gloom grew both darker and brighter.

It was winter, and the blue cranes stamped on all the fixtures had a comforting redundancy in that everything could be quickly identified. The delicate, spindly blue legs, the small head, long body and extended neck and tapering bill, the very indistinction of the blue with its suggestion of green spoke to the simplicity of the factory work despite its arduousness. The bird waded alone on the white porcelain much like the biology teacher was out of place among the heavy fixtures save for the purity of the porcelain, a blinding backdrop to the spindly bird.

Pat Lambkin had only been on the job a few days. He kept to himself. Few knew about him. The story hadn't gotten out yet.

Some wondered where he'd go, how he'd manage, but here he was already carrying toilets, sinks, urinals. How he got the job so easily nobody knew, but apparently he needed to support himself and keep his mind occupied. Too much had happened. He himself couldn't make heads or tails of it, but like the sink that had been dropped earlier that morning, his life was in shards. One of the pieces might have had his name on it for the swift ostracism he'd suffered from the community. Whether his fellow workers would read the local papers when they came out he didn't know, but throughout the shift he never smiled or acknowledged them, and certainly there was no prolonged eye contact.

The girls were never the same afterwards. The team plummeted after being undefeated in their first eleven games. He ran their practices. Then he was suddenly gone. At the Paris tournament they looked down the bench and he was not there. It was Paris, Kentucky, not France. It hadn't the distinction of the City of Lights, the museums, cafes, strolls along the Seine. This was Kentucky where basketball was king. Had they diversions, maybe they would not have taken it so hard. Had they read French novels, maybe they would have had a better understanding of human nature. His shadow hovered over the rest of the season. The practices lacked spark, while the head coach sat sprawled on three seats observing, his outstretched arms alone encompassing the varsity program. It was Coach Lambkin who organized the drills. His enthusiasm provided the momentum that prepared the team.

Coach Lambkin was wholesome looking, twenty-nine-years-old, and always dressed formally for a game in a white shirt and tie. He walked with a slight stoop because he was just over six feet and was marginally friendly. Nobody claimed to really know him. That alone should have been the warning, but it was as if his shyness brought the best out of the girls and made them try harder. By any yardstick he was a handsome young man, with the attractive vulnerability of not knowing it. The girls didn't want to let him down, as if they answered his shyness with an aggressiveness on the basketball court. Perhaps there was something hidden about him. At the time it seemed little more than the shyness that plagues many men around women. Maybe if the coach had been spoken to more, he'd have opened up. What he was hiding no one quite knew. They concluded it was his nature.

He was the perfect assistant to the head coach, infinitely compliant, with just the right measure of enthusiasm not to overshadow his superior, and willing to do everything for the girls. They all secretly admired him, his looks and fine size, despite a muscularity that was a bit soft. Maybe that attracted something competitive in them, like an easy victory over an unprepared opponent. But you can never tell everything about appearance, no matter how much you speculate.

Afterwards the season went to pot. The girls were never spoken to about Coach Lambkin once they noticed him missing on the bench after the Paris game, like a family member who disappears one day without a word. Another coach from middle school replaced him, but it wasn't the same. The team won only four of their remaining twenty-one games and ended with a losing record. Coach Lambkin was the sixth player on the floor, and without an explanation of his absence the ball was passed with a hesitancy, steps were lost as if minds were on something else.

Was he all right? Could he feed, clothe, shelter himself? Each interception, each lost assignment, each half-step asked those questions about Coach Lambkin's absence, supplemented by rumors the girls didn't know whether to believe. Neither the head coach nor the three assistants mentioned Coach Lambkin ever again. Among parents, no one knew for sure what happened. It was a conspiracy of silence. Any mention of the coach would bring a knowing or quizzical look, and a deeper silence. It got so bad that the girls just wanted the season to be over, and Angela, the star of the team, said she wasn't returning next year.

Maybe it was the contrast with the dress shirt and tie. Even though Coach Lambkin wore sweats in practice, his attire for games did not go with his summary absence, dismissal, or whatever it was. Some claimed that he still came to the games, saying they saw him in the shadows of the 1950s gym. They even thought they saw him motioning plays from behind the steel stanchions. Others roundly denied this though they admitted the team needed a shot in the arm. Still the girls could not let him go, though they felt more abandoned as the season wore on. Their practices with the new assistant never reached the pitch of Coach Lambkin's enthusiasm and hard work.

Some parents combed through their every impression, but they were all so positive that they ended pointing out his stoop, his marginal friendliness, his unparalleled politeness as hiding something. They were desperate for an explanation. Some brought up the earlier criticisms that he never played basketball himself and so was unfit to coach at the varsity level.

"After all, we entrust our children to these coaches. They can't just leave like that, walk out on us. We're a family and we have a tradition that goes back a hundred years."

"Go Jack Rabbits!"

When the charges came out they leaped on them.

"What's wrong with that man?"

Maybe that was the problem. Nobody knew exactly, but had Coach Lambkin been fired? Did he resign, or had he been asked to leave? It was as if a fireball in the night sky illuminated the Brandon faithful. Was this going to leave the small town in Kentucky in ashes? Nobody quite knew if Coach Lambkin was a bright nova or a dwarf star, or a meteor observed for weeks that one day lands smack in the town square. They refused to believe that he was just the assistant coach of the undefeated Jack Rabbits whose season went up in flames. Certainly Coach Lambkin was a rising star. But then came the rumors. The girls were doing what the boys basketball team who had a losing record had failed to. They were winning for the first time in years for Brandon High.

The girls had joked how Coach Lambkin couldn't find a girlfriend. They had heard that someone had turned him down. How he was engaged, and it was broken off. Virtually all of them felt a private glee wishing they could have been her replacement. Parents too were extremely fond of Coach Lambkin. Some mothers undoubtedly fantasized just like their daughters. So the news came as a personal betrayal, as if he had turned on them, as if each one had somehow been jilted by a coach so available to all of them. He inhabited their households like another family member. Unlike the head coach, Coach Lambkin gave of himself so totally. That is what threw salt on the wounds more than anything. They couldn't explain what

203

had happened, and as a result couldn't accept it. He appeared gentle, caring, not pushy, nothing like most men. Women warmed up to him feeling they could have their way with him, manipulate him even if he was the coach. All saw their own window of opportunity, a vulnerability juxtaposed with his authority that made him infinitely attractive. His six feet and broad shoulders, gentle hands, especially in the way he held a basketball; the extra length of fingers beyond the ball told of a facility for added caresses that might be reserved for them alone. In fact the girls fantasized about Coach Lambkin like a fleece pillow in their own beds at night upon which they could rest their heads. They had him all to themselves. His towheadedness and soft features, and the fact that he was always there attentive to their needs, made them nestle deeper in sleep at nights. The parents at home picked up on what their daughters transmitted. Despite the mild jealousy the fathers exhibited, it was quickly dispelled by the coach's gentleness, by their wives turning into eager embodiments of the school logo, volunteering and fundraising. Many didn't notice, but Coach Lambkin had a strong chin. There was good reason he ran the practices while the head coach sat eating peanuts or worked through endless bags of popcorn. Coach Lambkin kept the girls engaged in that detached manner that affected every girl personally, as if the practice was for each one alone. He made them all feel important and that was one reason for the team's success. Basketball he emphasized was as much a game of physics with its spectacular geometry involving forty moving hands and feet and a little round ball.

When the girls found out that Coach Lambkin was gone, almost by consent no one spoke, and barely shared the news with their parents. What had been such a fixture in their lives was gone. The space was wholly visible, the absence telling like gap teeth. The team lost its bite. No one sat in the empty spot on the bench Coach Lambkin had occupied because he couldn't be replaced. Perhaps a shearing had occurred, the ritualized slaughter that periodically occurs in small communities all across America. Scandal breaks out because of all the built-up pressure of everyone's waiting and heavy breathing.

The absence was as palpable as having no player come off the bench to galvanize the team. Nobody stepped up. The passing was lackluster, and the shots fizzled. Were the coach really seen in the stands, peeking behind a steel stanchion as some claimed, someone might have emerged as the sixth player. But he was simply gone. Still the skeleton of a team carried on, and it was reported that some of the girls were losing weight, starving themselves over Coach Lambkin's absence. It was something in their lives that they lost hope of filling. No one put up a defense of the coach as the accusations spread through the community.

Even though nobody knew the circumstances of his departure, he colored their dreams, their personalities, his reticence and the personal calm privately acquainted with all the phyla of the animal kingdom. The girls pictured the added propriety of his dress, his white shirts always immaculately pressed and his tie. He was the model of rectitude, of their own family solidarity. He was a pillar in the community in his small but supportive way as assistant basketball coach. He had them squaring up, keeping their elbows in when they launched foul shots, their feet set shooting threes, making crisp and timely passes. All the synchronicity of play was now lost. In short, their game was slow motion where the ball was repeatedly stolen and easy shots were blocked or passed up. The steady barrage of hearsay and innuendo was a disruption to everyone, and all related conversation was off limits at the players' homes.

Certainly the crassness of sexuality never came up with so many girls involved, but a dark cloud loomed over the town, the program, the rest of the season. Would the girls recover, would it affect the rest of their lives, or carry over to the next season? It was bigger than any individual, bigger even in the end than Coach Lambkin. It retained the awkward focus that throws everything out of kilter, so that no one knows what to do short of stoning in the town square. That is the buried element that has warped America since before Hawthorne, feelings just short of explosive buried in everyone. The love sacrificed for an undefeated team, and all because of the coach's gentle persistence, his abiding presence, his guiding hand, the nonthreatening posture that made the girls dig deeper in themselves to produce wins even by small margins. He was perfect for the job and brought out the best in the girls. The games seemed won for him even when the head coach got all the credit. Coach Lambkin was their bellwether. Winning brought the parents together. The mothers secretly dreamed of him, took pleasure in their own suppressed emotion, and by association found all aspects of the program infinitely desirable. Many didn't realize how they supported their daughters through the attraction to the young coach. He was only twenty-nine, so who knew what could come of it.

It is odd like the sparkle of precious jewels that sexuality, no matter the setting, or light so monitored, appears in the briefest glance, a fleeting smile, lost in grunting efforts to better reappear on the shiny sweat on the girls' young bodies, trickling down between their breasts, staining their sports bras, or glistening on their shoulders, or in the highlights of their hair, all that is so visible for what is deliciously suppressed. For it is confined to the basketball floor where the emotions are left, save those darting looks the girls give each other, or the passions in the huddle as they examine Ginger or Stephanie, the starters, to calculate why Coach Lambkin chose them. Each effort attempts to answer the question of their own suppressed desires for a twenty-nine-year-old coach, with moves on the court that will win him over. Purple and gold, their school colors, seem made for romance, for the pageant of both parent and child. It is a whirl of delicious inadvertencies, as if two things so apparently balanced, sex and basketball, don't mix but tantalizingly come in contact producing such rainbows under the gym lights. Surely each girl had the opportunity during the season to brush up against coach Lambkin, as their hearts beat in huddles over the excitement of being inserted into or pulled out of a game. Surely they imagined the consequences of revealing more leg or their breasts while bending over, or their flat belly even as their jersey is unconsciously pulled up to wipe their face.

"Was that Molly's bellybutton I saw!"

"Is that her nipple visible through the jersey?"

She knew he must have seen that. She could read it in the nervous movement of his eyelashes.

Coach Lambkin's pants are they too tight tonight, the bulge, all the girls notice it, and his round backside every time he bends for a ball. The ringlet of his point guard's hair when she raises a finger to push it off her forehead is matted with sweat. Coach must have seen that. Every time he blinks, two or three teammates interpret it as a wink at them. Everything is ripe for interpretation. It is all a steamy brew that sweat washes away leaving the pheromones for the nostrils. Some when they get home always find an excuse not to shower and go straight to their room. It is a soup of emotion stirred into a winning record. Who could argue with that?

But society sniffs around until it is satisfied. It is not to be underestimated. Who knows what it has a nose for? It will have its fill no matter what it has to squeeze the life out of. In the end there is a communal respiration that breathes for everyone, that substitutes a winning record for the fantasies of each individual. It could be said that deviants breathe for the women, give them a sense of positive liberation. They relieve their own impulses while chastening them at the same time. They lose no time restoring order. It is like people take the rod to themselves; frothing with indignation in a kind of panting excitement, thoroughly masking what they are attracted to.

"How dare he!"

The indignation comes in waves, whitening the lips with spit, balling the saliva. They don't even know they are striking out, but feel that it is right, hiding their own feelings pointing the finger at someone else. It emboldens them with greater authority by denying something in themselves, so they become guardians of the public trust. Their bodies tremble taking a pleasure that their indignation camouflages.

"The pervert!"

"What's wrong with him?"

"He's not going to get near my child again!"

"What is it, a hundred yards from the school. That's too close, five, ten football fields wouldn't be enough."

"We should take them to the nearest landfill and bury them with the other garbage!"

"What is it he's done?"

"I don't know, but I can tell you one thing, he better not touch my kid!"

"Coach Lambkin?"

"No, not him. He seemed so mild-mannered."

"Those are the kind you have to watch."

"I knew something was up with him."

"Yeah, he was too good to be true."

"He was so withdrawn and the way he stroked his tie, flattening it all the time. How many times do you have to do that? I used to think to myself, what's up with him? It didn't need it. That's always a dead giveaway. What they do with their tie, out in public, in front of everyone. You just have to watch them. You think it's all nerves, but it's something else. It was unconscious, but I noticed it! He walked so erect, but do you want to know something, I caught the stoop, the shoulders slumped inwards, just slightly. That's a dead giveaway!"

"But of what?"

"Of what he's done."

"But what's that?"

"I don't know, but it must be something, or they wouldn't be making all this fuss."

"He did everything Coach Simpkins asked of him?"

"That too can be suspicious. What did he want?"

"He was too quiet."

"They are the ones you have to watch, like I said."

"Fiona says he never made a pass at her."

"I heard he took part in their drills. Made passes to all of them."

"But that's the basketball, Rachel!"

"Maybe that relieved the need for intimacy, the passes he

208

exchanged with them! Public life always does. In fact it is meant to shroud us."

"It always does with those kinds."

"Frankie, what are you talking about?"

"It was the perfect cover. Don't you see? Coach and biology teacher. What better camouflage would you want?"

"It makes me mad."

"It makes me sick!"

"But he looked so harmless, soft and doughy, and all the girls liked him."

"That's because they didn't really know him."

"He was too good to be true."

"Like I said, Gina, those are the ones you have to watch out for."

"Maybe he thought he was above that holding court with all those young women. He must have thought he was untouchable."

"Untouchable?"

"Untouchable! That's a good one!"

"Something must have happened."

"They shouldn't have men coaching girls anyway. They don't know how to behave themselves."

"Most seem a model of propriety."

"But there's the rub, Alice, they 'seem!'"

"It shows they are hiding something. The more proper they are the more suspicious you have to be to protect your own child!"

"I never dreamed this of coach Lambkin."

"Sadie, that's because you're naïve. They are all like that underneath. You just have to remove the sheep's clothing and there you have it. They have to be watched. You can't take your eyes off them for a minute. Pick your kids up on time. Ask where they are sleeping on road trips."

"I hate to think about all that."

"And watch every movement on the court, their every twitch. I guarantee that will reveal something!"

"They're supposed to teach the girls fundamentals. No more. Just saying it sounds like a joke!"

"But they don't even do that."

"Linda, they were undefeated."

"What does that mean, Ethel, if all this is going on?"

"It's only Coach Lambkin."

"The rest of them are probably in on it too, only we don't know about it."

"We don't know a lot of things."

"I wouldn't trust any of them."

"We'll find out. It'll get in the papers."

"It's only a rumor."

"Sadie, will you stop."

"It'll get in the papers, I tell you. Just wait."

"All I can say is that nobody better touch my girl. Bill won't stand for it either. He told me that last night."

"There's no proof, Margarite."

"I heard, and that's proof enough for me. What more do you need? I never trusted my daughter with those men anyway. And going into the locker room with the girls! That's the limit. What do you expect? And then walking out of the locker room so calmly afterwards as if nothing had happened! It's like the cat that swallowed the canary!"

"I didn't tell you, but Stanley really got angry last night."

"Who'd put up with all of this? If I were a man, I wouldn't."

"They love the game, Rachel."

"It's not the only thing they love. We have to watch out for them, and they need to be protected from themselves."

"Don't they have to do background checks on these guys?"

"Lucy, he hasn't been charged with anything."

"It'll come out, Kathy. It'll come out. Just you wait."

We always pay others back for the emptiness of our own lives, for the sheer uneventfulness of all the years behind us and ahead. That's what living is, this desperate need to get even, to make up for the powerfully present inequities, for something

210

that we didn't get, something we think we deserve, though we are not entirely sure what it is, except by stirring up the pot. The gifts, the talent, the beauty, the brains, the persistence, and the discipline each lacks is almost palpable. The skewed allotments. It's almost criminal, we tell ourselves. Who could settle for a moment with what they've been deprived? We want recompense for everything we don't have. We want to even up this distorted creation. Settle scores. The inequality drives us nuts and never lets us settle on ourselves. Nobody settles nowadays, until their zest for life leaves, but still there is a quickening resentment at every turn. We'll do each other in in a heartbeat if the community joins us. Then what we lack will not be so painful. We can get back at people, at the very society we are allied with, at the whole shebang, at creation itself as if we have a hand in changing it. In one fell swoop we'll even things up, for not being tall enough, handsome, young enough, liked enough, for not captivating our own daughters like a stranger does. We'll get him in the end and boost ourselves, even the scales so we'll rise for our children who will look up to us for protecting them.

We don't look like birds of prey. You'd be hard pressed to find the raptor's beak on most, the claws. We look so harmless, just like ordinary housewives, but don't be deceived. Our indignation is terrifying; it can rouse mobs, summon lynching parties. The courts are too slow, juries are stacked and judges themselves are crooked. Even newspapers have to check their sources and we don't have time for that. We have to take things in our own hands sometimes, gang up, whisper, shift our eyes, point fingers, eventually take up the cudgels ourselves if it comes to that and the authorities don't respond. That is why we are together, sacrificing all our individual pleasures for the group. He's not interested in us anyway. We'll swallow him up like flakes of dry cereal, one stepped on by our collective weight, crushed underfoot.

"Still we have no proof!"

"I told you the way he stroked his tie is proof enough! I can see him now returning the basketballs to the rack as the

211

girls huddle with Coach Simpkins, his fingers extending so conspicuously over the balls. There is too much extra length not to come to no good. Okay, he's upright, relaxed, but that should tell you something. He's too clean-cut I tell you, and that hand on his tie is a dead give away. What do you think he does with it at other times? He is so servile looking, such a wolf in sheep's clothing. It's shameful how we can't tell anything. It reflects poorly on us. We should have caught it right off!"

"But we have no proof."

"Will you stop that. I'm getting tired of you, Sadie."

"She's right."

"We don't need proof, Melissa. You can tell. It's right in front of you. The tie's the thing that'll convict him. The way it hangs so openly, and he smooths it like that with his hand. Ugh, it's disgusting!"

"They should have run him out of the gym long ago."

"And that he is so clean-cut, wholesome looking. I can't get over that."

"You can't trust anybody, Janice. You have all the ingredients here. It's the devil's brew, all solid, respectable, fine upstanding members of the community, a coach, a teacher."

"In biology."

"You have to be suspicious of that."

"They shouldn't teach it in high school. It gives the kids too many ideas."

"Sure, I know why he chose that field. It shows he's a pervert who needs to name everything and look at what he's not supposed to."

"Don't you keep an eye on him when he's in the huddle with the girls? I sure do, and I can tell you a thing or two."

"What?"

"He's in for a surprise if he thinks he can pull the wool over my eyes."

"He thinks he can catalogue us, label us, pin us in cigar boxes and assign a name. That's what's going to happen to him, the pervert. Thinks he is better than us. We'll show him!"

"He's a rat. And around our daughters. The school administration should all be fired. I'd get rid of the lot of them. At Fountain Square we should start a bonfire. Burn them all at the stake, hold public hearings until they all confess. I mean if the authorities don't do it . . . !"

Most of the players were quiet. They themselves weren't sure their mothers spoke for them. They didn't understand the coach's leaving, felt let down, not threatened. He'd only made basketball passes to them and seemed interested in improving their game and nothing more. But the rumors colored what they thought. They brought about a contagion that was catching. They sheepishly thought Lambkin had some defect, a weakness, that they vaguely sensed in themselves, that contributed to the quietness and only redoubled the cacophony of their parents for being unspoken. It must have been catching, or why would he have gone? Left us? What was he running from? they thought. They felt abandoned and tried to concentrate on basketball. They thought their bodies under the uniform were recognized by few, certainly not by the coaches.

The force of attraction is often the unwitting nature of it. We don't know what we are attracted to immediately and suddenly there is an exposed midriff, the outline of the breast, a nipple peeking through, and it's a whole new ball game. Basketball becomes layered and heroics on the court take on a whole new meaning, deeper often than a pretty face or stunning body. Most attraction to the coach is relieved by dreams alone. Some would entertain nothing waking, for it would throw them off their game or embarrass them and they wouldn't be able to perform.

At banquets it is astonishing the way they dress up. You'd think they were not the same kids you see on the floor. Most look like prostitutes with thick make-up and bright lipstick and the most seductively inappropriate dress for a sports banquet. You wonder how their parents let them out of the house. It is as if it is their first chance to make themselves truly attractive to their coach, dispel the grunting, the clumsiness, the sweaty indignities on the court. It is as if the genie is let out of the bottle. And he is there before them with his flattop and incredibly muscular folded arms, rising to six feet, a eunuch almost in charge of a harem, a regular Mr. Clean who sanitized sexuality for the good of the team. So spotless is his behavior that subconsciously he brings out the prostitute in them. And the surprising thing is the parents pretend to notice nothing.

If players and coaches thought like that during the season, nobody would take the floor. They'd be too ashamed. The laws of attraction would prohibit it. It has to be done on the sly, or here in the open banquet to let the steam off of what might otherwise not be only sweaty associations. Perish the thought! Girls' sports wouldn't be possible. That sexuality can be so downplayed when sports take over is a surprise, despite rampant charges of lesbianism. All that is suppressed but still lurking under the surface. From the stands sometimes you wonder why a beautiful face is competing at all. But the coaches steel themselves like Lambkin did till the story broke. Still it was not the case with the team. That's why they didn't break their extraordinary silence and didn't rally to their coach's support. They who had dressed up for him, who dreamed about him, felt betrayed. He betrayed their trust with someone else. In fact privately they were dying to know who it was. The team felt isolated, abandoned. There was no bleating, just a public shearing of rumor, a network of whispers, finger pointing, and then it hit the papers.

"Ex-Brandon High School Coach Indicted on Sex Charges Involving Student," the headline read. The x branded him immediately. And then there was that large picture of Coach Lambkin, a file photo with his hands in his pockets. He was always so attentively laid-back in his dress shirt and the tell-tale tie. Behind him in the photo is the leg of a girl, the calf and thigh, and covering her lap is a basketball. The hardwood floor is behind. And the coach's face is a surprise to everyone. His mouth is open, and there is the suggestion of a light moustache above it, but in the middle of his open mouth the top row of teeth contains a gap, a wide dark gap to suggest the worst of sexual proclivities that go back to Chaucer's lecherous

Canterbury pilgrims, the pimply red-faced Summoner or the Wife of Bath. It looks like a player's little brother had blackened the teeth with a pencil or pen. I never noticed such a severe gap in Coach Lambkin's mouth. It is as if something had been missed by us all this time, as apparent as the picture now on the front page of the local newspaper. The teeth may have gapped overnight, at least that was what the newspaper conveyed wanting to identify him as the perp, providing space on his own face for such shenanigans. From the photo alone, you could tell the coach was guilty. Who needed to read the rest of the article, just look at the picture! You could tell he'd been fooling around. Pictures don't lie. It made you think the worst and understand what got the community talking. Stoning could conceivably follow in another era. After all, local standards have been violated. Individual rights are sacrificed for a reason. Deviancy has to be punished and the populace kept in line, or there would be chaos and everything will spin out of control. And then there are the parents to think about. What about them? Nobody remembered the gap in real life. We all had missed it. Still we had our suspicions. We are a deeply religious town and believe anything could happen. The mothers must have felt betrayed. Their own fantasy life was now rudely exposed. They turned away in disgust as at an infidelity. They felt betrayed as did their children.

The local grand jury, that almost always hands down an indictment, claimed the coach "committed the offense of criminal solicitation to the use of a minor in a sexual performance."

"Wow! That confirms it. He's gone, outta here!"

It was "a misdemeanor charge" that was "turned over to Clay County District Court." The article went on, "it was not clear if a warrant for his arrest had been issued." Police said the student "a sixteen-year-old girl claimed Lambkin offered her money in exchange for oral sex and said he would give her money if she would expose herself to him."

That was the last straw for the parents. They and the whole town were convulsed like their young girls over the charges. In the deep recesses of their minds they wondered how they had been left out and felt the cold shoulder so much that they grew numb towards the coach for having done such a thing with someone else, and not even a basketball player! The players themselves simply didn't know what to think. How had they been left out? How did it happen? It'd take the rest of the season to organize their response. They were understandably silent about Coach afterwards.

The coach has been ordered to have no contact with any child under the age of 18, and to have no contact with any city or county school systems, or any school property. Lambkin resigned shortly after the allegations arose. The paper read, "he taught science and was an assistant basketball coach at BHS."

It was no one on the team. Well, that was a relief. Or was it? Was that salt in the wound of the worst kind? There was a sigh of relief before the next level of condemnation kicked in. The girls could escape each other's jealousy at least. They would not be at their own throats. It didn't split up the team. That was probably good for them. The girls said they knew the student, Sheila Mays. She had been in coach's biology class. Another reason why biology should not be taught in high school with such impressionable young girls, some mothers repeated. Yes, everyone knew her.

"She's a flirt," they said.

"Slut," some whispered.

They had him on tape. They recorded the calls, the paper said.

But the players were reluctant to divulge more, if they knew anything. They gave their parents the idea they were both ignorant and knowing. What was really the matter was the magnitude of their disappointment. They had admired the coach for his propriety, his reticence, his quiet but tireless efforts getting them to improve. His rigorous drills, and the way he kept practices animated, the way he confined everything to basketball had made him almost unapproachable, and more importantly irreproachable. This seemed like a positive betrayal of the worst kind. And with Sheila Mays! Sheila Mays! She just didn't deserve it!

They had thought Coach Lambkin was above this. His tall frame was a pillar they could rest on. He was the stuff the old gymnasium was made of, durable, solid material that would not buckle or let you down. He and the whole succession of coaches who kept their distance from the girls they coached constituted the most dignified tradition, those who gave every ounce of their talent and energies, employed all their imagination to get the most out of the girls and suppress any untoward feeling that would compromise their trust so the girls could reach heights the coaches themselves never attained. And it was nothing more, any preference or predilection was quickly swept under the rug, hidden inside the coachly mantle of fairness and rectitude that made each coach profoundly impact the girls who passed through the program at Brandon High for almost the last hundred years.

Rumor and now the formal news wiped out the initiative of the team. Everyone knew the season was over. The personal loss was almost incalculable that the girls never vocalized. It was as if their own desires for the assistant coach, their private life, stood crudely exposed on the front page. Of course they knew better, but their feelings for the coach could, considering the circumstances, hardly be articulated. It shocked them into a permanent silence.

"I don't want to talk about it, mom!"

"Dad, will you stop!"

It was as if the girls themselves feared exposure over a coach that had appeared untouchable, someone who was dreamed about, wondered at, desired just because of the restraint he represented, for the pure glow that surrounded someone who doesn't assert himself. It was like an altar had been stormed and everything holy knocked down. But now he was tarred and feathered, and they couldn't look, only ignore the empty space on the bench, forget that voice missing in practice, and the passes thrown to them. The zest was gone and their performance in games was lackluster. The head coach couldn't rally them and never addressed that undercurrent of all

217

programs burdened with the tension of being so thoroughly above reproach.

Brandon High was having such a miracle season until the allegations and rumors of Coach Lambkin's firing that a ball of flame rose above the community like the bonfire at New Years where the gaunt visage of Coach Lambkin was reportedly seen inside a grim reaper's cowl of a heavy gray garment. So much did he focus the indignation of the community that the girls barely talked among themselves about a crime they had not committed but felt guilty for being excluded from because each one felt personally jilted. The snippets they shared with their family were immediately blown out of proportion, as mothers tried to erase their own guilty thoughts. For it was like looking in a mirror at the visible hurt on their daughters' faces, second guessing themselves about what they could have done differently.

Could they have been kinder to him, have shown him more of their own feelings? Had they been more flirtatious, would that have kept him with them, not caused him to stray with Sheila? What could they have done? That someone in the student body beat them to the punch, they who had given so much of themselves every practice, all eleven games they put their bodies on the line for him; it made them angry, confused, but they felt they had no right to their anger for what it revealed about their own feelings for the young, handsome twenty-nine-year-old coach.

But what was Coach Lambkin accused of? The charges were never entirely revealed. What made him so susceptible when his behavior towards the team was above reproach? Did all the tension of the social charade just snap? How could he go off the deep end, drown in such a sea of communal resentment?

The team quickly established that Sheila Mays was a flirt, even if her name didn't get in the newspaper. But how could the man they knew, dressed so impeccably in white shirts and tie commit such an indiscretion? What did he do? The papers could not have gotten the whole story.

True Sheila was in his biology class. True they discussed

reproduction like they did every year. True Coach Lambkin lived alone, had recently gotten engaged. True the engagement had been broken off, and it was reported he even had a girlfriend. For a time he had trouble getting a date, the girls whispered because he was too nice. They giggled over his difficulty, privately imagining he was saving himself for each of them. Someone so attractive and clean-cut, any of them would be proud to walk arm and arm with him to the altar.

The email he got from Sheila maybe struck him at the time when he was vulnerable. She expressed her shameless fascination with him, and speculated that he alone was going to make breakthroughs in the field of science out in the woods living in a solitary cabin where he would change the world. She told him he was brilliant, and a marvelous teacher. And then she explained her problems at home, relating that sometimes she didn't want to live. She speculated what he did when he was alone. He made the class so interesting for her and the other students, seduced his students into a love for biology that they'll never forget, and she mentioned how his basketball players all loved him. She said she pictured him making breakfast for himself and wished she could be there to serve him, pictured the glow of him doing his own laundry, washing out the cares and stains of the world, the playful suds on his underwear, iridescent bubbles bursting in the washer window, and his eating alone by candlelight and she just knew he needed a companion. Everyone loved him, she said. `She stroked his ego with the same care he gave his tie. He'd grab it lightly between thumb and four fingers, just under the knot, and then ease his hand down its length where it tapered off to the tip at the bottom. It was a mysterious ritual that couldn't help to enchant anyone who noticed it. Shelia was at the games, never missed a class, and turned up in Coach Lambkin's office one day. She even took to calling him regularly at home and asking for advice about squabbles with her mother with whom she lived. And that annoying younger brother of hers. She called so often that Coach Lambkin grew not only accustomed to her calls but even anticipated them. Sheila was tall, attractive, with eyes that seemed the exact opposite of Coach Lambkin's doughiness. They penetrated his gray eyes with one searching look, but he never felt threatened, only fascinated by her insistence. He observed her with the same intensity he observed the iridescent beetles or luminous butterflies from South America, noting their wonderful shapes. The shape of the breasts and bottoms, the profiles of all his girls without knowing it dissolved into one generic appreciation listening to Shelia talk about her problems at home, and her dependence on him was already like a needle through her body. It affected him with a pleasurable concern that he never allowed towards his players, or other students, and appealed to something of the collector in him. In fact he imagined he was acting as Sheila's advisor, and that day when she said she just got a tattoo of a crane and wanted to show him he didn't think anything of it, nor did he associate it with the logo on the blue porcelain fixtures made in Brandon where her father had worked before he lost his job and left the family. Crane served gas stations, schools, businesses, and residences all across the country.

"Where is it?" he asked innocently.

"I'm not going to tell you, but I'll show you when I see you."

"Okay," he said abstracted.

It never occurred to Coach Lambkin how badly she wanted to show her tattoo. She seemed a little jealous lately of the excitement over the undefeated season.

Sheila called the next night and brought it up again.

"Do you want to see it?"

"If you want me to. Where is it?"

"It's a secret."

"Come on, where is it?"

"Will you pay me if I show you?"

"Pay you?"

"Yes, pay me. It's blue with a touch of green."

"Okay, I'll pay you if you show me."

"To expose myself?"

"What? Okay," the coach finally said, "why not?"

"And will you kiss it?"

"Sheila!"

"I thought you were my friend."

"But I'm paying you, remember."

"Yes, for the kiss."

"Okay."

The coach didn't know he was being taped. He didn't know Sheila felt slighted by the undefeated season, or the rumors of a new girlfriend.

This was simply a dose of cayenne pepper, she thought, only mildly discomforting. She never imagined her mother would get hold of the tape and bring it to the school. The rest was history.

Within a week Coach Lambkin was fired and Sheila to escape the taunts of her classmates moved cross-town and changed schools where it is reported she has already been emailing her social studies teacher.

Postscript

Dora Maggio saw the man at the pool at General Burnside Island State Park videotaping children on a field trip. Dora didn't like the looks of it, the way he hung on the chainlink fence, the camera hanging from his neck. She thought he was up to no good. She saw him return to his car and that's when she wrote down his license plate number and called the police, but the man was gone by the time the authorities came. They sent Sheriff's deputy Casey McBride to the scene to investigate.

It was a hot day in Burnside and the refreshing squeals from the children gave nothing away of what was taking place outside the chainlink fence.

Deputy McBride went to the residence of Frank Crabtree and asked to see the video camera and tape. After Officer McBride viewed a portion of the tape, he returned to the Crabtree house with a search warrant to confiscate all the videotapes in the home.

Mr. Crabtree refused to produce the tape in question. On the confiscated tapes there were clips of naked children the newspaper reported, but there was no tape of the Burnside swimming pool, or the passing houseboats that Crabtree said he was unable to get his camera out in time for. McBride had seen no children on the tape he viewed.

Crabtree was convicted by the Circuit Court for "tampering with physical evidence and for being a first-degree persistent felony offender." He received a sentence of twelve years. The Court of Appeals reaffirmed the conviction two years later in an appeal.

All the citizens of Burnside felt relieved that the sex offender was behind bars.

The newspaper said that the seventy-year-old Crabtree had been prosecuted in multiple states for sexual assaults on children, so citizens felt vindicated placing the perpetrator behind bars for allegedly taking footage of the children at the pool and tampering with evidence. It was regretted that the fence was not enough to stop the prying eyes of such offenders. Citizens were disturbed that such men were walking around free.

"They should all be behind bars," someone bellowed at the city council meeting following the conviction.

But a recent development stunned the good citizens of Burnside.

"Sex Offender's Verdict Overturned, Crabtree Walks," the front page shared the headline with "Ex-BHS Coach Indicted on Sex Charge."

The State Supreme Court had reversed the ruling making Crabtree "a free man." Coach Lambkin's picture was there plain as day, right under Frank Crabtree's in *The Examiner*. The citizens of Brandon didn't know what to think except to keep their children, both boys and girls, indoors for all the sexual predators lurking in the community. Attendance at the Burnside pool dropped the next summer. Some suggested the pool be closed completely if there was not proper surveillance, and that schools should close their doors too until the matter was properly addressed to prevent future incidents. A wall was proposed to replace the chainlink fence.

"They need to lock them up and throw away the key!" a Brandon City council member replied and was seconded by two other council members. His comments headlined the next issue of the paper.

The assistant DA had said two years earlier of Frank Crabtree after his appeal failed, "I hope he draws his last breath in prison."

After Crabtree's release, Commonwealth Attorney, Eddie Haste, said that he was frustrated at the order from the Supreme Court, adding he was very disappointed in the Court's ruling. He added that Crabtree had "a long history of sexual crimes and now he is free to go back into the community again."

Crabtree's lawyer Stanley Hoch said his client was "wrongfully convicted" and had lost four years of his life. He added that the charges were an "attempt to get a man society didn't like off the street."

"What's this world coming to, Helen?"

"Sometimes I don't know, Harold."

The Betrayal

It was like he was visiting them. They would come sooner or later to him; inevitably their numbers would one day swarm over his body. That's why he was apprehensive of what he would find. In the back of his mind he knew they'd be there, but denied them.

He averaged under ten miles an hour to reach the George Washington Bridge, and then on to the Cross Bronx Expressway. Traffic proceeded at a crawl. He found himself in the slow lane the closer he got no matter how many times he switched lanes.

The power of New Yorkers in their sleek black cars all looked like intimidating versions of limousines zooming north from their high-powered jobs. The Spanish machismo like a high octane gasoline powered their cars to their representatives in the Bronx for the World Series that night. They drove at breakneck speeds and Jack too was caught up in the final throes of World Series fever, the electricity racing to the city. Until promptly the traffic slowed close to the bridge.

Nothing climbed his arms or legs as the radio announcers cheered the Yankee fans over the Phillies. The faces of their own family were erased by the likes of Alex Rodriguez, Derek Jeter, and Hideo Matsui dominating television and radio and splashed on billboards all over town. They substitute for the forgotten masses. The exaggerated attention to their heroes makes everyone forget their own family. After Rodriguez homers, death rattles become as inaudible as baby rattles as fans dance around their living rooms and shout from windows.

"Dad died when Alex took his shot!"

The lanes constantly converged, and Jack is squashed out each time; his headlights like a bug light up the city as dusk descends. The antenna on his car barely clarified competing signals.

He had put off the visit for five years. Two years before she forgot where he lived, his children's names, and his occupation, so he didn't know what he'd find. The World Series will substitute in a league all its own, where the players are more real than we are. Jack was nobody compared to Ed Kranepool whom he ran against in the school yard of PS 36. Jack was the fastest kid on Watson Avenue and Danny Lieta who knew Eddie set up the race.

Eddie who later starred for the New York Mets left Jack behind in the schoolyard of broken windows and Bazooka bubble gum wrappers.

It reminded Jack of Dr. Kramer telling Ollie's mother when she was ninety that the bones in her two legs were already turning to dust.

Remembering that, Jack raised his fist and knocked on her door not knowing if she'd remember him.

The door slowly opened and there she stood a ghost of herself. Her face had collapsed around the mouth into countless lines. The teeth were gone for years, but she had stopped wearing dentures for visitors. Her wig was off. All traces of vanity had fled, and her skin was sallow and the remaining wisps of hair permanently white.

After they hugged, the heat of the house overpowered Jack with the smell of the cat box and rotten eggs immediately confirming his suspicions.

Cat food and litter crunched underfoot in the hallway and into the kitchen. The carpet in the dining room was startlingly soiled. The cat's dishes were yellow with egg yolk. The kitchen floor and the soiled table made Jack stifle a gag reflex.

The coating of egg over everything was explained by the raw egg Ollie gave Tiger every day.

Ollie's face around her mouth was a black hole that had the cavernous look of the Norwegian painter's famous portrayal. Our mouths are tunnels for the abiding question of whom and where we are, signaling the horror of our diminished understanding. Ollie had been so particular about the cleanliness of her mouth, always running her tongue over her gums even in the absence of teeth.

Jack feigned a kiss like the ones that she had always given

225

him.

"The traffic was bad," he said.

It was an hour and a half before the World Series, and he had chosen the worst day of the year to visit.

Jack set his two bags down.

Ollie didn't ask him to take them upstairs like she usually did.

"It's all right if I spend the night?" he asked.

"Sure," she said.

When he had called about visiting he said he was going to get a motel room, but she said he could stay with her.

He glanced at the living room before going upstairs. The carpet he saw no amount of shampoos could have cleaned it.

The knickknacks were in disrepair. The house had gone to pot. Cockroaches scrambled across the kitchen floor and over the countertops. Jack's worst fears were realized.

Ollie didn't ask him to put his things upstairs because entering the bedroom he found no furniture, only four empty blue walls. The pictures were missing as was the beautiful dresser with the long mirror, the set of high drawers, and the queen-sized bed. There were some clothes on the floor in a neat pile and the half-opened closet looked rifled of all but a few garments. Everything was in the den, but there too the closet had only a scattering of clothes.

The TV in the den could only get a shopping channel and the television Ollie insisted could be watched in her bedroom was missing. She told him about three or four times to turn it on. She didn't have a radio either.

So there was no help for the World Series. It could not come out of thin air with its soothing irrelevance to displace the conditions the house had fallen into. He went downstairs and said, "The furniture's gone!"

"Margarite's with them," she said.

"Who?"

"Cheryl and Joe."

Margarite had died over twenty years earlier. Ollie at first

226

resented her sister coming to live with her when her mother died, but then grew guilty and she came. When Margarite died Ollie said she missed her even more than Harold, her husband.

"So Cheryl took it?" Jack asked.

"I guess," Ollie said.

Jack's eyes rested on the china cabinet and three large platters, but the dishes were all gone, replaced by papers plates.

"Did she take the dishes too?" Jack asked.

"No, they broke," Ollie said.

"All the dishes?"

Ollie smiled.

Ollie had always kept her house immaculate. Harold was proud of his home, she had always said. He was a handyman who made cabinets in the basement, polyurethaned the doors that still looked fresh after fifty years, and complied with all Ollie's wishes shopping for knickknacks and the most beautiful furnishings during trips downtown and out to Jersey.

There were marble lamps and end tables from Italy, the finest Italian sofa and chairs whose plastic coverings Ollie hadn't removed for years after they were purchased. The furniture was now bare, and the fabric hopelessly soiled and matted with cat hair.

All her life Ollie had a physical dislike of dirt and cleaned her house like her teeth with an immaculate precision. Why she agreed to have all her teeth removed was a mystery. Maybe it was the fashion just like braces are today.

Jack was a teenager when they bought the house and knew every piece of furniture that arrived because he accepted delivery that summer after high school when he was staying there.

Ollie had been like a mother to him.

All the windows in the house were tightly closed, so he cracked one in the den upstairs. To get some air himself and assess the situation, Jack told Ollie he'd get some Chinese food.

"You don't have to do that," she said as he looked in the cabinets.

The dishes were all gone, only the cabinet by the door had

a few cups and small plates and bowls. He opened the drawers and found each one thick with cockroach specks and eggs dropped everywhere. The counters were filthy and so he wiped them. He was shocked that every drawer and cabinet was hopelessly fouled by cockroaches.

The insects had been tolerated for years. They are always waiting in the dark and dirt, in the moisture of basements, feeding on paper and glue, whatever commercial materials serve their appetites, before moving upstairs to share the real food. They now inhabited the cupboards, the toaster, and were there a radio they'd have invaded it for the warmth around the replacement bulbs.

People are commensal, sharing their crumbs, their foodstuffs, as if expecting company. The singular tooth marks of rodents on almonds are not so obvious, but they rarely miss a nut. They thrive on what we discard, wait for our garbage. Walking around uncrawled on requires constant surveillance, sprays, traps, and even the construction of actual motels. It is a monopoly board of cohabitation. Daily life beats back the tide of insect and rodent populations poised at every entrance, window, uncaulked pipe. Once entrance is gained their populations explode. Moats and waterways are their highways. They love the damp all of us ready for them, the hordes at the borders. The least putrescence draws them.

Ollie's house is one tiny triumph in their million-year history. Our infinite capacity for waste sustains them. We set the table for them, while we think we are eating alone. They wait for us to lose interest in ourselves, in our surroundings; their success depends on our dropping our guard, not raising the black flag, capitulating to armies of scurrying cockroaches, shiny oily brown infestations waving their antenna through the least openings and raising their wings like celebrating pennants. They'll crawl up our arms, inside our clothes, invade our drawers and mar our written records, not to mention foodstuffs, until we forget to brush them off, or our movements slow.

"Oh, Grandma, a water bug!" a grandchild will naively say,

not realizing what is in store for all of us.

Sometimes when we are unattended they'll mass at the ordure of the backside or hide in a crease of fat and we won't know they are there, our mental acuity dims; their crustiness becomes a permanent amber that we don't bother with. Our hand rubs against the carapace, like shiny brown jewelry we have not taken off; or we'll call, "Is this Janie Lynn's barrette?" envisioning in her chestnut hair what is only a burrowing cockroach. They supplant all our fastidiousness about a clean house. The furniture, once unmolested and protected by plastic, is now stained, and their brown wings surprise us suddenly taking flight.

Insects are not articulate for nothing. Their well-defined bodies exist when our arguments for order and cleanliness break down. Their oversized mandibles meticulously replace our best arguments, as does the efficiency of their sorting foodstuffs, glue, or paper, or a thin slice of sclera taken from a host. They mass at the city gate. They need no formal invitation, no treaty. They are always waiting for an internal breakdown to move in, for a crisis of will.

Visits such as Jack's seem milksoppish by comparison; they know nothing will change, that he'll leave in a few days. Their swarming reduces his visit to a short campaign. He might as well have not visited so far as they are concerned; despite how many he's already killed downstairs and in the bathroom, it is little more than skirmishes to them. Their sheer numbers of replacements baffle mathematicians.

Jack's outrage knows no bounds for a day or two, but they know he'll be gone, and they'll have the house to themselves again. In fact they've haunted drawers and cabinets for a thousand years anticipating every change of owner. They relish social catastrophes. They know we'll one day lose the desire to brush them off. The drool from the mouth replaces memory of the itch caused by their tiny feet scampering up our arm or down a leg.

"Do you want anything to eat, Ollie?"

"No, I've eaten," she says.

229

Jack gets Chinese food for himself, but as he reenters the house the smells overpower him, and he loses his appetite. He wipes off the kitchen table and manages to find a bowl. It is sticky with old egg.

He pours in the egg drop soup and gets paper plates. He wants to heat up hot water for a teabag, but there is no pot. He is afraid to look inside the tea kettle.

Finally he sits down to eat, but quickly realizes his regret at having gotten egg drop soup. He finds he cannot eat it with gusto. Ollie again asks him about his family, where he lives and how many children he has, and what work he does. She doesn't seem to notice Jack eyeing the two cockroaches crawling across the wall.

She talks about Margarite living next door with Cheryl.

"Margarite's dead twenty years," Jack says. "She's not living there."

"She's not?" Ollie asks puzzled.

"No, Ollie."

"How old are you, Ollie?"

"Eighty-nine."

"When were you born?"

"1915."

"Let's see, that makes you 93," Jack says, and the correction makes no impression on her. Jack recalls Michelet's saying, "Women never get old."

Jack looks up and sees more cockroaches on the wall. Then he looks on the floor and notices them scurrying all over the cat's dishes. He's already killed about twenty on the counter and watched them disappear into the coffee maker.

Jack gets up and gets a paper plate. Everything feels soiled and he digs one out of midpack. As he eats he loses his appetite completely.

Afterwards Ollie asks if he wants coffee.

"No," he says.

The refrigerator has large bowls of butter for some reason, some old punch, and a fresh quart of milk.

"I'm really thirsty for some juice," Jack says. "I'll go and get a few sponges and cleanser," he says. "Do you mind if I clean up a little?"

"No," Ollie says.

Jack then looks under the sink and stops counting at forty containers of insect spray and an astonishing array of green, blue, yellow, brown, and pink cleansers.

Yes, Jack had been there the summer when each lamp, marble end table, when the sofas and chairs were delivered when Ollie and Harold were at work. Their condition now shocks him.

The knickknacks remained though many were broken. The head was off the largest ceramic cat down the basement, but on the table upstairs he noticed an absent elephant tusk, the missing cougar's tail, chipped birds' beaks, cardinal crests removed, and the legs of any number of animals were gone. The old Chinese man that Jack had got Ollie lost his fishing rod, a policeman missed his nightstick, a housewife her skillet, one dolphin its fin. Come to think of it, most of the limited edition of Rockwells were missing. The birds up on the valence for the curtains, however, were all intact.

Ollie, such a meticulous housekeeper, had come to this. The knickknacks didn't replace the missing husband or her sister, no matter how she expanded her collections, though they had kept Cheryl and her baby away for fear that she would break them. In fact even when Harold and Margarite were alive, the regard for the knickknacks and the animals often replaced the attention for people.

The world is so perfect in Rockwell, with all the timely difficulties universalized and every unseemliness addressed with honesty, integrity, and the hopeful optimism that provides the cement to society even when a figurine gets broken. Rockwell's illustrations, and the series of animals, made everyone's life simpler just looking at them; they unify all the loose impressions within the genius of one man. His representations gave perspective that made the world more hospitable. It simplified life and froze its reality as something attainable by all. Living sometimes becomes unbearably messy, people can be frustrating, but he reassured us that everything could be corrected with a kind word of discipline, a gentle scolding in the end, a look of understanding indulgence at what's spilled or broken. Even the taunts of the little black girl on her way to school could be absorbed with a social grace that recognized that everything is going to turn out for the best and society will progress. He captured life and its petty concerns and sometimes big problems like prejudice, but he handled them with a dignity that preserved the fabric of society; despite the little boy's stealing, the tall policeman was there to kindly take him by the collar, tempered like Granny's reaction when the cat overturns a saucer of milk. Nothing couldn't be corrected with love and hard work. Never did Rockwell chart the decay of old age, save happily on grandma's rosy cheeks, floral patterned dress and rectangular spectacles, as her two outstretched hands hold a platter of turkey high above the table at a sumptuous setting at Thanksgiving where everyone is happy.

But the cockroach up the wall, its antennas waving, that was another dimension, or two or three congregating, or a swarm of them on the floor at the dry egg, a regular infestation, that couldn't be beaten back with the imagination or wasn't depicted with the kindliest paintbrush. In short if it was never depicted, not released by the *Saturday Evening Post*, it didn't exist. Not even Edward Hopper's loneliness could reach the sheer neglect. We look in vain for the cockroach on the wall, for specked drawers, their eggs under the coffee maker, five or six crawling the walls, or peeking out from behind a tin. All the representations are idealized. Real life doesn't intrude outside Bellows' brutal boxing matches. There is no dirt. And nobody has established how long a person should live after the dignity goes. Nature has established no boundaries beyond the symptoms of illness. The loss of pride, dignity, is untouched outside the relief of dementia. It is no longer the golden age seniors experienced in the sixties at centers around the city, where no one said an unkind word or upset the platter of turkey. Everyone was served on time. A full stomach was the main thing. The dead birds endeared us to each other as traditions of slaughter always do. For nobody recognizes themselves on the platter served up.

This is exactly why the World Series is such a relief to the loss of control of the bowels, to the uncleanliness of the house and the vagaries of dementia. Baseball gilded every degradation and that is why it was so important for New York with its long tradition and huge population. The celebration enables people to forget everything for a few days.

The way the night descended, and the traffic patterns slowed to a crawl told something larger was taking place down on the field, a Rockwellian America that includes everyone, players from Haiti and the Dominican Republic, from as far away as Japan. The dining room is emptied now of people, and dishes no longer filled the cabinets. But there are paper plates. Margarite was still alive next door in a Rockwell world even though dead twenty years. The Rockwells that are missing have done their duty. P.T. Barnum is a part of America after all.

This was the America Jack revisited despite his apprehension. The cockroach under the clothing rarely shows itself and the flower print dress gives away nothing. It's looseness and the way it falls is perfect. The kindly old Rockwell face and the rectangular spectacles will never show that Ollie can barely see to clean the house she once kept immaculate.

Jack half suspects the dry cat food on the floor is dropped intentionally, scattered like for the birds on the top of the steps, half to get the attention of those who neglect them. Jack senses something stubborn, hints of anger in old age, at people, though there is no proof outside the wretched conditions in which Ollie lives, and the interest she has lost in herself. All houses capitulate in time. The white flags of memory droop and we drift into filth and neglect, become part of our hopelessly deteriorating surroundings. This is what shocked Jack. Your own children should be there so you won't be abandoned to the indifference of strangers, but Ollie only had her adopted niece and a stepson living in Georgia.

"Tiger," Ollie calls when the conversation is at a lull and she's repeated the same questions too often. "Where is Tiger? Is he in the house?"

"He's under the dining room table," Jack says looking at the orange cat, not knowing what to make of Tiger. He is a shocking bag of bones.

"How old is he?" Jack asks to fill the silence.

"He's eleven," Ollie answers.

Despite his thinness, Tiger had all the food and raw egg he wanted. Jack was reluctant to touch the cat, but finally did pet his ratty coat and felt the rachitic spine. The feel of the bones was distinctly unpleasant.

Jack then got up and changed Tiger's water bowl, then went and turned the thermostat down to 75 degrees.

When Jack asked Ollie about the bed, she said Cheryl probably took it for Magarite, and the dishes Jack asked?

"They broke," she repeated dryly.

Jack fooled with the TV again but couldn't get reception and couldn't locate the set Ollie said was in her room. The lack of radio meant he'd have to pass on the World Series. He didn't want to listen in his car.

"No radio. What do you do all day, Ollie?" Jack asked. "Does anyone come?"

"People have their own lives," she said.

"Cheryl and Joe go shopping once a week for me. I give them $40 dollars, and I give Joe $75 to clean the house for me."

Jack went out and bought orange juice and sponges to clean the floor and looked for a bucket. He imagined already the dirty water of our lives with the dead bodies of cockroaches floating on top. Unlike people they seem lighter.

Why bother talking in the first place if living adds up to this, a host for insects, the moving in of thousands for the one lover that you denied, for pain when he moves away, for the second childhood, for the resentments that surface after being buried a lifetime? Is it worth it for the antenna waving through the cracks, for the smells, and the backside we eventually forget to wipe.

"Wipe that smile off your face, Kunkel," he was told in the school and it echoes all his life till it ends an unwiped posterior.

The mind forgets the face of a loved one and the experiences of a lifetime leave blank stares that hang suspended for years.

Who knows one day Kunkel will lack the strength to bring his arm up to clean his own body. There will be no one to come to his assistance.

Jack returned with the juice and sponges.

Being outside in the air was refreshing; the moisture he knew would invade his defenseless lungs had he remained in the city.

He returned and rustled through the basement, noticed the lost head of the waist high porcelain cat again and found a white dishpan. He filled it with water and cleanser, soap and Pine Sol, and after sweeping up the kitchen dropped to all fours to scrub the floor.

He had asked Ollie if it would be okay.

For the next couple of hours, he scrubbed the floors and ran the sweeper over the carpet. Ollie was agreeable to his working, but he could see that she was nervous sitting at the dining room table not knowing what to do with herself.

The cockroaches scattered at the approach of cleanser. They scurried from the foamy lather. The cat's bowls he cleaned and then scoured the sink after finishing the floor. He swept up all the cat food in the hallway and changed the litter box.

He knew he was a weekend warrior, come a few days and then he'd leave.

The cockroaches on the counter were bold. He smashed them with pleasure for fouling everything, for dropping their eggs so promiscuously, for their fearless pertinacity, used as they were to not being crushed. What he was combating was a million years of behavior virtually perfected.

He knew he was beating back what would eventually swarm

over him and all mankind. He squashed the insects so he wouldn't get Ollie's attention, and tried not to convey his disgust. Man is doubly lost for that appellation "kind." In effect we are as much of a horror as the massed insect world. Of course we can stand, even marvel at, a katydid, but let ten, twenty, a hundred scurrying insects come and the marvel turns into a nightmare. Foodstuffs, clothing, sheets, newspaper, nothing is immune. They'll eat up everything in print, all our written history. Learning will be devoured by their voracious appetites. Books they start by spotting the pages, fouling every fine sentiment with their leavings. They embody our own abandonments with their stench. We can't help leaving each other, forgetting the face of even a loved one. Insects wait to ruin everything. They know their time will come.

What was remarkable was that Ollie, despite her bad eyesight, knew they were there, but soldiered on ignoring her disgust. It was as if all the dirt and debris of her past was seeping back into her, reclaiming itself after a lifetime of fastidiousness. The filthy pants were the tip of an unwashed body. What would have inspired horror a few years ago now was overlooked on the wall.

Maybe all the specks recaptured the peccadilloes of a lifetime. Maybe their transit is a slap in the face for the preoccupation with cleanliness, the disgusted mouth and nose turned away from dirt and dust that will have its due, one day totally inhabiting our lives. Maybe we'd soil our surroundings like cockroaches do our kitchen drawers if given half the chance, but clean them too quickly for recognition. Maybe like everything they catch up with us and spite our cleanliness, slowly turn everything upside down so in the end we don't even notice.

Jack despised his mother writing his name on his clothes, and the orphanage had name tags on every garment. His mother even put his name on books she gave him: "Presented to Master Jack Sylvester Kunkel. Love, Mother."

It made his skin crawl towards the lack of identity that the insects speckled, erasing letters, eating paper, eliminating name tags, controlling our environment.

It wasn't Elizabeth's house any longer. No, Cheryl and Joe were displacing it, removing the furniture and dishes, her dignity. The cockroaches had taken up permanent residence multiplying at will, despite the cleansers and spray. If she could find her checks she could easily clean the oily insects, the *aburamushi* as the Japanese call them. Through it all her white hair, her toothlessness, her wig persevered. The past was buried in her appearance, and the present, well, she kept asking him where he lived, how long he was married, how many children he had and how old they were. The present was a problem for her, how to lift a finger through the pile of dust she would soon become.

Jack went to the closets on the second floor to get clean sheets for the bed in the den. Nothing was folded, just jammed into the shelves. He got some sheets that looked clean to put on the bed when Ollie came up the stairs and said the bed in the den is too small.

"Use my bed."

Jack declined, but she insisted and so he put fresh sheets on her bed. She said she would sleep downstairs on the couch.

The honking of horns on the street signaled the World Series was over and the Yankees had won.

The next morning he was awakened by the cooing pigeons on the ledge outside his window. He looked at their plump bodies and remembers the dry cat food at the entrance. Ollie always fed the birds and strays in the neighborhood.

Jack went downstairs and noticed Ollie on the living room couch squirming uncomfortably. She couldn't sleep as the couch was hard.

"I'm going out for rolls," he said.

"Okay," she said. "I'll make coffee."

When he returned with rolls and a newspaper, he asked if she made coffee.

"No," she said.

Cockroaches scampered out from underneath the coffee

maker as he poured fresh water in the beaker after washing it thoroughly.

Jack put out paper plates and asked Ollie if she wanted orange juice.

"A little," she said as she looked at him.

Ollie sat down at the table.

"It looked uncomfortable on the couch," Jack said.

"It was okay." Ollie then looked at Jack as if studying him and said, "Who are you?"

"I'm Jack, Ollie."

"You're not Jack."

"Yes, Ollie, I am."

"You don't look like Jack."

"I don't know who else I'd be."

"You don't sound like Jack."

"It's me. I'm Jack. Don't you remember, you recognized me last night."

"You're not Jack Kunkel."

"Ollie. I know you dated Ray Rice. What, was that fifty years ago?"

"Anybody could have known that."

"I know you used to have a dog, Tuffy."

"Someone could have told you that."

"I used to live with Mrs. Layman, your mother."

"You're not Jack Kunkel. Someone could have given you that information. I don't know who you are."

"I'm Jack."

"Jack is soft spoken, not like you. He's shy and compassionate."

"It's me Ollie. If it's not me then I don't know who I am."

The body will escape identification without a name. Start to fool with the name, let amnesia set in, and self-doubt creates a flimsiness of identity that is paper thin. No documents will prove who you are if you yourself are not sure. If a name doesn't identify you, then what does? The finger pointing at you? That's him! but then you need everyone present synchronously,

238

or a picture that says, That's him! Still we don't know beyond the object of the finger even if we deny or admit who we are. "Is" requires real time. He is the one going downtown, who sat across from me, who just left the room. He is the visitor let into the house the night before, but at the breakfast table the next morning is suddenly unrecognized. The tall one, for his height identifies him, the blue-eyed one, the one over there with the flat feet, or pug nose, the shy one, identified by his compassion, but that is gone now. Names are thin threads of alphabets that when undone insure our loss doubly. But the features reclaim us, though a hundred have the same chin, or nose. A compatibility that despite a moment of doubt can be duplicated. Of father and son, they say, "It's the same face!" The fear of confusion spawns identity, but even parents throw up their hands at twins, not knowing who's who.

"How old are you Ollie?"

"I'm 87."

But would her being ninety-three change her identity?

Margarite, though she died twenty years ago, is still next door. Jack is not Jack anymore despite sitting at the kitchen table.

"I'm going to stay another day, is that all right?" Jack says confident that Ollie will remember him by nightfall.

All she knows now is that he's not Jack.

We can't insure our identity outside insisting we are whom we think we are. We're not George, or Martin, unless enough people recognize us as such, or we are coerced by their collective identification into a name change.

Jack Kunkel is merely a name significant for its ordinariness, validated by knowing himself as such. But when others have doubts, so do we.

But most people don't have a name that you know. So are they nameless? To us they are. We can't get a handle on them. Jack do this, do that, and the other thing. That confers rights of identity to be so ordered, or imposes a burden of being yourself trapped in their expectations. Ordering others also consolidates your identity, insisting someone do what you want.

Cruelty insures identity. Names insure we will never step out of our skin. They are like collars with the spikes poking inward every time you respond to your name, Jack, and your head perks up. Jack Kunkel is afflicted, but Ollie doesn't go along with it. Deep down there is a certain relief to Jack, a reprieve from being himself, from performing.

Jack met a girl from Atlanta one summer whose father was a minister. When she'd do something that her father disapproved of, he'd say, "That's not you, Augustina," and that made Jack think, Who is "you"?

Names are the collars serving to keep us on a short leash. People have a stake in us being Jack or Augustina to get their will of us, to keep us shy, compliant, compassionate. Our names are chains in the backyard. "Kunkel, come here, boy!"

Billy Jack. That's who you are today. Come to New York to save the town! you daydream. But then the reality of your lack of courage has you called Thornton, employee in a bank for the chances he never took, for not contacting Ollie's niece. When the robbers come under the guise of relatives, they are always in cahoots with weak names. Jack could be the town drunk, or the auto mechanic that'll intentionally loosen bolts on the tire he suggested you replace.

We bully each other with names. After "Georgie Porgie, puddin' and pie!" how could he ever grow up and assert himself? Jack was always a little embarrassed at the name Ollie, despite her alternative use of Elizabeth, until one day he looked it up and found one origin to be Estonian. Her mother was Russian. Why had he always thought Olga German? Ollie was too kind for the Tartar underneath.

When Jack was growing up he'd walk up Castle Hill Avenue with Ollie and by the time he got the eight blocks to Westchester Avenue, at least twenty people would exchange greetings with her and she'd stop and talk with six or seven.

She was the most popular person on the street. She knew everyone's names for their having come up to Dr. Ostrove's office where she worked as a receptionist. He was the dentist on Castle Hill at Watson Avenue next to the grocer.

Ollie's warmth and friendliness brought in business, her remembering everyone and inquiring about their family put them at ease.

She always said she needed people and during the holidays sent out and received hundreds of Christmas cards.

Where are all the people on Castle Hill that she greeted? A lifetime of them has been reduced to Jack Kunkel whom she now insists is not who he is, and a niece and her husband who neglect her and steal from her, and her dead sister whom she imagines still lives with them as an excuse for her house being ransacked. How can a lifetime of friends, family, and acquaintances be so completely reduced to this skeleton crew of a hollow-cheeked man visiting a house overrun by an infestation of cockroaches? Does it have to come to this? It's conceivable but still the mind, its sense of decency and proportion, revolts against it.

Ollie plays into Jack's faulty sense of his own identity. Who are we anyway? Is Jack the little boy Ollie's mother took care of for five years before he was dumped in an orphanage? Now that's a can of worms the briefest speculation can go fishing with and come up with not even an old boot. The hooks are everywhere when it comes to identity pulling at us. We needn't revert to senility or Alzheimer's. We can still take our place in line, get a table at a restaurant, receive a grade, get a license or diploma with our name on it. That's me! But the identification goes the other direction and we disappear nominatively from the face of the earth. Oh, we may remain with a caved in mouth, the teeth all gone, significant hearing and memory loss no matter how many times things are repeated, and we may not be able to recognize anyone, even ourselves looking in the mirror at our own face, the hair having turned a stubborn white that we refuse to recognize as us, all our teeth gone leaving a hole radiating wrinkles. Who is that in the mirror? Can we be faulted for forgetting? It's not us, for sure. It must be someone else. Cathy! Cindy! Rachel! We don't know her, but surely it's not us.

Elizabeth Novak. What an important name until she lost

241

it marrying again. George her first husband got killed in the war. He was handsome, all the pictures showed Elizabeth had made a good catch. Jack remembered as a child meeting Ollie on Watson Avenue wearing George's military helmet. He was ashamed at her loss. And Harold her next husband ramrod straight in posture was a fireman, an officer, the handsomest man in the firehouse. Ollie with her buckteeth and intelligent eyes always got the best-looking men around.

But now who was she, that receptionist at the dentist's office who put everyone at ease, who knew hundreds of patients and the names of their children and spouses, who developed friends with incomparable ease and social grace? Was this white-haired woman whose teeth are now missing still her, who no longer wore her wig, and who remembered nobody?

"Ollie, I'm going downtown."

"Okay," she said.

"Will you let me in, or do you have a key?"

"I don't have a key," she said.

"I am going to the Fountain Pen Hospital."

The very thought of it would make anyone confused. Animal hospital okay, but fountain pen hospital with overnight stays and solutions to an inoperable nib, to unstopple gills and restore flow, or to simply replace the faulty converter whose tired hydraulics don't work anymore. The parallels to people are uncanny. Does the point need ground down a micron to recapture the exactness of stroke? Maruzen did it in Tokyo for him. Will they perform the same service, or need the pen stay a week?

Jack gets chills imagining a Thai doctor once who swabbed the opening to his penis with a Q-Tip so thoroughly with the cotton fibers for the pleasure he must not have gotten lately. He grit his teeth just thinking about it. Jack is old-fashioned and still sits at his desk every morning hoping the mock effervescence of a fountain pen will translate into ideas, approximate the ineffable, but even that sometimes needs hospitalized like an unnamed desire he pursues without knowing it, for what causes the discomfort, melancholy, depression, or double vision may be in the pen itself. The pen hospital could conceivably straighten him out, maybe advise him with some pointers about taking care of his instrument.

"No, I don't want a cartridge, they're too easily spent, I need a converter.

I write with my pen; I'm not a collector or affixing a signature. But my identity doesn't even come from a story or play, either."

A play! What foolishness at my age, Jack thinks. Grow up! You're an adult for heaven's sakes.

Jack says he needs one sick pen fixed and is in the market for a new one, or even a rehabilitated one, one having convalesced in the dutiful hands of the staff. He imagined the clerks in white uniforms and napkined hats with peaks, hands gloved, and the doctor severely gray, impeccably dressed, with the bad breath that comes from the seriousness of pipe tobacco. Jack didn't want to mention the hospital to Ollie, set off false alarm bells, and confuse it with his health or hers, for it was his pen that needed help, for it scratched. Maybe it was simple pruritus that the pen transferred to his dry skin!

"I'll eat downtown," he told Ollie after identifying the hospital as a place he could get his pen fixed.

Jack saw that the kitchen floor needed swept again though it wasn't filthy like the night before.

He had brought back the newspaper and saw where Hideo Matsui knocked in six of the seven runs in the last game of the World Series and realized that was a mind bender. What happened to the national pastime? Who was this Hideo Matsui? Who could keep up with the world at ninety-three? Yes, the Yankees were in the World Series again, but with Japanese players? We defeated them in World War II. Foreigners hit our World Trade Center and now they are overtaking our national pastime!

"I don't know if I can get in," Jack said.

"I can come to the door," Ollie said.

Will you remember me? Jack wanted to say, so he went upstairs and got Cheryl's telephone number.

243

Why is he here? Is he still the little boy Ollie was so kind to? He remembered the centrifugal force that pasted him to the wall of this giant revolving barrel even after the floor dropped on the ride at Palisades Park. Do the stubborn remnants of the past make us human? And what does that make Ollie who has forgotten him? Without memory are we no better than fence posts, worse for the lack of connectivity, the call to arms of termites, despite the creosote to stop the galleries of emptiness, the lacuna in memory.

He is afraid he'll be locked out. We are all strangers he knows, even to ourselves. We take all acquaintance for granted, even inhabiting a body we half-understand.

He remembers his youth aged five to nine. Every weekday he'd visit Ollie for his "allowance" of ten cents, and she took him every year to Palisades Amusement Park, and the butterscotch pudding and hamburgers and French fries she'd make for him after he was placed in the orphanage and visited her. He'd remember her shaking the French fries in a brown paper bag and his telling his mother that he wouldn't go with her on vacation if he couldn't visit Ollie for one of the two weeks.

Familiarity breaks down the barrier, but ill-remembered sets more up. Nothing remains between people. The memories are fickle despite our emotional clarity. The glowing light we bathe others in in the end makes up a drowning past. Was he really that little boy Jack that Ollie's mother took care of, or is all identity only a passing phenomenon for the convenience of others, trapped in time? We are on shaky ground unless constantly seconded, but when everyone forgets us our own identity begins to slip through our fingers.

Though Jack is afraid that he'll be locked out, he knows all familiarity can change by morning, for in the end we are all strangers.

He recalls the owner of "Three Guys from Brooklyn," a grocery stand in Lower Manhattan, who asked him for a ride up to the Bronx because he was afraid to travel on the subway. Jack talked about his relation to Ollie and how he kept in contact all those years and the man praised him for that as he dropped him off in the West Bronx.

One day soon after when he stopped in the grocer's the man pretended not to know him. They had spoken about forty minutes inside the Volkswagen in the front seat, but then he treated him like a complete stranger. Jack knew that foreshadowed a certain substance we all lose not being recognized. He realized Ollie's age contributed to not recognizing him, but still he resented the betrayal of memory. If we are not the substance of others' recognition, we are mere shadows. If there is no one to share our past, we might as well not exist. Our mind at twilight becomes a horror show of outlines fading into the night. They have no more reality than we do, beyond the sensation of bumping against their bodies. We end up wraiths attended to by a world of paid strangers.

"You don't look like Jack" went to the heart of his identity and Jack had to admit that he never had confidence in his own face. It never had the certainty it had for others. He had to admit he never knew it, didn't like it, and was perplexed by a too steady look in the mirror. He examined himself like a total stranger. He could form only a dubious idea of what he looked like. His mind could never reconcile the distance at which he saw himself. He knew there were eyes, but they were incapable of looking at himself like someone else. The color even was baffling, devoid of significance. We cannot consciously look at ourselves. There is an immunity of gaze that will never be connected to our intelligence. And his nose and ears, and chin, he'd never seen them in the round, but sensed their length was exaggerated. His lower body was all right, but even that would trail off like those pleasures he could never explain. His desires always seemed somehow divorced from him, estranged most when they gave the keenest pleasure. Was it still him? It wasn't George now, or Harold! He was at the most concrete moments a phantom of himself, a genie let out of a bottle whose musculature was no more real than the folded arms were not him.

245

He tried to catch himself in three mirrors, but still lacked the advantage of every pedestrian on the street. So no, he didn't know who he was if someone who knew him decades later said he didn't look like Jack Kunkel. It wasn't his voice.

Maybe he wasn't Jack. Maybe getting caught in World Series traffic generated a phantom existence, or he had died already, or never lived except in others' triumphs. A whole life could be the briefest dream, trapped as a fan, excited by someone else's breeze.

"Are you hungry?" Jack asked after Ollie let him in that night.

He thought too of that odd intimacy of the subway. How close he was especially during rush hour to other human beings that he could study their pores, every dark spoke of their eye color, the breaks in the skin causing scarring between pores, each hair follicle, even the ones slightly inflamed, or the cases of full-blown folliculitis on the neck. And they could study him, and still neither were more real for inspecting each other. No words were spoken regarding this visual feast. You almost imagine one or the other cleaning the bones, the sucking noises in the din of the subway before they latch on to an advertisement to divert attention from visually devouring the person next to them. It is a cave man gesture in the bowels of New Your City, more real than your mincing look away from strangers. They are faces without the confusion of familiarity, or the exhaustion of getting to know them, free of the accountability that exchanges names, and ferrets out information, free of feeling. Who'd want to bother with yet another Rosita or Pepe? They remain beautifully anonymous on a subway, like upright cockroaches gripping the subway strap.

In the end there is no reality but in numbers. Populations swarming to the gills so the oxygen supply is compromised, waiting for a ninety-three-year-old to let down her guard. They have already moved up out of the basement, into the sheets in the closet, the foodstuffs in the kitchen cabinets, taken her furniture and dishes.

On a train Jack once took with his children in Tokyo they were exposed to the danger of an exploding population as his two young children got crushed by the rush hour crowds, tighter and tighter as Jack pushed back to protect them. What we don't recognize doesn't exist except as part of a crowd, the swarming hordes, the multiplication past counting that will leave tooth marks in every other almond in the food supply.

"Do you want pizza, or a sandwich?" Jack asks Ollie when he returns that evening.

"Boloney," Ollie says, "a boloney sandwich will be fine."

Jack goes around the corner and walks up Tremont to a deli for sliced boloney, tomato, pickle, and a soft croissant.

When he returns he goes in the cupboard and gets a paper plate and plastic cups. "Do you want orange juice?" he asks and takes some himself.

Ollie gobbles up the sandwich as if she hasn't eaten all day.

Afterwards Jack cleans off the table and countertops. Does he gain identity staving off dirt, keeping back stickiness, smashing cockroaches, hearing the crush of their carapaces? He kills a few bold ones, shows them a new order is established, at least for three days. What's his need? Should he allow them to crawl over everything? Does killing them again answer to some frustration in his own life? Should he alone be responsible for stemming the tide of multiplying insects?

Ollie seems not to notice. She asks to be taken to the bank tomorrow saying she can't find her checkbook. That's what she's been saying for years.

Jack notices her niece's name on the stock information from Morgan Stanley. Ollie asks him about his family, job, where he's living over and over again. He tells her again her sister Margarite is dead. She never really accepts her own mistreatment of her sister when she wanted her independence, and didn't take her in, told her she wanted to live her own life.

"Well, I'm going to bed," Jack says.

"Good night," she says.

Jack goes up to bed and hears Ollie coming up the stairs.

"How come you're in my room?" she asks at the door. "I want to go to bed."

"Oh, I thought you wanted me to sleep here."

"I'll get out sheets," and Jack goes and pulls out the bed in the den.

Jack then goes to the closet where some sheets have dried lightweight cockroaches on them, like pressed flowers. He looks until he finds two that look clean.

Ollie seems to have gone to bed and turned out the light. About three Jack wakes up and goes downstairs for a drink of water. The kitchen in the dim light is overrun with scores of cockroaches scattering in all directions. Jack is overwhelmed but has no desire to incorporate their movements, the lopped off heads, the squashed bodies, the damaged antennae and crushed eggs into his dreams. He knows he'll have them standing upright on a subway, studying their coloring, every segment of their bodies, how an appendage, a feeler is violently pulled off, the near transparency of a wing. He is simply glad he remembered to wear his shoes down to the kitchen.

Before he had squashed what like looked like a silverfish on the den wall, and a centipede with innumerable appendages. He tried to imagine that he'd gotten everything. He had opened the window when he first arrived and the outside air had freshened the room somewhat.

Jack returned upstairs forgoing the drink of water.

Suddenly Ollie is standing at the door of the den.

"Jack, I'm sorry. I took my bed that I said you could have."

"No, that's all right. You were not comfortable downstairs."

The next morning Ollie asks, "Who are you?"

"I'm Jack."

"You're not Jack."

His identity is again swallowed up by her faulty memory.

Who we are is someone remembering us in the end.

Jack tells her he's getting rolls at the bakery and will make coffee when he gets back.

She doesn't want cat litter she tells him.

Still he does her laundry.

With the sheets he sees nine pairs of pants.

"Who are you?" she asks again when he comes upstairs.

"I'm Jack."

Jack pulls away from Ollie not remembering him.

Her mouth is a hole without dentures that can only end in a scream.

Up in the bedroom Ollie asks, "Where's my wig?" in a panic. "Someone took my wig!"

"There are three on the end table," Jack says.

They sit in the kitchen for breakfast.

"Are you going now?" Ollie asks.

"Yes, I'll be heading to Albany. Things will have to change, Ollie."

"I want to call Cheryl," she says and picks she up the phone, dials, and yells out, "Cheryl, I need you!"

She calls twice. "Joe, I need you to come over!"

"You should go with Charles in Georgia."

"I don't want to leave. Are you going to call him? He's like a bull. He'll come up and take me away. I prefer to stay in my own home."

"But you're being taken advantage of."

Charles already came up to take her, but she changed her mind at the curb outside her house and yelled "I want Cheryl!"

She sees clearly her options.

"He comes like a bull not understanding things. This is all right. I don't have long to live."

Jack weighs this in the balance.

Should he call the State, social services? The juggernaut once started will not care but to fulfill its mandate to follow its rules and regulations. The struggling limbs of the investigated can already be seen protruding under its huge wooden wheels. It seems benign until you calculate the ponderous jobs behind it, factor in the hefty pensions and salaries behind their decisions. Their own sense of power augments their smallness.

Ollie'll be taken out of her home.

Jack is angry at Cheryl and her husband for taking advantage of her.

Her sister Margarite loved Cheryl and Ollie complained how she just "takes, takes, takes!"

Love gives and is the fertile soil for greed. What if love of all emotions started the awful greediness of mankind that then took on a life of its own, morphing into so much that is unrecognizable? Ollie chastised her sister for giving all her money to Cheryl and now in honor of her memory allows her to take everything. Her niece's name is on stocks, checkbooks, the cabinets emptied of dishes, the rooms absent of furniture. All Ollie has left are the knickknacks, though some are missing, and most of the Rockwells.

"I want to stay in my home," Ollie says pointedly.

Should he call? The cockroaches crawl around his decision. How low can you go? Her pants are filthy. She changes them only after Jack does the laundry.

Will she eventually be crawling through the cat litter scattered over the small tiles of the entrance, a ninety-three-year-old Kurtz who loves animals, birds, and stray dogs and cats?

Is this the horror that awaits all of us? Does the State have to muscle in? It is her home.

The dried egg will end up under her nails and on her face. "Look, Ollie has egg on her face!" her siblings cackle ninety years ago. But she's almost ninety-four.

She used to take a healthy cocktail of vitamins every morning. Is she immune to the degradation? She has no bruises on her body, but the way she wolfed down the boloney sandwich is disturbing. After your metabolism slows you can live on nothing. The very air sustains you and the dried body stubbornly resists disease.

Does Jack merely want to get back at her niece and husband, outraged as he is by the naked rapacity?

He never sees Cheryl or Joe, and he realizes he doesn't want

250

to contact them. He is afraid he will tell them off, then realizes they don't want to see him either.

Cheryl dropped in only when he was downtown.

He doesn't want to make it bad for Ollie. He's leaving and so cleaning the short time is a luxury so he can afford the indignation, the fall from the middle class life to the edge of hygiene. Cleanliness is more than it's cracked up to be. Give anyone a few days, weeks, and they'll deteriorate beyond recognition. It can start overnight. We are always on the verge. Washing, simple movement, is such a leap of faith and effort of the will. Every day is a triumph of movement. Matter, the unspeakable weight of even what's light, we are constantly beset by how to lift it, push it out of the way, realize it won't budge, but to find the wherewithal to keep trying, that is the mystery, our sheer persistence. That we ourselves move is a crowning achievement; Ollie's going downstairs to the basement, or up to her bedroom, is a triumph, still climbing up and down after ninety-three years.

Jack, do you really want to take her out of her home? I know you want her niece and husband shot, but think of her. Picture her lying in a pool of urine, in her own waste, not able to move for days. It happened before. Yes, that's a triumph! Or the eighty degrees the house was when you entered, do you want her dehydrated on the floor? Let her go her own way.

Shouldn't I do what's best?

Best for whom? So there's a few cockroaches.

The place is overrun!

His Sunday best wingtip shoes and the suit Jack wore weekly in the orphanage were spanking clean, showing the orphans off at the church service in the community theater. That's best, but God got away, suits get away, despite the cleaning mania.

Ollie was like a mother to him, warm and loving, afraid when his mother took him that he'd not get enough to eat.

His mother didn't believe in three meals a day, ate sporadically.

"I'm never hungry," she crowed until she went to people's

251

houses when she'd scarf down everything in sight and never refused anything.

She took Jack to Russian and Spanish films, to the ballet and opera. Just what it ended up he was drawn to, but he would always want to see Ollie. She was the mother he wanted who took him to Palisades Park every year, who gave him a daily allowance of ten cents; she was the one he went to the summer he graduated high school and stayed in contact with.

Now he was ready to betray her at ninety-three and call in the State. Would her stepson do anything, or was he too angry at being refused at the curbside when he had come up to take her to Georgia? Was Jack getting back at the niece who received government checks for being disabled and who never worked a day in her life? Her husband Joe was a smooth talker, the custodian worker whom Ollie paid to clean and go shopping for her.

But Ollie barely recognized Jack. Was he the little boy who couldn't wait to see her, or stay at her house when he worked in the city, whom she showered with kindness, this woman whom he was about to betray? What's left from dementia? He was already a stranger to her half the day.

Who are we to manipulate each other's life until, as Ollie said to her cat Tiger, out of the blue comes, "I love you."

The scrawny, bent, pitiful excuse of a cat that she knew manipulated her, an animal whose bones protruded hopelessly out his orange ratty fur as he sat there pathetically wide-eyed, assured of the love Ollie lavished on him. He was as if the backbone of what was now Ollie's hopeless bent spine. Did Jack want to take Tiger away from her by calling the State?

"Oh, Tiger," Ollie sighed.

Was her life like the aftermath of the World Series that except for the parade and celebrations left the city more bereft, unlike the parties Ollie hosted at her mother's apartment when the furniture was largely hardback chairs and even a sofa was a luxury? They are a shadow of memory no longer. All the participants are dead. Games were played, masking a teasing sexuality, and at Christmas Jack remembered the mirrors under the Christmas tree that simulated lakes for skaters. He remembered the snowy towns and all the tinsel and colored lights. It was a whole world that Ollie permanently moved into her own home and enlarged year-round purchasing all her knickknacks. Her mother's apartment was immaculate, if sparsely furnished. That's where Jack lived until the day, hoping his mother would never come, she finally did arrive. He'd pass food to Ollie under the table, so he would not have to eat what he didn't like. Her own mother was too strict with him, Ollie always said.

Ollie was always so outgoing, understanding, warm, and loving. The old woman before him signaled the ruins of his childhood, like the dreaded arrival of his mother who when he was sick gave him penicillin shots after boiling the used needles on the stove. One Christmas his mother bought him a shoeshine kit and wanted him to make money on the streets.

His mother was dead over ten years, but Ollie was left of a past only he contemplated where in his mind the long arm of government was now reaching through, breaking and entering a home she was accustomed to that was already pillaged by her niece and overrun by cockroaches.

Jack thought of the little boy taken away from Ollie's mother and placed in an orphanage where love was replaced by the daily competition of twenty-one boys. Could this be Jack's way of getting back at his own uprooting as a child, taking Ollie out of her home? Was it right to roll the juggernaut of the State through her front door to stop the vandalism, or were there other axes to grind?

Was Jack ready for that, or had his future already betrayed itself? Was he too going to eventually lose his own teeth, his bearings; his books wouldn't even have the pretense of being boxed up but would be thrown away. His wife and children would claim water damage, dust traps.

"Who'd read them anyway with all these markings?"

His work would be placed in black plastic bags like leaves gathered for the garbage truck to take to the nearest landfills. He would be shipped off to a nursing home for the faces he couldn't identify by morning. No one would have access to, at midnight in the nursing home's dim light, the glimpses of his children. Only alone could he remember them, without the pressure of their expectations when the connection couldn't be made, and everyone stood around a stranger until the visits stopped altogether from him not recognizing them. Their laughter at night was crystal clear and their smiles never-ending before the rivalry gave way to screams and meanness. His wife would have gone on to someone else, and his children would scatter to other states. The insects poised on his arm, maybe not cockroaches, but a semblance of them, would be a welcomed visit. His nerves would be so shot that only with difficulty would he scratch the itch on his arm to remove them as if his body were someone else's. An attendant in passing might brush them off. The scabs that thicken from breaks in his skin would remind him of sitting on the steps on Watson Avenue tearing them off and eating them. They now slough off unnoticed.

He'll finally raise his eyes to his daughter Cassie to say, "Ollie, is that you? Did the State take you away?" hoping she is still in her home and he hasn't reported her.

The Untold Story of the Awaji Puppet Master

The dolls take on a life of their own no matter how crudely carved. He saw them as members of his extended family. He could only relieve himself of their care by visiting his neighbors' houses to distribute their upkeep, extending their lives, telling their stories, especially when his own house became so cluttered that his family started to leave him after the increase of so many dolls. You could call them puppets, for in Japanese they meant the same thing. They are thought to be invested with a soul and most are made with human hair. You couldn't criticize the dolls in front of Kenji even though their lives only took shape with a script. He couldn't help carving them in that frenzied period of creativity where he produced dozens upon dozens of dolls so they soon surpassed a hundred. Though there wasn't room in his own house, he made room at the expense of everyone else, his wife, children, and grandparents who had to double up because of the crowded conditions.

Princesses defending lovelorn samurai, woodcutters, farmers, orphaned children looking for better homes, women bearing a grudge over a doting lover, corrupt policemen, bitter nannies, jealous brothers and sisters, bent, broken old men, young women stuffed full of romantic notions, even one shogun and surrounding daimyo were represented. Kenji didn't know what to do with them all, so he traveled from house to house telling stories about them, amusing neighbors who grew to expect his visits. The dolls stood mute, their faces stolid despite intricate moveable parts that waited to be worked. It was understood that they were no different than real people worked on by complex emotions. The doll was left in its new home where the household waited for Kenji's return visit to extend the narrative of its life. Soon dolls were distributed all over the countryside. Finally one day to broaden his audience Kenji traveled to town, and later to surrounding towns, to give performances that relieved people's daily lives for the endless possibilities on stage. They became like members of the household waiting for the next chapters of their lives when Kenji visited and they were taken off the shelves or out of their glass cabinets.

Compulsively he told their stories to the greedy ears of his neighbors and the surrounding towns. Each doll had a real life, and tales of which they had to be relieved. Kenji was burdened at night gathering story lines compulsively spun like so much silk. During the day he'd carve new dolls and at first his family helped with the costumes and painting, but soon the dolls accumulated so that the household was overwhelmed and the crowded conditions made everyone uncomfortable and irritable. His family shrank before the enlarged roles of each new doll taking its place like a person. Kenji stopped his work on the farm to produce the dolls that he felt obliged to show to the world. Stories crowded in his mind, an overproduction of ideas not unlike mental patients who cannot stem the tide of their thoughts, that soon Kenji barely had time to attend to his daily needs. His hygiene suffered, he lost his appetite and sleep. Outside the narratives he produced, his own life seemed to dwindle. He was convinced the dolls all had souls that he was responsible for having brought to life, releasing them from the wood and putting words into their mouths. Each wood curl brought a hip, a nose, an elbow to life, and a story to justify the existence of the emerging character, whose roughness was sanded away, ever smoother, and with every doll Kenji's skills improved. That they truly became his family, he knew each time he touched their hair. The hairdos multiplied as their garb billowed with evermore intricate designs for the obi as they entered different strata of society. Those lucky enough to go to court, rise above their station, were the envy of all, until it was found that even their private lives resembled in many ways those of the lowliest farmers.

Still Kenji felt bound to make each doll distinctive and that kept him busy looking for new turns to their personality. Like in every family there were pickpockets, liars, women of ill-repute, damaged intelligence hidden away, spiteful black sheep, broken athletes, characters too smart for their own good, but all mixed up for each performance. Kenji discovered an originality he never knew he possessed, constantly probing inside himself to bring together what he also drew from real life. He got little rest, bound to use every hour of each day until it cut into his sleep. He felt solely responsible for giving birth, for the life lived afterwards even when his doll's actions were criticized by local residents and in distant villages. Despite a certain belief in each doll's autonomy, in the free will they exhibited, he himself didn't always know where their stories came from and felt sometimes they were imposed on him. In his most private hours he suspected something demonic was at work directing his labors. Though he saw clearly the aspirations, disappointments, pettiness, food squabbles, the obvious favoritism, and sweepingly profound jealousies, the envy everywhere, the urgency of reprisals, there was something infernal driving all this social entanglement that in the end he knew was not for the good no matter how compelled he was to reveal it. Everyone was drowned in this stunning soup of emotion starting with his own family, even the critical relatives that he saw infrequently, then the neighbors, as if on stage they were all performing underwater motions that would one day do them in. In fact everyone around him provided examples of a naked human nature with which he quickly clothed his dolls. It often made audiences squirm seeing themselves represented, barely looking to see if others noticed the same thing. Perhaps Kenji never entirely admitted where his ideas came from and never admitted that he himself was uncomfortable with the characters he created on stage. He like his audience groped to determine exactly their origin and to figure out what they would do next. Maybe he didn't want to see what he saw, except through his dolls. They protected him against real life that so troubled him that he needed this representation on stage.

His performances extended from nearby villages to towns to eventually reaching the prefectural capital. His stories were simple, crude at first, but he quickly learned what made people laugh, the narrative twists between a nervous laugh, or a powerful guffaw, to a helpless cachinnation that infected the whole theater. He knew about the dead silences when he had touched a nerve, or when a long silence was called for, or those moments when the audience was sometimes as puzzled about his intent as he was, or when everyone held their breath. Early on he left the theater satisfied that the dolls had indeed come alive, that he started to make beds for some of them, elaborate chests, stuffed colorful futons so they could rest at night, and for the women he provided vanity tables with double mirrors that reflected the trouble they took over their own beauty. He sometimes rose in the middle of the night worried about the debut of a new doll, about her match, or a costume he had not properly visualized, groping for a missing twist in a story. He sought details that would bring startled astonishment, audiences to their feet, for Kenji now regularly played in theaters to standing ovations; the makeshift country theaters with crude curtains in Awaji had become ornate tasseled varieties of rich brocade at the larger theaters. As audiences grew the pressure correspondingly weighed on Kenji to leave everyone helpless with laughter, or frightfully receding into their private lives with tears in their eyes, drawing a solitary line down their cheeks. The housewives could see so vividly the romance absent in their own lives. This challenged Kenji's talents as the venues enlarged. He felt the pressure to keep everyone dreaming with his love stories, reaching for their handkerchiefs, daring them to cross boundaries that would have been unthinkable before. He didn't avoid the betrayals and the heartache.

Gradually Kenji's own household grew so cluttered with his creations and his nights now became so full of carvings and storytelling that no one could keep up with the costumes that he drew as he left the house at first light to hunt for new ideas, to give life to dolls that were already draining from him any semblance of vitality. The life he created in his own image became one he didn't live. He was often seen wandering in town at the earliest of hours.

People always knew that their life stories were being told.

Even the dolls they adopted after each performance became like family members and were treated with extraordinary respect and protected under elaborate glass cabinets that looked ornamental. They were dolls for children, it was said, but they were not to be taken out of their case and played with. Years later few knew their derivation went back to Kenji Watahari, the puppet master. Of course, the respect came from the fact that all Japanese thought dolls had souls. That everybody went in disguise was a principle in this honor bound culture, but from time to time there erupted an unspeakable violence showing to what extent the society concealed what lay beneath that extraordinary politeness. The dolls in fact were an embodiment of that veneer, revealing only in glimpses a society stripped to its bare bones, with everyone for a brief moment naked. Life couldn't function without the infinite honorifics that masked the real motives keeping everything civil, and so the bare wood was clothed with elaborate costumes and scripts that reinvented themselves. Despite the occasional disturbing story, or gesture, or downright evil character that made everyone glimpse themselves. The tension from this was the nucleus of Kenji's art, the trembling honesty in all the stories he told, of art in general that exposes motives, so we see into ourselves what's hidden the next moment. Nevertheless the glimpses remain through half-smiles, feints, frowns, or partial gestures, the almost raised hand to the bold salute, the signaling of horror or exultation, or that brief moment when chills race down the spine at the total estrangement, or the contagiously radiant brotherhood on everyone's face, or finally the outright betrayal leading to a stupefying violence.

Kenji had created a world from a population of simple farmers that branched out to greedy merchants, hidebound bureaucrats, snooping newspapermen, lonely samurai, their ever-loyal retainers, members of the floating world, geisha and women of easy virtue, lonely housewives, and even blind masseurs. Yes, Kenji worked his helpers relentlessly night and day as his family members dropped away. The dolls multiplied, their bright green and orange kimonos, the stunning blacks embroidered with gold for funerals were so strikingly color coordinated to bring out the utmost solemnity. Or the exception sticking up, the one nail, that was invariably hammered down.

Kenji's entourage grew when he began to yell at them, scold them for the smallest infraction, for what was out of place and didn't meet his exacting specifications. A kimono color that wasn't deep enough, a complexion insufficiently pale, the sash too low or high, the coiffure that didn't meet the classical expectations, a gesture that lacked crispness or wasn't phlegmatic enough. Kenji indeed became the Little Emperor, an epithet whispered in hushed voices and despite the help he had bringing his characters to life, still they all came from him. Characters absolutely danced around his head. He drew too from his frustrations with everyone around him, secretly alienating them when they saw themselves so clearly on stage.

"Just look at them!" It was as if nothing ever happened, Kenji reviled one night in a drunken stupor, experiencing himself a period of creative drought attacking everyone around him. "They are my creation," he said, "you are all my creations," as he waved his arm feebly while his head drooped towards his small sake cup. "Mine, all mine," he mumbled as he passed out.

And there was no one who dared argue with him. He knew it. The intrigues, the hatred, the jealousies, the craving for power, the silent usurpations, all the hidden life in the briefest gesture, or the shallow optimism that kept everyone in the troupe going. You'd think nothing happened in daily life until unexpectedly there was a full-blown violence from a clash of wills, or an inflamed corruption surfaced, like a carbuncle that rallied everyone, that required the quick attention of a lance, a word, a witticism. All the bowing and self-belittlement in the culture told a history of heads cut off, lost limbs, digits shortened a joint at a time, lives snuffed out at the least sign of displeasure. Society inherited all that without fully realizing it until Kenji brought it on stage.

All this Kenji caught and placed smack between people's

eyes so they were dazzled, so spouses trembled at what they saw; employers were exposed right before everyone's eyes, the secret betrayal of a brother or sister revealed, and the children mystified by a world they didn't understand, full of intrigue and violence. They learned how to bow with such art and so low, ever lower until their foreheads touched the tatami mat. The performances captured everything so that audiences consolidated, completely captivated on those evenings.

Kenji saw how art influenced lives, how they anticipated his monthly visits, saw the control he had, and the power of the performances over them that it was frightening. It showed too how the Awaji farmer got so irremediably absorbed by his puppeteering that he almost lost his mind to what he had developed. Who imagined that a rural farmer from Awaji left to his own devices could create such a world? Much less be the goal of even the most meager talent. Kenji didn't himself realize this transformation, or the resentments that build up along the way, the hidden angers. The silences he rarely interpreted, the quailing before his direction he never saw as a threat to him. His itinerary was always set weeks in advance so he remained up all hours of the night now carving new performers, adding to his troupe dolls that came alive under his direction as his helpers faded the better they did their job bringing the puppets to life. Kenji's bullying commands made his helpers grow stiff, wooden, so they lacked the initiative working the moveable parts of dolls that spoke up and seemed animated with a spirit their handlers lacked. They kept their disgruntled silence to themselves the more remarkable were the words out of the dolls' mouths. Kenji's commands too grew louder, more shrill, with his celebrity, as he treated his workers, even his admirers from the capital, more and more harshly, as dispensable blocks of wood themselves fired only by his imagination. Their own mouths slack except in admiration rarely worked like the moveable parts of the puppets, for they never contradicted anything Kenji said, while his wooden creations came to life. Kenji's dismissal of so many of them alienated an army of people, even though there were always novices waiting for the chance to take their place. Kenji truly lived up to his Little Emperor title for his authoritarian ways, for the increasing cruelty towards his helpers.

No one could match his direction, fit the perfection of his ideas, the way he moved the puppets or taught others to. Even when he ceded control to the three puppeteers masked in black who worked just one puppet, it was as if the minds of the three shrank under his direction to one harmonious whole. The characters grew real right before the audience's eyes, despite his tongue lashings midperformance, replacing the handlers with characters whose emotions outsized them. Chikamatsu's creations too filled their meager lives, given up to the theater, leaving them with the feeling that they were little more than props in a grand scheme. The violence on stage, the cruelty, love, jealousy, pettiness, bitterness, the small acts of kindness, the outright tenderness, the gratitude, the rages and hatred, overshadowed their own lives that faded into insignificance. They never could match what transpired on stage, from those first performances in their homes, then at neighboring villages, to larger towns, finally in the prefectural capital. It was even said as Kenji's reputation spread that the troupe would one day travel all the way to Kyoto.

✻

Kenji had created a world, so wide, rising like each morning sun, intimate as the twilight and the first stars, before being replaced by pale moonlight that I want to say was so spectacular that one night Kenji as we knew him disappeared. Some say he so occupied the spirit of his dolls that he had nothing left over. He so informed the movements of every puppet, and those of each puppet master. The crews worked the one doll, though he knew every feint and dodge, the sets, the dress, the motions of each moveable part, the words out of their mouths, stylized to an art form that now surpassed itself to represent life so that all his creations as everyone claimed were indeed in his own image. He gave them their stories, their gestures, their costumes, their faces. The eerie spell of lives other than their own worked on people. Some even whispered that he was much more than an Emperor. For every emotion, every gesture, the least honorific, or bow, was managed by him, so his handlers knew what string was pulled tight, loosened, exactly how much slack to allow the jaw, the reach that hid a limp, or curtailed a sneer, the suddenly stiffened defiance, it was all his.

All but the most immediate family he had frightened away, for the air around him had become unbreatheably thick, that most left and didn't know that he had stopped eating and was growing thinner, became a specter of his former self. His assistants had to bend down to hear him talk. Still he knew the power of a whisper, the lower his voice the greater the deference, the deeper the bow to hear it, that finally they had to imagine what he said. They started to follow commands he never gave. While his scripts had been as sacred texts before, now they were embellished, words changed and so did the costumes until they felt they had a free hand.

The morning audiences by admirers stopped altogether, the need to recheck an already established itinerary, or to make sure of a gesture or correction in the script, the more removed was Kenji who had taken to bed. His youngest daughter Yoko of all his four daughters stayed with him. Yoko was now managing productions. But without the firm hand of Kenji. Even she could not stop his pulling his hair in bunches over the least thought, viewing long strands stretched before the bulging, upturned whites of his eyes, then suddenly his champing down on the hair.

"Here, put this on a doll," he said.

Perhaps he suffered too many lives that were now overtaking his own that he recoiled with a vengeance into himself, too many story lines continued wrapping around him, tightening every day, choking off the last of his contact with the world.

Yoko couldn't discourage his trips to the stream running through the bamboo behind their house, his dropping on all fours and crawling on the pebbles of the bank, digging into the stream's bottom, clutching handfuls of tiny stones and soil, sifting it through his fingers mumbling to himself, "Hourglass, hourglass, tell me the time, before my body disintegrates in lime."

The pebbles streaming towards the water glistened, dull and shiny by turns like the characters he had created. It was as if this was the end of the entertainment, the world he had given everyone, one he could no longer support. There would be no more carvings, freeing characters from the wood, no more scripts or costume designs, no detailed drawings for each scene, nothing that gave life as his own ebbed away into the stream behind his house. He was alone now, so chockfull of all he had created that all he could do was sit in water every day. He could barely feed himself, but drifted away from all he had done, from his fellow man, the villagers, his family, from each character he had enlarged on the stage, firing up whole towns with their thriving theaters. He was a bag of skin and bones crawling on the banks of a shallow stream where occasionally a ray of sunlight poked through the dappled leaves exposing the bare silhouette of his body crawling in the spotlight. He was watched over by his daughter loath to interrupt this last performance of her father. Every last scrap of dignity was now gone from him crawling and sifting tiny stones until he'd stop and observe something so methodically. He was a creator who had disappeared into his own body now indistinguishable from the landscape, his arms thin as the surrounding bamboo.

✻

One night there was a revolt at one of his performances without his presence. Something depicted onstage struck too close to home, mirrored an actual event in the life of the village, and brought back bad memories. We don't know who started it but there was a collective uprising after an interminably long groan, then vicious heckling that got out of control and then an attack on the dolls themselves. The audience rose up to a person, rushed and grabbed the dolls from the handlers and proceeded to tear apart the mechanical pieces responsible for their gestures, dislodging the moveable jaw, what worked the mouth and the things it said, wedging their fingers into the eyebrows so they would never convey a suggested assignation, all the nuances of meeting, tore ears off that heard the whispering, and ripped away the strings that the dolls were worked with, right out of the hands of the three handlers and wrapped them around their necks as they pushed the handlers dressed in black to the floor. One got his hands on the fine clothes of the princess and proceeded to pull off her dress to expose her sex that ended almost undefined. There was no deep crescent between the legs but only a faintly drawn pencil mark and unlike the rich heads of hair from Kenji's family their sex was bare. The rags of dress soon lay torn on the stage and the wooden skeletons that only suggested bones underneath were thrown down partially splintered.

"So much for uncovering our secrets," one audience member scowled.

"Yes, look at theirs!" another chimed in.

"Let's burn them all, and the whole theater!" another said.

"Sticks of wood is all they are. It doesn't matter what they say."

"They don't reveal us. They don't speak for us."

"No. We're alive, and they're mere matchsticks."

"Matchsticks! Let's set them on fire!"

"Gather all of them."

"There are more in the back room."

"Yes, let's go," as another male had his trousers torn off and someone it seems had drawn the outline of his sex but failed to give it three dimensions."

"It's flat," one man said and laughed to himself in ridicule.

"How could he court the princess?" another said.

"He's a fraud, we've all been tricked by this show long enough. Let's have a bonfire!"

"But what of their souls?"

"Souls, ha, they have no souls!"

265

The three handlers in black were beaten to a pulp like limp pieces of material. They barely moved, as if they couldn't get over their torn, exposed dolls, master puppeteers no longer. The rest of the troupe had fled.

The tiny makeshift theaters where the performances were given the countryside over were set fire to one by one that spring, reduced to charred rubble as if the realization of what happened on stage spread to audiences everywhere who now wrote their own script. It was the people's reprisal for what they considered years of misrepresentation, even if they were seduced by Kenji's craft, they resented that, and now their naked emotions rebelled for being on display throughout the island of Awaji for so many years. Even the idea that Kenji was the Little Emperor faded. In village after village they extinguished their main source of entertainment, cutting off their noses to spite their faces. Erasing what had been a meeting place for amusement for generations. Burnt to the ground was theater after theater. Not always did the handlers die, but many received serious burns when they were not discovered in the rubble. The dolls were irrecoverable. Since it was a communal uprising the authorities felt disempowered by what they considered a moral outrage for having the worst of themselves depicted daily on stage. So they did nothing to intervene, and never prosecuted the wrongdoers.

In fact the fires were said to resemble a spontaneous combustion among the village folk that so few understood and to which their wooden structures were always so vulnerable, even vast temples and one that housed the giant wooden Buddha had burnt to the ground. It gave an eerie presentiment to the night, the burning of each theater. Few outsiders knew that the patrons had turned on their entertainers. The people seemed possessed, like the demons that everyone still believed lurked in the countryside after hours when through the darkness a fire would suddenly start. People were stunned when this happened the first time, but after the second, third, and multiple times it surprised no one that they thought it was inevitable, fate, part of Kenji's narrative and the cultural bias of *shoganai* that accepts the inevitability of human nature depicted on stage that finally had caught up with real life like a meteor observed in the night sky. The collective power took over and the buildings were torched, the dolls ripped apart and burned like a pile of sticks, their individual narratives incinerated before everyone's eyes. Some saw the wood catch fire and the billowing garb exaggerating the flames and imagined they could hear screams from the dolls that compared with high pitched imitations of the most unearthly suffering, with a lover throwing himself off a cliff, a young man finding his woman mutilated, or dogs having torn a grandfather to pieces, even the horrid secrets of incest buried for years ending in a horrid cry, or the unnatural enamorment towards animals, then the unspeakable cruelty with the appearance of ghosts or demons that represent human beings at their worst. It was as if with the fires the narratives continued an apocalyptic extension of the scripts, that the burning and destruction was meant to happen. Some thought of the creative certainty of such theatrics and trembled at what had come to pass. They knew the gaps that Kenji's creations had filled. It was only natural that they'd turn on what depicted the underlying horror to restore their dignity and stop this probing into their dark secrets, restore their society to the unparalleled politeness that erased anything untoward, hid the violence and all those ugly emotions just below the surface.

They just got tired of seeing themselves depicted year after year. The whole arrogant parade of characters that thought they could capture their human emotions. Who did Kenji Watahari think he was? The Little Emperor, yes. Well, we'll show him a thing or two!

Meanwhile Kenji's house standing before the bamboo remained unmolested while theaters all over Awaji went up in flames. The handlers, the promoters of Kenji's vision who had contracted with him, were tracked down one by one and beaten, even those who felt they had been mistreated for their work not coming up to standards. People from the audience who had wanted to participate but were turned away for lack of talent, who never survived auditions, now turned on the troupe and helped to identify the handlers and crew. Like secret police they ferreted out every participant. No one who had ever been associated with a production was spared, for people remember every slight so when the mob takes over the communal indignation gathers, like birds rising all at once, grabbing what is within reach, attacking at the least provocation. Their grievances were in the end relieved. Sitting in the audience for years, being the pawns of puppets, the butt of jokes, of an inventive mind that saw too clearly into them, who wouldn't get fatigued by that?

"Puppets, can you imagine that?"

"How degrading!"

"It's not even us but claims to represent us!"

"Not ever real people, but wooden representations in all their showy garb, their gaudy finery, and scripts that weren't really us now that we think about it, but they duped us into thinking these exaggerations showed something, duped us into laughing or crying or leaving with sorrow, pity, or anger. They showed nothing when you come to think about it but inflated parodies, yes, that's all they were, parodies of us!"

"They were making fun of us all along! Puppets! now really, how could they ever be who we are?"

"We want our lives back!" one person shouted during one of the first fires.

"Yes, we want to be who we were, peaceful, loving, kind, courteous, obedient, cheerful, thrifty, brave, clean, reverent, and harmonious, not the opposites that form the substance of all this drivel."

"That's all it is, stagecraft, that should be wiped out and not allowed in the city limits."

"Nor on the countryside to contaminate us!"

They sensed that acting robbed them of something and left pale imitations the next morning for what happened on stage the night before. Yet they had gone back time and again. They knew they could never live up to how a fertile mind depicts them, no matter how much he drew from their daily lives, their dreams and desires, no matter how he tooled into their dark underside. His angling into their souls, making them better and worse than they really were, they had had enough of it.

"I can't take it any longer," and the community agreed in shouts of collective assent before they stormed the stage.

"All we see are naked examples of ourselves."

"Yes, it's obscene!"

"They're only sticks of wood who have no sex themselves. Traipsing like they are god's gift across the stage!"

"Naked still," someone said, "they should be ashamed!"

"Yes, but with less privacy than our daily lives. It compensates for what's hidden by our politeness and bowing. Otherwise we'll never be found out except for what's so rudely exposed on stage."

The crowd hardly paid attention to this analysis.

"We show no one what we are thinking most of time," he continued.

"Get him!" someone quickly yelled. "He's one of them!"

"We don't want to see ourselves," he argued.

"Muzzle him," someone screamed, and they descended on the young man beating him black and blue.

There were periodic revolts, even in twentieth century literature that ended in burning buildings, never so overt but just as startling.

The Temple of the Golden Pavilion was burnt to the ground by that monk, he even with his stuttering spoke for the rest. Mishima didn't make his stutter universal, but knew he had tapped into the destructive impulses of the common man haunted by beauty, but not able to do anything about it.

Most of us can't get the words out, so the jealousy of that permanent stage festers, the temple reflected so calmly in water that we are reduced like those who left the theaters in Awaji, swept away by each performance just like the monk, Mizoguchi, Ditch Mouth, who at first quietly swept the grounds around the temple. No wonder he hatched a plan to burn the temple to the ground, spite everyone for his own impotence, for not being able to reconcile the beauty with the ugliness in his own mind, unlike the clubfooted Kashiwagi who embraced his ugliness. Both had antecedents to the earliest puppet theaters and the villagers on Awaji who one night almost changed the course of history. But people are stubborn, they need their entertainment. They can pass all the laws they want keeping the theaters outside the precincts of the town, on the other side of the river, but the theater comes back, people return out of the burning rubble, through the mist, through the charred past to start building anew. They pick up the pieces of burnt puppets resolved to reconstruct them.

Still, the monk spoke for all of us, who want, despite art, no actual temple, even if it is stubbornly reflected in our mind, in the pond, the beauty lodged there that Mizoguchi had to eliminate by burning the real one to the ground, but still it stayed, didn't go away, came back, just like the idea of the theater. Mizoguchi was not unlike Kenji crawling in the stream behind his house. But he sat calmly on the mountain side watching the pavilion burn then took out a cigarette and had a smoke while Kenji crawled away from his productions.

Mizoguchi rose above his act like life always does art, while Kenji descended into the stream behind his house. Both fires were not unlike the remarkable *Snow Country* when the projector room at the local cinema caught fire and Yoko throws herself off the balcony and the main character Shimamura, an aesthete, can't help himself but mourns not her death but the beauty of the line of her body disrupted by a misaligned limb. The Milky Way goes into him with a roar as he looks up. So too art disappears in a rush as on Awaji Island theater after theater is burned to the ground so that almost no dolls survive today from the hundreds made, except those crude reproductions hidden in those houses that were unmolested.

Kenji's vision is almost lost in the vague annals of Japanese history on what was once a resistant population that turned on their own entertainment and burned theaters and homes to the ground so that Awaji Island today is only a faint replica of where a people glimpsed their naked selves and revolted.

Kenji wasted away to nothing, and today no one knows even where his original house stood, or whether it was later burnt to the ground.

Postscript

A real puppet madness occasionally seizes the Awaji farmer. He wanders from house to house with little one-handed marionettes, going through a favorite passage, himself both singer and puppeteer, when someone asks him in; he may even bring his house to ruin with his puppets, and he has been known in an extreme case to go quite insane.

—Junichiro Tanizaki *Some Prefer Nettles*

About the Author

Richard Krause's collection of fiction, *Studies in Insignificance*, was published by Livingston Press, and his epigram collection, *Optical Biases*, was published by EyeCorner Press in Denmark. Aforisticamente (@wordpress.com), an online website of aphorists from around the world, translated 70 of his epigrams into Italian in 2012. Krause grew up in the Bronx and on farms in Pennsylvania. He drove a taxi in NYC for five years and taught English for nine years in Japan. Currently, he teaches at a community college in Kentucky.

Acknowledgements

These stories were published in the following magazines:
"Gregor" *J Journal*,
"Crossing State Lines" *J Journal*
"Hamid, the Water Carrier" *Indiana Voice Journal*
"The Splinter" *Hackwriters Magazine*
"Baseball" *Cold Creek Review*
"The Alumnus of the Year" *The Alembic*
"Out of State Plates, or Decapitation 101" *Scarlet Leaf Review*
"Spoons" *The Heartland Review*
"The Coat" *The Oddville Press*
"The Tension of Suspenders" *Indiana Voice Journal*
"Another Zoo Story" *EXPOUND*
"The Child Molester" *Red Savina Review*
"The Watchband" *Brilliant Flash Fiction*
"The Betrayal" *The Long Story*
"The Untold Story of the Awaji Puppet Master" *Eastlit*

CPSIA information can be obtained
at www.ICGtesting.com
Printed in the USA
FSHW010300180319
56376FS